LANCELOT'S CHALLENGE

Also available through Mirador Publishing:

The Prophecy
Vampire

The Knights of Camelot Series:
Lancelot and the Wolf
Lancelot and the Wolf and Other Stories
Lancelot and the Sword
Lancelot and the Grail

Lancelot's Challenge

Coming Soon:
Lancelot's Burden
Lancelot's Curse

THE KNIGHTS OF CAMELOT

LANCELOT'S CHALENGE

BY

SARAH LUDDINGTON

Mirador Publishing
www.miradorpublishing.com

First Published in Great Britain 2012 by Mirador Publishing

Copyright © 2012 by Sarah Luddington

All rights reserved. No part of this publication may be reproduced or transmitted, in any form or by any means, without permission of the publishers or author. Excepting brief quotes used in reviews.

First edition: 2012

Any reference to real names and places are purely fictional and are constructs of the author. Any offence the references produce is unintentional and in no way reflects the reality of any locations or people involved.

A copy of this work is available through the British Library.

ISBN: 978-1-908200-90-7

Mirador Publishing
Mirador
Wearne Lane
Langport
Somerset
TA10 9HB

The unconventional twist to the Arthurian Legends leaves me open to a great deal of hate. I want to say 'thank you' to those who support me when I wilt under the pressure. Especially my knight, because without him I wouldn't have the courage to continue Lancelot's story and it needs telling. He finds the silver in the darkest of my clouds.

Me on Facebook

Me on Twitter

CHAPTER ONE

"Bloody hell," Arthur said. He cursed roundly and for some considerable time.

I didn't bother speaking. I just looked down at the army walking below us and wondered what we'd done to deserve yet another impossible fight.

"Our tactic is sound, Arthur," I whispered, fearing enemy ears, although the chances of them hearing me over their own feet were slim.

"I just didn't want to have to kill this many people," Arthur said. He rolled onto his back and stared at the pale blue dawn sky. The cool late summer air was sharp in our noses.

"It's not your fault Lot won't give up," I said trying to console him. I wriggled backward off the crest of the hill before standing.

"Everyone else has stopped this insanity, why won't he?" Arthur asked, following suit.

"Because he's a proud old buzzard who hated your father and he wants to punish you," I said, with more patience than I felt.

Arthur cursed again. He'd been doing a lot of that recently. "On the damned throne for almost twenty years and they still want to pick holes in my bloody leadership and punish me for my father's mistakes," he muttered while hauling himself into Willow's saddle. He'd gone very blonde over the summer and for a moment I glimpsed the young man, not the King.

I stared up at him with Ash's reins loose in my hand. The old warhorse tended to fight me less these days. I guess we'd both mellowed with age. "Maybe we should try to sue for peace again?" I asked.

Arthur threw his hands up in the air. "If I thought it would do any good I would, but the old goat wants me dead. Aeddan might not be funding our enemies any longer but

Lot still isn't giving up and I don't understand where he's getting the money. His barony isn't worth enough."

"Bloody big army for just his purse," I agreed, mounting Ash. He pirouetted but didn't buck.

"I think he's ransomed Camelot in the hope he wins against me and can pay off the mercenaries." Arthur walked Willow through the narrow valley running parallel to the wider one Lot and his army occupied. We passed makeshift camps, with simple canvas tents and just a few small fires. Our troops were stirring and for some this would be their last morning, their last meal. I shook my head trying to rid myself of these thoughts; they wouldn't help me fight.

"There are a great many more of them than us," I said.

"They don't know Camelot's bankrupt," Arthur said. His unhappiness made his face as miserable as his tone.

"You aren't bankrupt, Arthur, you are merely without funds until the harvest and those who owe you pay you," I tried to reassure him.

"I thought we'd know unity and peace once Aeddan had gone." Arthur kicked Willow and we began to canter into the main part of the camp.

I had naively thought the same thing. No Aeddan and all our enemies would vanish over night. Unfortunately, we were wrong. Some vanished, it was true. We'd lost enemies who were directly controlled by the fey but others still pushed, thinking Arthur remained weak. Since we'd come home the previous autumn we'd been in a constant state of negotiation or war.

Arthur finally lost his temper and declared war on Lot, no longer prepared to compromise or concede land. I stood by his side at all times and in the end, I realised we had no option but to fight. So, here we were, just before harvest, heading up a small army because we couldn't afford to buy in help and once more facing overwhelming odds.

Some things never change.

Arthur rode straight into the middle of our army. Only two thousand strong but the core consisted of his own men and my Wolf Pack. Since our return from Albion I'd retaken possession of the Pack and Captain Moran helped the transition, muttering about retirement. I feared the day I would lose him. My new sergeant, Helis, proved a good man but he'd never replace Tancred. One of the other new additions to the Wolf Pack came as a surprise. Captain Moran agreed to allow Kadien to join our ranks. After a few initial hiccups and some unfortunate conflicts, she'd passed the necessary tests and became a cadet. This meant she was supposed to stay out of the fighting but we needed every man we had on the battlefield. Half the army were in love with her, half feared her and I just tried to remain professional toward her. Something I found increasingly difficult.

My eyes found her among the guards outside Arthur's command tent. It wasn't as grand as it sounds. We didn't have time for the bells and whistles, a flag with a table under it and a large bivouac. A fire grate, able to cook half a side of venison, with a heavy black skillet and cooking pot, sat cold and empty. We wouldn't be eating this morning. Arthur slid off Willow and I dismounted more slowly. He started telling his commanders about the size of Lot's army and pointed to a map. We were going to shadow the slow moving mass of men until they reached a point where their valley joined another, two rivers combining into one. At that point, the army would stop and be surrounded by hills. We'd destroyed the bridges of Watersmeet, making life more difficult for Lot. Once they were penned in, we'd sweep around from our valley and attack. The opposing forces would be kettled in the valley and against the rivers. It would be a blood bath and one I wished we could avoid.

"Sire," I interjected quietly.

Arthur turned to me instantly, "What is it, Lancelot?"

I gazed at Kadien, who chatted amiably with some of the other guards. I'd given her guard duty over Arthur in an attempt to keep her out of trouble. And now, "I have an idea," I said. Arthur raised an eyebrow. I continued, "Give me ten of the Wolf Pack including Kadien and allow us to push for Lot independently of the main army. If we kill him, or ideally capture him, the fight will end and lives will be saved. We can't sneak in and kill the man, we've tried, his personal guard are too good." I'd almost lost Gawain and Yvain on that foray. "But we can become the arrow that strikes to the heart of the enemy."

Arthur frowned. "What makes you think such a venture is viable?" he asked. I understood his careful tone. He asked why I had to place my life in such danger. Since our return from Albion, we had been given the space to let our love breathe. I often found myself alone but I'd grown used to isolation, and it didn't stop Arthur from loving me. It also gave him a voice whenever I suggested doing something dangerous.

"If we can protect her long enough, Kadien can and will reach Lot," I said with absolute confidence.

My protégé had some remarkable physical strengths that came from her full fey heritage. Her acrobatics in Albion were the least of her abilities. She climbed, ran and jumped better than anything other than a cat. I'd tested her one day, to see which of us could race around Camelot's walls first, me on Ash or her bouncing from walls and rooftops. Kadien won. She'd bought me a small dagger with her vast winnings to say thank you for her rescue. I carried the knife with me everywhere. Being lighter and smaller, she also had her own fighting style, using finer blades than most of us. Yvain trained with her most often because his own quicksilver forms were closest to those Kadien found natural. Captain Moran made her learn the traditional training with the Wolf Pack but those that wanted to could also learn from Kadien. I caught him writing down her methods and encouraged him to improve her abilities with his own pragmatic approach. Almost nine months later Kadien, near the end of her cadetship, had been forged into a formidable weapon.

"What is the plan, in detail, Wolf?" Arthur asked, clearly very unhappy.

While I'd been thinking, the scents on the air grew sharper. Horses, leather, body waste and sweat. I heard the birds, some distance from the camp and the coolness of the morning felt wonderful in the shadow of the hills. "We form a basic arrowhead. Kadien rides with me. The team engage

Lot's guard and Kadien breaks through. You know she can do it, Arthur and you know it will save lives," I said.

"It is a good idea," Gawain said, knowing why Arthur scowled but pushing for my side regardless.

"Yes," said Arthur, "it is but it doesn't have to be you." He pointed a finger at my chest.

I grabbed his hand. "Yes, it does," I said. I tried to be kind. "There are only a few horses she's trained with that can perform tricks like this, Ash being one and I am not prepared to send her in without my back up."

I saw in Arthur's eyes he wanted to accuse me of loving the girl too much and he was right, I did care more than I should but I wasn't going to back down to save his feelings. I wanted to save lives.

"If you must, then do it," he conceded and his shoulders slumped slightly. "Go find your arrowhead while I finish up here. We'll place you at the head of the army, go into attack en masse, then you and your team break off and head for Lot."

"Thank you, Arthur," I said.

"Don't thank me, just come back to me in one piece," he said.

I smiled slightly to myself and strode into the mass of people moving quietly through the trees. The sharpness of the world did not fade, I moved with fluid joints and a sense of dislocation. The calm before the storm of battle. We had our own sentries posted in various places in case Lot sent men to seek Arthur. We were not expecting him to do so, as Geraint led his own men into acting as a decoy. They sat in the middle of a large heath, pretending to be the King. When the time came, they would sweep down toward us with readymade bridges and rush to attack Lot's army. It would be a dangerous gamble. If Geraint didn't make it in time, Arthur would be wiped out.

I forced my fears back and focused on my plan. "Kadien, with me," I shouted.

She broke off from the men she spoke with and said, "Yes, Sir." She instantly came to my side.

Her long hair, braided back tightly then covered with a

scarf which she wound all the way around the long length of the plait, made her face appear even more beautiful. The hair emphasised her blue eyes, but the black scarf just took the distraction of the hair away. Her flawless pale skin and bright smile made my skin feel hot and tight. I wanted her so badly but I had promised myself I'd never touch the girl. She deserved someone better and younger and not in love with their King.

"We are going in at the head of the army, then breaking off and I'm sending you in to kill Lot." I spoke quickly and didn't look at her so I could hide my fear and longing. I did hear her swift intake of breath.

"That is a great honour, my Lord. Are you certain I can do it?" she asked.

I stopped in my tracks and finally looked into her blue eyes, so like Arthur's. Her strength and utter faith in me made me flounder. She stood only a few inches shorter than me and far too close. I wanted to reach up and trace the strong line of her jaw. Instead, I smiled. "Kadien, if I didn't think we could do it, I wouldn't be sending us in there."

She nodded and all her doubts instantly fled. "Fine, Sir, we will do it."

Her attitude toward me had changed over the months, from cheeky comradeship to deference, as she learnt exactly what I was capable of as the leader of Arthur's armed forces. I missed the cheeky version.

I spotted one of the Wolf Pack I wanted in our arrowhead. "Lionel," I called, "Find William, we have a job to do."

I reached down and offered Kadien my arm to help her up behind Ash. He stood still and sighed heavily as her weight joined mine. He'd grown used to her acrobatics over the time we'd been training together and he allowed her to move smoothly around me. I think, to be honest, the old tart enjoyed being taught something new and being the centre of attention.

Within a short time, nine of us were on horses at the head of an army only two thousand strong to face over ten thousand men. Geraint had another thousand and a huge quantity of men stuffed with straw to look like a fighting force sat on a hill. The odds were interesting.

With Kadien, I rejoined the King's company, my chosen few arrange behind us. Arthur sat on Willow for a long time surveying the men around us. When he spoke, the world held still to listen. The sun's rays, just cresting the hills, no longer cooked us in our armour. The breeze grew quiet and the horses still.

"Soldiers of Camelot, today we are facing the impossible. I won't hide it from you. I've seen the army over that hill," he gestured behind us. "It scares me, so I dread to think how you will feel when you see it and I'm supposed to be the brave one." He laughed and a chuckle spread through the ranks. Then he became silent and pensive. Finally he spoke again, "I will not lie to you either, I never have, we are going to be lucky to survive. But we will," he raised his eyes and his voice. "We will survive because I have the best damned army at my back and I have the best men at my side to lead us to victory. We will survive and win because we are the finest of men and we deserve peace. We've fought a long and bitter war of attrition these last years and we are all tired. But this," he pointed with savagery at the hillside. "This is it. I have drawn a line and we will stop them from crossing it. Do you know why? Because I want all our families to be safe, happy, well fed and content. Because the Pendragon family includes you and your families. We are one and I will fight by your side today to ensure Camelot is not auctioned to the highest bidder. Lot has betrayed us and me. He has bought in troops he will have to pay with our blood and sweat. They will strip your lands, steal the food from your children and I will not be able to stop him. Don't let it happen. Focus on your enemy and take them apart, one at a time. Together we are unstoppable."

Willow reared perfectly at this point. I watched men draw themselves straighter, grip their spears more tightly and continue watching their beloved King.

Arthur projected his voice but made it sound conspiratorial all at once, "I am sending our greatest knight and a handful of others into the centre of this fray. Lancelot du Lac will see to it that we face a leaderless army, a rudderless ship, and when that happens, let loose men, let loose the passion in your hearts and fight for your families, your land and your homes. Let us, together, smash that ship on the rocks of our determination, pride, skill and honour."

"Good speech," Yvain murmured quietly. The men reacted well. Spears and swords banged softly against shields and the ground in acknowledgement of their King's words. Arthur rode forward into the ranks and began shaking the hands of his men, Willow stepping through the crowds carefully. The men touched him as if he were divine and could protect them from the spear, sword, arrow and armoured knights of Lot's army.

"It makes me want to throw myself at the castle walls," I said watching him with great pride.

"He could tell you anything and you'd throw yourself at the castle walls," Gawain said on my other side.

Once that would have been true, now... Well, now I knew the truth but I consciously allowed his words to stir my soul, readying me for battle.

We would have cheered but to do so would be to give Lot's scouts a target and we couldn't be the target. Not with the odds this bad. I turned Ash and signalled the order for the ranks to form up. Arthur returned to my side.

"Be careful," he said. He held out his hand and I gasped his forearm as he grasped mine.

"You to," I ordered.

We nodded. Not a moment for sentiment to weaken men's hearts, but a moment for bravery, for war.

CHAPTER TWO

Kadien wore light leather armour and carried two short, light swords. We'd argued for hours about her using heavier armour and wearing a helmet but she wouldn't cave in and almost resigned her commission over the right to wear her own design of protection. I'd spent many days training with her lean hard body moving around me as I controlled the horse and we'd finally developed a fighting style which suited us both. Now, she sat behind my saddle and lightly rested her hand on my armoured thigh. I couldn't feel it but somehow the heat of her hand made my cock start to twitch. With the rest of us in our traditional armour, mail, plate and surcoats, with thick layers of padding underneath, I wished the sun would vanish behind a cloud. We'd all be cooked long before we reached Lot at this rate.

I used to feel excited about facing an enemy with Arthur at my back but now I lacked the spirit for such warfare. I felt solemn, not excited about this fight. I no longer suffered the nightmares and my adoptive daughter, Rhea, ran rings around me, giving me a focus when I struggled with life. My love for my friend meant I coped well enough with living in Camelot, though I did escape into the wild wood at every opportunity. Now, though, I thought Arthur had made a mistake in challenging Lot and, although I understood why he'd done it, I didn't like it. This was about men's pride, not a noble awareness of what was right, the protection of our society and those within it.

Kadien interrupted my sad thoughts. "How do you want this to happen, my Lord?" she asked.

I sighed. "Please, Kadien, Lancelot is my name." I hated the formality of our new roles and wanted her to relax around me.

She perched her chin on my shoulder. I couldn't see her clearly through my helmet. "What do you expect from me, Lancelot?" she asked with emphasis.

"I expect you to live," I said and reached back with my gauntleted hand to hold her thigh where it sat tucked under mine. I twisted in the saddle so I could see her clearly with my visor up. "I want Lot stopped but not at any cost."

She smiled. "I can do that." She bounced slightly and her smile turned into a hungry grin. I had learnt a great deal about Kadien over the months. Arthur's mother and her own were half-sisters, so she and Arthur were half-cousins. Nice and complicated. She'd been raised on the great plains sweeping through Albion. The tribe she'd been a part of didn't like her heritage. Her mother had been used by a fey from another tribe, making her a mixed race child. She'd been trained by her people but with resentment. All the women fought and rode among her people and Kadien wanted to prove her worth from an early age. She didn't suffer fools gladly and when one of the older boys tried to use her young body she'd killed him; with that and the family debt, her fate was sealed. Her kin sold her into slavery and she'd been bought by Nimue. The fey queen knew her relationship to Arthur, distant as it was, and felt it would be usable to an arch manipulator.

When I'd found her and she'd chosen to help me defeat Aeddan, she'd been a slave for ten years but had lost none of her spirit or fighting talent. Since she'd been in Camelot she'd bloomed into a strong, beautiful woman, but she remained carefully distant from all men and did not welcome casual contact from anyone. I respected her privacy, knowing her slavery must have been very hard on the free spirit she represented.

My hand still on her thigh flexed and I smiled in return. "Just be careful," I said.

"You worry too much." Her hand sat on mine, and for the first time she didn't fight the contact. Her other arm circled my armoured waist and she leaned into my body. "I'll come back to you, Lancelot. I promise."

My heart rate trebled but she melted from the contact and dropped her gaze.

I wanted desperately to explore that one small intimacy

we had shared but I knew if I pushed she'd bolt, so we rode in silence.

The army slowly moved into place behind us and the men I'd chosen fanned out either side. We moved far more quietly than Lot's men and with so many professional soldiers rather than mercenaries, we were a better team. The odds were bad but under Arthur's inspired leadership, our men would prevail. I hoped.

I flexed my fingers, curling them into a fist. The damp nights sleeping outside did nothing for my old wounds. "I'm too old for this," I groused.

A small chuckle behind me caught me off guard. I'd forgotten Kadien. I felt myself flush with embarrassment. "Shut up," I grumbled.

"I didn't say a word," she chirruped happily.

"Just wait until you break a few bones."

Kadien reached forward and took hold of my right hand in her own. "You are not too old, my Lord, you are just tired." Her voice softened and her long slim fingers, in their heavy leather gloves, pushed between my own.

My breath hitched and my pulse raced. "Kadien," I began. I wanted to babble at her, I wanted to take advantage of this strange moment and tell her she moved my heart. I wanted to tell her I had room for both her and Arthur if she'd just give me a chance.

"My Lord du Lac," an outrider galloped toward me on a foaming horse, cutting through my thoughts. Kadien faded from me without actually moving anything other than her hand.

The horse, trembling with effort, skidded to a halt beside me. The man wore Geraint's colours. This could not be good news. "My Lord Fitzwilliam sent me. Lot has reinforcements on the way. They are coming down behind our forces. He has to come off the hill far more quickly than planned. You need to move up your own attack."

"Fuck," I reviewed Arthur's plans and made some adjustments. "If we go around this valley at double time and join with Geraint we can face Lot head on inside the hills but the rivers will be at our back, not his."

"I don't think we have much choice," Kadien said. She instantly understood the threat we faced. From a slim chance to no chance in heartbeats. The fortunes of war.

"We should run," I said.

"If we do he will just come for Camelot and the city cannot survive another siege," Kadien reminded me.

"Then our mission to take Lot down is even more vital. I will not lose this day." I squared my shoulders and spoke to the messenger. "Go to the King, tell him what you told me and tell him we are moving up the pace and heading for Lot. He needs to divide his forces when Lot is pressing hard into our ranks and chase them toward the river. We need to take chunks out of his army and dispatch them. Strike fear into the enemy."

"Yes, my Lord," the scout said, saluting.

I shouted orders to pick up the pace. Those with horses, the Wolf Pack and knights, began a slow canter. The regular soldiers and auxiliary started a loping run. The noise increased but not by much. Pennons snapped in the breeze and the spears of the foot soldiers bobbed behind us like a moving forest of wood and steal agony.

"Lancelot," Kadien said so quietly I barely heard her through my coif and helmet.

"What is it?" I asked sharply, my mind already in the midst of the battle I was about to face.

"I'm scared," she said and her body leaned into mine for the first time in months.

"I know," I replied, "but you must banish your fear and live just in the moment. Empty your heart of everything but the fight you will face. You exist only for this, for war. Nothing else in the world matters and you face a glorious death if he chooses to take you." Over my own dead body, I thought. I'd fight Death for Kadien as hard as I would for Arthur.

"Is that how you do this, over and over? You live only for death?" she asked.

I pushed my visor up and smiled grimly. "I am trying hard not to but when I find myself surrounded and forced to fight, it is an easy path for me to take. I am a warrior. I am resigned to dying on the field of battle but I won't make it easy and I will fight for those I believe in and love."

"Like Arthur?" she asked.

I nodded. "Like Arthur. Focus on your goal, Kadien, and allow nothing to distract you. Remove all who would prevent you reaching Lot."

"Thank you," she whispered close to my face and I felt her lips press briefly to my cheek. "Even if I do die today, I want you to know, you have given me a better life in the last few months than I've ever known."

She couldn't see it, but her words made my eyes swim with unshed tears. I wanted to pull her off Ash and force her to return to Camelot, to wear dresses and learn to make embroidery. I also knew she'd never forgive me for such chauvinistic cowardice. There were no words of love I felt able to give in that moment without giving her more to fear.

In the end I simply said, "You are one of the best cadets the Wolf Pack has ever had, you will do this and we will win."

I sensed her arms tighten around my breastplate but couldn't actually feel the hug through the armour. I patted her arm and wished I could kiss her lips and eyes to take the fear away.

A messenger returned from Arthur. "My Lord, his Majesty has asked that as soon as we sight the army we charge into the attack. We are not to give them time to prepare."

"Inform him we will do everything he needs us to do," I said.

I forced my mind away from Kadien and concentrated on the upcoming fight. There would be knights leading Lot's army, just as there were for Arthur. We would engage the knights and then slide around the side. Lot would sit somewhere in the centre of the army. We would be fighting against men on foot and those who served the pretender to Camelot's throne on horseback. If we managed to carve a hole in those ranks, Kadien would be able to move through the men like mist and reach Lot. The weapons we'd face would be spear, hauberk, sword, archers, shields of the good fighters and possibly some more basic weapons such as staffs. Many of those Lot controlled were his levied men, farmers and herders, no real threat to us. The archers would not shoot into their own ranks and the mercenaries should be focused on Arthur, not protecting Lot.

Arthur, damn I wished he'd let me do this alone. He might be one of the finest warriors I'd ever known, but whenever he rode into a fight, he frightened the life out of me.

Once more, I fought for control and chased my thoughts back to the fight. For once I felt the fear curl in my stomach, the same nerves which attacked Kadien. I did not want to die today. I wanted to love my new life. A life where I saw the colour of the sky and smelt the scent of roses. I wanted peace and time to explore the world around me and those I loved. My heart had brought me at last to a place where I understood war and death were not the path to strength and greatness. I could be more. I wanted to be more than Arthur's weapon of choice.

The hills we followed started to peter out and I saw the rivers glinting in the distance. Rosebay willowherb sprouted tall and pink but we were forced to squash it flat as we rode on. My breath sounded harsh inside my sallet and I watched young birch trees shiver in the summer wind as we galloped toward the confrontation. I knew we would soon face Lot's men. I gave the final orders to those around me, the young knights formed up tight around the ten of us from the Wolf Pack and we prepared to circle the final hills.

Everything calmed. Ash carried Kadien and I around the final ridge and the ranks of our enemies spread out before us. Just as I knew we would, we faced the finest knights of Lot's army. Fortunately, they wouldn't be a match for Camelot's. No orders were necessary. We moved as a single organism and picked up our pace to a full gallop. I carried no lance. With Kadien on Ash the manoeuvring would be too hard, but I did carry a spear. Every other member of our advance party also carried long range weapons. The smell brought with it so many memories. Horse sweat, churned earth, fear and strangely, joy. The noises around me were of more than one hundred hooves hitting the dry soil beneath our onslaught. The harsh breath of the horses and the prayers of men who used them. The chime of metal against metal as men set themselves deeper in their saddles and the sound of wind rushing, exhilarating me.

I released a great whoop of joy. My fears were now a desperate memory as I swooped toward my foe. No matter how I loved life, I loved the challenge of war. It lived in my blood and bones. My vision closed down to those I faced and Geraint's men rushing over another hillside toward the rivers they needed to cross to reach us. I felt all those men, all those souls around me and my brain started negotiating the path before us, which would lead us to Lot.

Twenty paces and the horses would engage. Orders were being screamed. Bows strung in panic. Ranks trying to change formation from marching to fighting. Ten paces and I saw the eyes of the foot soldiers who would die when we crashed into their ranks. Five paces and I marked the knights I'd take down first. Ash plunged, his head down, his own armour adding to our weight and protection. Suddenly we were there in the centre of the battle lines. My spear snapped on the first engagement, tearing into the chest of a horse and catapulting both the beast and his rider back onto others. My sword, already drawn in the left hand, changed sides and I engaged a man wearing Lot's colours. I felt Kadien shift behind me and knew she now had her back to mine, a simple loop of leather the only thing other than the strength in her thighs keeping her on Ash's back. She screamed her own battle cry and we started to carve into the heart of the army. My sword smashed into arms, faces, chests and legs. It cut where it could or broke the bones lying under inadequate armour. Ash snapped at the horses who drew too close and kicked out at any men foolish enough to attack from the ground. He became a living weapon, as did I. The rest of Arthur's men now joined the slaughter and I knew we needed to peel off and head for Lot.

"Wolf Pack, to me," I bellowed, doing my best impression of Captain Moran. My men disengaged from the chaos and we fought our way free of the front ranks.

The valley, the widest in the area, contained the only road, along which Lot obediently marched his troops. I forced us onto the rough verges, which still remained bizarrely free of the enemy, and charged along the ranks. A few arrows spat towards us but hit nothing. We drew level with the flags surrounding Lot. I heard his mighty voice ordering his men into tight ranks, preparing for our strike. The sun froze above my head and the wind stilled. The clouds ceased their journeys. Kadien moved behind me, her legs shifting over Ash's back as she readied herself. It felt like she moved through treacle. My right hand flexed on my sword and I felt the sticky mess of blood and guts covering my blade and hand. I carried a shield on my left side, its weight a comfort, the wolf's head emblazoned on the front was now chipped and scarred by fresh blade cuts. My breath sounded loud inside my helmet and I smelt Ash's sweat. I saw everything in those slow moments. I watched four loyal knights lowering their visors and turning their horses to face us. I saw Lot's hard face, his faded red beard and long grey hair spilling out from under his coif and helmet. His pale blue eyes focused on mine and I saw rage. No fear - Lot had never been a coward - but I did see recognition of a pivotal moment in his quest for Camelot.

Those frozen moments ended when Ash threw himself into the foot soldiers trying to protect their Lord. The world sped faster than before, compensating for those slow breaths and my body fell into the patterns of death dealing. Five of us reached the knights protecting Lot, they turned to hold our backs and flank. Kadien screamed her strange war cry and Ash shift his hindquarters around. She rose behind me, a deadly angel in black leather and launched toward the horses of the enemies. Using them to spring forward, her short light blade slashed even as she fought for her balance before lunging toward Lot's great bay horse. I watched him slash at her and she twisted in mid air, thrown off her target. She landed among the frantic legs of the horses and I bellowed in fear, slashing through my opponent without even glancing at him so I could reach her.

I shouldn't have allowed fear to control me. Kadien

pirouetted where she crouched and used the long slim muscles of her legs to power herself upward. It looked as though she flew for Lot, like a great cat landing on the back of a horse. Her feet touched the bay's hindquarters and he froze in confusion. Lot twisted to rid himself of the pest at his back, but his armour prevented the movement. He tried to drag his horse's head around, to turn and force her off. He gave his back to me. Kadien slipped her blade into his neck, between the joints of his armour. I plunged my sword between her legs and under his back plate. Kadien shifted and threw herself at Ash, landing lightly enough and slipping back into her original position before I even managed to draw my sword from the pretender's back.

CHAPTER THREE

Lot slumped forward, great gouts of blood pouring from his neck and back. Now was not the time to celebrate, we needed to move.

"Retreat," I ordered loudly.

I saw one of my men slumped over his horse, another under the hooves surrounding us. Three of the four of Lot's knights were dead or dying. William grabbed the horse of our wounded comrade and we carved a path out. An easy task now the word began to spread of their leader's death.

Kadien whooped and yelled calling out her victory as we galloped back down the ranks toward our own men. I looked for Arthur. His flag should be somewhere near the front. The fight remained fierce and I couldn't find him, but I did spot Geraint's tall form and his red hair.

"What the hell?" I asked myself. Why was Geraint fighting without his armour? I caught sight of Willow. He stood still, riderless but attacking anyone that came close.

I forgot everything else. "Arthur." I kicked Ash and joined the fight, trampling many under his hooves. I focused only on Willow. Geraint carved his own path from the other side. We reached the great war horse at the same time. Kadien shifted off the back of Ash and landed beside a bloody, mud splattered body. Golden tangles and finely engraved armour peeked out from the mess. Bile rose in my throat and my vision darkened. Were clouds covering the sun?

Willow, his flanks heaving and sweat foaming on his thick neck, blew hard but calmed the instant he recognised Ash. Men were fighting in a circle around the horse and his fallen rider. The Wolf Pack fought tooth and claw against the press of men trying to reach Arthur and finish the job.

"Geraint," I yelled over the noise.

"Move him, Lancelot. I'll hold your back," he bellowed,

swinging his mighty broadsword into a hapless mounted soldier.

"He's alive," Kadien called, her fingers pressed to his neck. I almost tumbled from Ash in my desperation. Now I felt the hands of fear on my neck, tightening their grip and shortening my breath. Anything, I could face anything but losing Arthur. Not like this, not when we'd killed Lot and peace was just moments of insanity away. I knelt by his side, now protected by Ash and Willow.

I didn't bother to call his name. His eyes were closed and his cheeks grey. Blood covered him, flowing from a deep wound in his chest, the hole in his armour ragged, the metal torn and twisted. I hooked an arm under his neck and another under his legs. He would only be slightly lighter than me but I rose in one movement and cradled his still body.

"Kadien, get on Willow," I ordered. She nodded briefly and leapt up onto the huge warhorse. I lifted Arthur as high as humanly possible but couldn't place him in her arms. Kadien leaned outward and down. She wrapped her arms around Arthur's chest and pulled back, grunting with the effort. I managed the final push and he lay against her body, bleeding everywhere.

"Ride." I smacked Willow hard on the rump. He turned, Geraint went with them and I set to, against the enemy around me. I don't know how long I fought, or how many I killed and maimed. The man who loved his King to the edge of obsession wept and took his rage out on all those around him. How dare they try to extinguish the sun and leave the moon without the grace of reflective light?

"Lancelot," a voice yelled. "Lancelot, for God's sake man, you've killed them all. Stop. It's me, it's Gawain."

My arm ceased its circle and pulled the strike aimed at decapitating my friend.

"We need you." Gawain approached slowly, hands down, sword pointed to the ground. "Arthur needs you."

I blinked, light blinded me. I didn't have my helmet on and the air stank. Ash walked among bodies, snorting, his sides dark with blood but not his own. It did not flow. Blood did flow from several wounds in me, my armour appeared to be littered with holes of various types and something warm trickled down the side of my face. My hands and arms were drenched in sticky redness. Bodies, dozens of bodies lay around me.

"Arthur." I turned and ran. I held my sword at its mid length to keep it from tangling with my legs. A body rose from the mass and I simply smacked the pommel of my weapon into his head. He wore the russet colours of Lot's men. I felt no pity as his scream choked off when he realised his jaw was broken.

I found the medic's tent, pulled by the strings tying my heart to Arthur's. The white canopy sat near the smaller of the two rivers. Men littered the ground, some acting as nurses, others groaning in their agony. Some very still and some already lost. I'd given my share to Death this day, but Lot's men also gave their own bounty.

Geraint stood, a pale sentinel outside one small tent. He, Kadien and others from the Wolf Pack were silent, sombre and unwilling to look at me as I charged toward them.

I didn't pause and no one stopped me. I strode into the small canvas space and stopped. Neither Merla nor Merlin were with us on this trip. Merla sat in Camelot, heavy with her first child and unhappy with Gawain joining the fight. Merlin said he would not be needed, so refused to come despite Arthur's threats. We'd taken it as a good omen. He kept making some vague comments about the fates of gods, but to be honest I hadn't understood and thought he might actually be losing his mind.

Arthur lay on a table. His armour cut from his body and the mail shirt also in tatters on the floor. His gambeson acted as a blanket to soak up the blood. A man, Willard of Malmsbury, crouched over his chest muttering.

"Well?" I asked. My throat wouldn't allow another word out.

Willard actually jumped and dropped a fine needle in the process. "My Lord, I didn't hear you," his myopic expression didn't inspire my confidence. With not a hair on his head and far too many out of his nose, he looked more like a diseased mole than a medical man versed in herbs and surgery. Merlin had informed me repeatedly that Willard could do anything that was necessary. I'd gut the old wizard if he was proved wrong.

I tried to remain calm and keep my tone measured. "Tell me of the King's condition," I said. My right hand began to cramp around my blade. It started to bite into my hand, through the gauntlet.

"He is gravely wounded, my Lord." I grabbed his throat with my left hand and he gurgled, "if you could wait outside."

I pulled him half way across Arthur's inert body. "Just fucking tell me if he is going to live."

"He..." the man squeaked.

"Lancelot, put him down. If you break him he can't work and he can't work if you scare him so much his hands are shaking." Geraint stooped slightly in the dull, hot interior.

I dropped Willard of Malmsbury. "What happened?" I did not move from Arthur's side. I asked the question of both men. Geraint answered and waved at the medic to continue work.

"From what I've been told, Arthur raced into the fight. He tried to engage as many men as possible to keep them from turning to fight you and the others." Geraint ran a hand through his greying red hair, his expression grim and skin taut.

"He led the charge himself?" I asked. Geraint nodded. I breathed deeply, "That was not part of the plan."

"I didn't think it would be," Geraint agreed. "Anyway, some freaky lucky shot from a boy holding a dropped lance took him in the chest. He never saw it coming, not on his left side and from the ground. It's carved a line through Willow's shoulder too. The broken tip went straight through his amour and into his chest."

"His heart?" I asked quietly, my own growing cold.

"Missed, just," came Willard's assessment. "We have a messy hole in his chest and wood splinters everywhere but the heart appears undamaged. I'm having trouble with his lungs and one or two of his ribs are badly broken. I'm trying to find a way to hold them in place before I stitch him up."

I didn't understand his words. How the hell you held bones in place under the skin I couldn't imagine. "Will he live?" I asked, forcing the words out.

Willard did peer up at me then. "Honestly?" He glanced at Geraint assuming he'd be safe with the bigger man in the tent. "I don't know. I will do everything I can, but it is a killing blow. His chest is a mess. Even if he survives this, there are countless other things that might finish him off, fever being the real problem. Right now, though, I need peace and quiet. I'd also like a steady pair of hands. Send the girl in," he said bending back over his patient. I caught a glimpse of white bone and metal inside Arthur's broad chest and bile rose in my gullet.

The day wore on and grew old around us. I sat outside Arthur's tent. At some point someone brought me food and water. Someone else insisted I remove my armour and they dressed various wounds. Yvain sat near me, also wrapped in silence. Kadien joined us when the medic finished but soon found the stress of remaining still proved too great. She vanished to find Ash, to clean him off. I waited. I waited to hear Arthur's voice querulously ask for my presence, so I could tell him Lot would no longer be a problem. That we had peace in England. We could unite Britain under his leadership and hold her course steady against all comers. We'd defeated men and fey alike, now we could rest. We could hang up our swords and spurs and grow old and fat in each other's company. I'd sacrificed everything to be here with Arthur, I couldn't lose him now.

Instead I just watched the river, and the crows gather over the field of battle. I heard men's screams and moans. I smelt smoke and death on what was once clean pure air, rushing through these hills and valleys. It crashed into this massacre and carried the stain for leagues.

Dusk started to rise majestically from the east, sweeping over the sky to give the sun its last glorious display of the day. Night would plunge headlong through the heavens releasing its panoply of stars and the moon. I would sleep at some point. I would sleep and the wolf would be alone. No white hart.

I wondered about that. Whenever Arthur's life lay in the balance, I'd dreamt of the threat and prevented it, so why not now? Why had I not woken last night in a cold sweat knowing what danger lay ahead for my King?

"If he dies, Merlin," I muttered, cursing the old man in my head.

"If I understood that bonding the two of you went through, if he dies, so do you," Gawain said referring to our strange connection forged when we were last in Albion.

"Perhaps, no one is certain," I replied, half wishing it would happen. A life without Arthur didn't feel like a life at all, merely an existence. Only one other thing gave me true meaning and I'd thrown that away.

"Lancelot." Gawain moved to crouch in front of where I sat. "Merla has taught me a great deal over the time we've been together. We might be able to help Arthur."

"There is no one here of real power," I said. "Kadien is full fey but her gifts are not healing or summoning. They are physical. Merlin, Merla, even Else cannot help from Camelot."

"But you can," he said, placing a hand on my arm. As Gawain grew older he looked more like his uncle every day. It made my heart ache to see Arthur shadowed in my friend's earnest expression.

"What are you talking about?" Yvain asked drawing close.

"Merla says Lancelot has real strength and talent from Aeddan. No one has thought to teach him because he's already one of the most powerful men in the country. He can't heal Arthur but he should be able to call someone who can," Gawain spoke with some excitement and I had the feeling he'd been trying to find a way to tell me all day.

"You want me to summon fey who can heal Arthur?" I asked.

"It can't hurt to try," Gawain said.

"Hurt? They are fey, of course it will hurt," I snapped. My grip on my temper and my patience started to fray.

Willard chose that moment to leave the tent. He straightened his back and I scrambled upright. I ached all over from the fighting, then all this time of tense stillness.

The bald, small man peered at me through the growing darkness. "I have done all I can, it is now in God's hands."

I swallowed. "God has no business on the battle field," I said. "Just tell me if he will live."

Willard blinked rapidly and his stooped shoulders slumped further. "I think, if I am honest, you need to prepare yourself for the worst."

CHAPTER FOUR

I thought I'd collapse in a heap if I ever heard those words in relation to Arthur. I honestly thought my heart would stop beating the moment it knew it would lose him.

Instead, something else happened.

"Yvain," I said and turned to my companion, "go and find Geraint. Arthur will need him with us."

"Yes, my Lord." Yvain raced away from me without question.

"Gawain," I said. "I want Arthur moved onto a bier the four of us can carry and I want you to dredge your memory of every fact or piece of law Merla has given you."

He nodded and moved off, barking orders to the Wolf Pack about building a litter and finding torches.

Kadien appeared like true fey magic at my elbow. "Can I help?" she asked.

I took her hands in mine and realised she'd been the one to feed me and clean my wounds during the day. "Can you summon?" I asked, hoping I'd been wrong about her talents.

She shook her head. "But I've seen Nimue do it. You could even try calling her, she could heal Arthur."

I laughed, a short bitter sound. "I don't think Nimue would like to heal Arthur. Kill him and me but not heal."

She didn't waste time arguing with me. "You need to focus on someone or it won't work," she said.

"Rafe, Tancred or The Lady of the Lake are the only full fey I've known except Merla. She could heal him, she healed me," I said. "Can I call her here?"

Kadien's eyes grew sad and doubtful. "No, she is with child and a human baby at that. Merla has given up the ability to move between worlds with ease. She would be able to heal him but only with time and he doesn't have time."

"You know this?" I asked. I realised a fine tremor now

ran through my right hand and it felt so weak. I couldn't feel Kadien's fingers properly.

"Lancelot, I am sorry," her eyes filled with tears. "I can feel his soul fighting to stay with you but it can't. His body is too weak."

I dropped her hands and walked into the tent. Arthur lay on the table, bloody rags all over the floor. A huge wad of mosses and cloth lay over the hole in his chest. His hand slipped into mine and I bent to his perfect face. I lay kisses on his brow, his eyes and one kiss which lingered on his lips. He didn't move. His breath remained shallow and I felt too much heat coming from his skin.

"We are not going to lose each other now," I whispered. "Just hold on, my Hart, and I will find a way to save you. I swear it."

Noise and movement around the tent alerted me to the preparations I'd set in place. Geraint came in. "What's going on?"

"I'm going to call someone from Albion to heal him," I said.

He internalised the succinct news. "You can't," Geraint said.

"I am Aeddan's son, I can and I will," I told him. I placed Arthur's hand on his stomach. "We are going to carry him into the water and I am going to call out for aid. They will come, they must. He saved Albion from Aeddan. I will summon them as Merla summoned my father when we were at the henge."

"Lancelot, you..." Geraint struggled to find the words.

"If I don't, he will die," I said. Oh look, I could say the words without screaming.

Geraint stood and stared at Arthur a long time. "I wish Eleanor were here," he finally admitted.

"So do I," I agreed. "But she isn't, I am and I have to try."

"I don't like it. I don't trust it and they will want something in return, they always do. Sometimes I think you lost Tancred because you needed Rafe's help and the deal was struck without conscious thought. That's what worries me about fey, they steal the thoughts out of our heads and use them against us," Geraint said.

"I don't know about that," I said, surprised Geraint had concocted such a complex theory about Tancred's loss. "I do know I will have to offer them something. So, I need you there to act as my head because my heart will give anything to save Arthur."

Geraint nodded. "Agreed, we will do anything we can to save him."

The stars began to blink on, sweeping over the sky like a huge handful of diamonds scattered onto the cloths of heaven. They watched impassive as the Wolf Pack dismantled the King's tent and we gently lifted Arthur's still body onto the litter.

The rushing waters of the river met about one hundred paces from our position and I judged this to be the place of power we needed to help me call into another world. Kadien agreed; she told me I had to trust my instincts over all other things. They would guide me in the magic.

Men and torches lined the path Gawain, Geraint, Yvain and I would walk. The army formed ranks behind the Wolf Pack, who held the torches. Kadien led the way and other knights brought up the rear. She'd released her hair and from somewhere found a simple pale dress, which hung from her shoulders to her toes. She looked ethereal, fragile and utterly beautiful. We proceeded down toward the river at a steady pace and I realised something in me had started to shift already.

"Sister River," I whispered into the still silence. "Sister River," the sound hissed around the crackle of fire from the torches. The gurgling laughter of the river brought back so many memories. A perfect picture of my home in the woods. My sanctuary when grief broke my mind and I hid from the world in my madness. During that time I'd become connected to the world around me in a way I'd never known. I heard the spirits of the trees. Felt the souls of the animals even as they died to give me life. I knew by instinct every twist and turn of that forest. I lived completely inside each moment, never remembering the past and never thinking of the future beyond basic survival. I needed to touch that place in my soul once more and the river would help to carry me there.

The water rushed and bubbled, chasing itself downstream, held in form and shape by soft banks of mud and stone. I heard a shimmering giggle in the reverberation. A breath of sound harmonising with the language of water. Something lived here at the Watersmeet and it welcomed us into its embrace. I walked to the edge of the river but Geraint paused, holding me back.

"Lancelot, I don't know..." his doubt jerked the line pulling me into the water.

"Arthur needs us," I said, unable to turn my eyes from the dark water highlighted by flickering torchlight. I pulled on the litter and Geraint found himself dragged into the water. The step down was not far and the riverbed felt smooth under my feet. I turned and walked backward into the river, so I could watch Arthur and ensure the others came safely. The water soaked through my bloody hose and soon numbed my knees. It kissed my thighs and I felt my balls begin to retreat from the coming cold. Geraint's breath hissed; he didn't understand the cold of Sister River. You had to welcome the frigid gift of life.

Yvain remained his placid, unflappable self. Gawain pulled faces but soon pushed the cold from his mind when he focused on his uncle. I reached the centre of the river and we stopped.

"Lower him," I said.

"The cold could kill him," Geraint said. I saw the fear in his eyes and I smiled to give my friend comfort.

"The cold will not kill him. I need him in the water, please trust me," I begged.

Geraint took a deep breath and nodded. We lowered the litter and water rushed over the surface of the wood and touched Arthur. The strong current pulled at the blankets we'd covered him with for just a moment. It pushed against our legs then calmed, grew still and became a gentle flow, not a rushing torrent. Gawain cursed softly and even Yvain shifted, unnerved by the sudden change in the water's behaviour. I merely smiled. We were made welcome.

I dropped to my knees and water rushed over my shoulders. I lay my head back and Sister River whispered directly into my ears and tangled through my hair. "Help me, show me," I said only to the stars and the river. "I cannot lose him. We cannot lose him."

The water swirling around me grew warm, caressing my skin. I lowered myself further into the gentle stream, the water closing over my head. With my eyes open I saw a pinprick of light further upstream. The red of torches graced the surface but this light grew from the depths of a body of water far more massive than this small river. I closed my eyes, my breath beginning to burn in my lungs and reached out with my mind to the light. The wolf stirred and raised his black muzzle. He stood, lifted his great head and howled for the white hart. The light grew, racing toward the wolf. My lungs forced air out of my mouth and I shot to the surface, gasping for air.

Bright white radiance flooded the entire field of battle. Men gasped, some dropped to their knees in prayer. I walked forward. Light gushed, growing brighter and brighter, until I squinted in pain. From the centre of the harsh glow came a figure. Clothed in white, petite, her skin like frost and eyes pure black, The Lady of the Lake walked toward us on the surface of the water.

I heard Kadien frantically praying to whatever gods protected the fey and Geraint cursed.

"You couldn't have called someone less terrifying?" he asked, finally managing to say something coherent.

I ignored him and focused on the figure towering over me on the surface of Sister River.

I bowed, "My Lady."

"Who are you to call me into the world, son of Aeddan?" Her lips did not move, but her voice echoed softly inside my mind.

"I am nothing before you, my Lady," I said aloud and I lowered my head.

She paused long enough to let me know that I was

indeed worth nothing. "What do you want, son of Aeddan?" her voice sounded a great deal harsher. It hurt my mind.

"Please, my Lady, I may be the son of Aeddan but I am also my King's Champion." I wanted her to see me as me, not as the bastard spawn of the fey king.

"I care nothing for your King and you have yet to prove to me that you are something more than the bastard son of our dead King," she said. The dour look on her cold face didn't bode well.

The words also hurt, especially after everything I'd sacrificed because of Aeddan, including Tancred. "As you wish, my Lady," I said. I kept my temper because I wanted Arthur alive. She'd not provoke me into a fight.

"You have used your connection to Aeddan to call me, what do you want?" she asked.

I moved sideways and swept an arm toward Arthur. The water caressed him but did not cover him. "My Lady, my King is dying. I beg you, help me and heal him." My heart pounded. I regretted calling her; she didn't strike me as someone who'd help Arthur.

She remained silent a long time and then said, "What is your King to me? Why would I save him? Why would I not place you on the throne as my cousin Nimue wished?"

Oh, fuck. This didn't even occur to me. No one else moved and I realised they didn't hear her. If they had, Geraint would not be standing, awestruck and very still.

My mind raced. I am not a negotiator, I am a killer. "I am not born to be King, either here or in Albion. But I am your servant in all things if you can find it in your heart to help me with this. England needs to be stable and Arthur Pendragon is the best of men. He is the only one able to guide this land forward. We know that the world of men and fey needs to be separate. You also know this, my Lady, or you would not have helped the Morrigan forge Excalibur."

"Do not presume to know my motives, Knight of Camelot," she snapped. Her words acted like a whip inside my head. I flinched and nausea rose. Sister River grew restless and bubbled around us. The others in the river shifted and I heard their fear. I ignored them, focused only on the image before me.

Being used to the vagrancies of a royal mind, I did not rise to the bait and argue with her about her motives. When she spoke her voice had calmed, but felt like stone, "If you are my servant in all things, Lancelot du Lac, you will become just that. I will heal your King, Arthur Pendragon, but in return you give me a year and a day of your life to use as I see fit."

I heard gasps around me, everyone heard that offer.

"You can't," Geraint said instantly.

"This is madness," Gawain cried out. "Arthur will never forgive you for leaving him."

Only Yvain remained silent, as he studied me carefully. "If he doesn't agree Arthur will die."

I raised a half smile in acknowledgment of his observation. Next, I focused on Kadien. She stood half on the bank and half in the river. I'd not needed her to call The Lady of the Lake and her shock at my ability made her wary. I wanted to ask her advice, even though I already knew my decision, somehow I wanted her sanction and understanding. Tears rose in her eyes as she read my decision in my eyes. I wanted to tell her so many things in that moment, instead I turned to Geraint.

"Look after Arthur and Guinevere. Don't let him come after me and help him forge a peace for when I return. Tell him it will be worth it and that I love him. Look after Rhea and tell her I'm sorry." My voice remained level and strong as though I gave orders to my Wolf Pack.

"Lancelot, this is insane," Geraint said. "You don't know what you are walking in to or what she really wants. You wanted me to be your mind because you knew your heart would drag you into making a mistake, this is a mistake."

I did raise a smile finally, "So what else is new, my friend?" I turned to the vision of the woman before me. "You know my decision, my Lady. You will have my service for a year and a day in return for healing Arthur Pendragon."

She smiled and held out her small hand. "Come to me, Knight of Camelot."

Now! My heart cried. You want me now?

I would have to leave Arthur before seeing him well again, before I could say farewell. My heart quailed at the loss.

"May I see him healing first, my Lady?" I asked.

"That was not our bargain, Knight of Camelot," she said. Her eyes glittered dangerously.

Fucking fey. "As you wish," I said. I stepped forward, lay a kiss on Arthur's brow, turned once more and walked toward the outstretched hand. I reached up and my fingers brushed hers. My large palm engulfed the cool skin before agony shot through my body. I screamed and the world shot black.

CHAPTER FIVE

I woke to a rough wool blanket tickling my nose and scratching my face. My right hand actively hurt and my body ached. Memory returned in fits and starts, until, "Arthur."

Pain bloomed deep inside my chest and I finally caved into the anguish of his loss. I paid no attention to my surroundings. Dozens of soldiers might be bearing down on me to end my life. They were welcome to it. I just wanted to indulge my heartbreak.

Grief always comes in waves and the initial horror eventually faded. Exhausted and utterly bereft, I sat up on the small cot. To call the room I occupied sparse was an understatement. I'd seen monks' cells which were more comfortable. A kind of strange grey green light filtered into a small window set just above my head height. I'd need to stand on tiptoe to look through the glassless hole. The bed smelt clean enough if you liked the stink of sheep; a sheepskin acting as the only form of luxury. The bed itself appeared to be roughly hewn and tied together; it didn't feel very sturdy. Other than a chair constructed in the same way, nothing else but a plain natural white wool robe kept me company. No rugs sat on the stone floor, no tapestries hung from the walls.

I stared hard at the door, wooden but bound with metal. It didn't quite remind me of a dungeon door. My code as a knight, the bit that made me unable to actually give up, drove me to my feet. I walked to the door and tried the simple round handle, twisting it to the right. The door did not open.

"Not exactly a surprise," I said. I went to the window and looked through, peering upward like a child, too small to see. There wasn't anything but a cold breeze. The strange greenish light seeped over a paved courtyard and a plain stonewall. I sat on the bed and realised the mattress felt very thin. "I'd be better off on the floor," I muttered feeling sorry for myself. My stomach announced its displeasure. I'd ignored it for too long and it needed feeding. "Marvellous." I sat back on the bed and hooked my feet up, with my back against the rough wall.

My mind instantly circled back to Arthur. The entire time he'd been lying in that tent I'd held myself in suspension. I'd worked hard not to think about the consequences or the reality that we were not immortal. I prayed he would be safe, which brought me to my bargain. A year and a day as a servant to The Lady of the Lake. I'd left Rhea, Kadien, Guinevere and Arthur. I'd thrown myself into the deal without thinking about the consequences to any of us. I'd just wanted to save Arthur's life.

"Always the most important thing," I muttered, banging my head lightly against the wall. Unfortunately, it was true. I held Arthur's life far above everything else, including my own sad existence.

"And now you have to live without him, again," I told myself. I realised I'd already begun slipping into old habits from my time in the forest. Not helpful especially when it made me consider Tancred. I missed him and thought about him every day. I'd given up something really special when I'd chosen Arthur and although I didn't regret it, sadness left a hole in my soul. I also wondered if I'd see him again now I'd been forced back to Albion.

I soon realised all thoughts, including those about beautiful young cadets and sergeants, were leading me down dangerous paths. So I simply lay on the hard mattress, stretched my stressed muscles and stared at the ceiling. Time vanished into whatever hole it lives in once it's done and I hovered on the edge of sleep. Strange images of the wolf caged, bound by a collar of chain filled my lucid dreams. He paced and pulled on the cruel tether, growling and biting at the links, which merely vanished into a mist he couldn't penetrate. He did not sense the hart or other members of his pack.

A noise woke me instantly. Relaxed I was not.

A strange snuffling and shuffling filtered through the

heavy door, before a key turned in an unseen lock. It finally opened and a small stooped man waddled in carrying a tray. My mouth filled with saliva. He placed the tray on the chair and I moved off the bed, causing him to shuffle backward quickly.

His legs were squat and stout. His arms were also short and his fingers stubby. His face appeared half formed. One side might be called handsome, the other drooped and bone masses under the surface almost hid his eye while showing his teeth. His body looked twisted under the natural coloured wool robe. He wheezed as he moved.

"It's alright," I said. "Please don't be scared. I'm not going to hurt you." Even I didn't believe me. I don't have a very sympathetic tone. He merely grunted and left, the key turning quickly. "So much for making friends," I muttered, moving to the tray.

I considered the plate. No doubt I'd eaten worse but it was hard to remember when. I did like the look of the large jug of water though and drank several cupfuls quickly. That instantly woke my bladder up. I peered under the bed and breathed a sigh of relief. A covered bucket squatted under it. I picked up the wooden spoon and the bread. The coarse flour did not bode well. The thick, almost cake like pottage appeared to be made of something grey, which might once have been peas and beans. Still, a warrior lives on his stomach and I needed food. I dug in and tried to think about roast swan from Camelot's kitchen.

Meal thankfully over, I returned to my bed and waited. The light did not change outside my room but I grew tired so slept again briefly. The snuffling noise returned and the strange dwarf man returned to remove the plate, jug of water and soil pan. He left a washbowl and rough towel. He grunted and pointed at the robe, pulling on his own.

"You want me to wear that?" I asked considering how it would feel next to my skin.

He grunted and shuffled off. Out of sheer boredom, I undressed, washed and changed into the robe. Just as I thought, the damn thing itched and scratched. "What is this? Fucking goat's hair?" I moaned. I hooked it off my back, the scars sensitive to harsh treatment even after all these years, and slipped my shirt back on. The tails covered my arse and genitals, making life more comfortable.

I'd just arranged everything to my satisfaction when the door opened. The Shuffle man, which is how I considered him already in lieu of a name, stood and gestured me to follow. I obliged, curiosity once more motivating me. It shouldn't have; the corridors we used were all the same, grey stone everywhere and no decoration. No windows either and I soon lost my sense of direction with the twisting and turning nature of our shuffling amble. Eventually, we came to a new door. The swirling patterns carved on the surface were very fey and my heart ached suddenly for Rafe's fine home. Shuffle knocked, twisted the large handle and waddled inside. I followed, my eyes instantly drawn to the fireplace and its welcome warmth.

The Lady of the Lake stood to one side of the fire, the flames colouring her pale skin and the heated air moving her black hair. The mantle of the fire rose above her head. She really was very small. The room, overly large and cavernous, contained little furniture and nothing of personal interest. The walls were the same grey stone. There were no tapestries and few candles or torches, leaving great swathes of space in darkness. There were no other doors I could see and a great chair, heavy and dark with age, sat to the right of the hearth. The chair appeared to be carved from the roots of a mighty tree, the seat and arms worn smooth but the rest rough. She did not turn when we entered and Shuffle wobbled toward her, bent his knee and almost grovelled on the floor. She ignored his presence.

"When you are in my company you will kneel," she said quietly. Her voice contained a strange quality. I heard it deep inside my mind and through my ears with a slight delay.

I did not like to kneel to anyone but Arthur and instantly felt my hackles rise. I heard a slight snap of fingers a moment before searing pain felled me. I found myself on my knees before a pair of very small black slippers.

"When you are in my company, you kneel," she said, her tone once more quiet but extremely firm.

I gritted my teeth and rose to one knee, my right, not the way I would kneel before my King. "Yes, my Lady," I said as calmly as my hammering heart would allow.

She shifted her feet slightly as though her body relaxed now she had my acquiescence on this small matter.

"How do you find your room?" she asked.

"Sparse, my Lady," I said tonelessly.

She made a small sound, "It will help to focus your mind on what is important."

I made no comment, there didn't seem much point. Only Arthur mattered.

She paced for a while and I let the fire work its magic on cold muscles. Even kneeling as I was, I felt relief from the stiffness incurred through the fight.

"You are to become my personal guard," she announced suddenly. "You are meant to be the best but I will make you better. You will study and train when you are not needed for other duties. I plan to forge you into a weapon beyond even Excalibur."

I opened my mouth to say I could not be a better warrior, then realised it was not true. I could always be better. "As you wish, my Lady," I said. "There is just one boon I would ask," I said and finally raised my head. She stood over me but it felt like looking into a child's face. Her features were small and perfect. Her mouth a red bud in her snow white flesh. Her black eyes pits into places I did not want to visit but her nose was small and delicate. Her skin appeared untouched by time or blemish.

Her eyes narrowed with contempt when she realised what I would ask. "Your love for your King disgusts me, so no, you cannot have contact or see him. I will break you of such disgusting lusts and this will forge you into the most powerful of weapons."

A chill swept over me and clutched at a place deep in my guts. Nausea made me weak. Arthur and I were never challenged about our love, no one would dare. I'd almost forgotten how perverse many considered our relationship. I wanted to rise up and lash out, I wanted to destroy the vow I made to this woman and I wanted to return to Arthur.

I felt a hand on the back of my head, small fingers tangled through the mess of rough strands. "If you leave or rebel against me," her hand tightened viciously on my hair and she twisted my head to the fire. The other rose slowly and an image grew inside the flames. I did see Arthur. He sat up in his bed, pale but whole and talked with Geraint. There were tears on his cheeks. The Lady's hand, reaching toward the flames, closed. Arthur clutched his chest, his eyes widening. Geraint rose, yelling, he knocked over his stool reaching for my King. I whimpered. The Lady continued her lesson, "If you do not obey me, Lancelot du Lac, I will crush his heart. I have you both now, thanks to the power inside Excalibur and the healing. Fight me and he will die. Obey me and he will live." Her voice never rose but the strange echo inside my head felt like needles inside my brain.

"I understand, my Lady. Please, I beg you, release him." I choked out the words and watched the image fade as Arthur relaxed, free of pain.

She released my hair and patted the top of my head. "Good. I am glad you understand, Lancelot. Rebel and he will die. Fail and he will die. Succeed, he will live and you will return to him in a year."

"Thank you, my Lady," I said through gritted teeth.

"Leave now." She waved a small hand once more and Shuffle came toward me. He beckoned and I saw a look of deep sympathy in his one good eye.

The Lady of the Lake turned her back and I fought my instinct to think about how efficiently I might kill that small body. I stood, bowed and followed Shuffle out of cavernous room. When the door swung shut behind us, I reached for his good shoulder, pulling him to a stop. He flinched and cowered, whimpering in distress. I released him in surprise. Shuffle gambolled away from me and stood well out of arms reach, staring up at me with a reproachful look in his eyes.

I'd kicked a puppy. "Sorry, I didn't mean to frighten you," I said.

I knelt down so the crown of my head sat below his own. He blinked, his good eye a beautiful shade of green. "Please, I just want to talk. I want to understand."

He sighed, a shifting of his uneven shoulders and opened his mouth. I stared between stained teeth and saw the terrible stump, which once was a tongue.

"Fuck," I cursed.

Shuffle closed his mouth and turned away from me. He walked slowly down the long hallway we'd used earlier. The Lady, it seemed, liked her men quiet and well trained. I rose slowly off my knees and followed Shuffle thinking hard. I realised I'd saved Arthur's life from the wounds he'd received but left him terribly vulnerable to my own weaknesses. If I wanted Arthur to live, I'd need to become whatever kind of man this woman wanted me to be and obey her orders.

CHAPTER SIX

Shuffle turned left at some point and we ambled into a large yard. I breathed deeply, outside for the first time but it didn't smell or feel like outside. The sky remained a strange shade of blue green, which filtered throughout the atmosphere, tinting everything. It smelt like a tide withdrawn from the shore and the cold air bit viciously at my bare skin under the robe. The yard consisted of grey stone and almost completely blank walls. They rose high overhead, maybe thirty feet and looked smooth. I wouldn't want to have to climb them. In the yard, I found a large range of training equipment. Dummies made of straw and wood, with swords, spears, mace, war axe and other weapons, which must be fey because I'd never seen them before.

There were other items clearly designed to improve balance, core strength and agility. I realised The Lady really did plan on making me the best of warriors. I sighed heavily. I enjoyed training, but this looked more like slow torture and I wasn't eighteen anymore.

I heard a noise from behind me, instantly bringing my senses onto full alert. I stepped forward and turned in the same movement. A sword hissed through the air where my head had been moments before. A man, dressed in black leather and fur, recovered quickly and lunged the point of the blade at my chest. I dropped and rolled to the side, toward the swords. As I rose, I pulled the nearest out of the rack. A short stumpy blade but sharp on both edges and well balanced. I'd seen similar in the Land of the Dead. The fight began in earnest. The man did not speak but attacked remorselessly. I'd never fought anyone so damned fast and I found myself scrambling trying to fend him off, my breath coming in short gasps. A nasty feint to my knees forced me off balance. My opponent caught my timing perfectly, switched the direction of his blade and slashed open my chest in one movement. The shallow cut instantly filled with blood.

I regained my balance and prepared to fight on but he stepped back, well out of reach and dropped his sword before turning to his right.

"I cannot teach him. He knows nothing." The man's voice held a strong accent, making his words dance and slide. His dismissal of my abilities stung far more than the cut on my chest.

I looked to the direction he'd spat his words. A balcony rose above the training ground. The Lady stood there; she'd been watching the fight.

Her cold gaze didn't waver. "He is the best they have, make him better," she said. "Do whatever is necessary."

The man sighed deeply, clearly in despair. "This will not work, he is too old. He is too slow and weak. He lacks everything I demand in a student."

"Erm," I said, about to defend my honour.

"Silence," they both barked.

The Lady remained quiet for some time and I wondered what my fate might be. I almost hoped for kitchen duty if it meant I didn't have to train with this freak of nature. I studied the man who'd beaten me so soundly. Smaller than me by a good two hands and clearly strong under the clothing, but not bulky. More like Captain Moran without the scars. His hair shone almost green in the strange light because it was actually white. Not white through age though, I think it had always sat on his head like a drift of snow. His eyes were grey and his skin held no real colour either. Against the black of his clothing, he appeared a shadow of himself. His hands were small and I realised the blade he'd used to defeat me resembled the one we'd had made for Kadien, long but narrow and lighter than anything I would use.

The Lady finally passed her verdict, "You will train him and if he fails at any point I will send him to my farms to serve out his time with me."

My new instructor did not appear pleased but he bowed saying, "As you wish, Lady."

Frankly, I didn't think a farm would be a bad thing. I almost said so until the Lady of the Lake addressed me, "Lancelot du Lac, if you fail in the tasks you are set you will be sent from this place to my farms. I farm only one thing, ore from the earth herself. It burns through the fey forced into servitude. You will last longer than most. You might even survive the year, but you will not be the man you are now. Think well on this when next you fail." She turned her back and left the balcony.

"You will call me, Sir," my instructor said. "And now we train."

He swiped the sword from my hand and picked up a wooden blade. It felt heavy and I guessed the core contained lead. He pointed to the tallest wooden dummy. "Show me a reason I shouldn't feel anything other than complete contempt for you."

Damn me, he reminded me of my step-father. I walked to the dummy and began to practice sword forms, weaving the blade to strike knees, thighs, waist and head. I combined these with thrusts to the major organs.

The Bastard began shouting orders. "Relax your shoulders; relax your hips and flow into each strike; soften your knees, you look like a stork. Use your body not just your arms you clot," and so forth. I'd been training all my life; I did all the things he asked but somehow my versions were not good enough. In no time he'd taken the sword from my hands and we'd begun open hand training. I found myself trying to punch through a slightly padded wooden board nailed to a stone wall. My right hand soon started to swell and I knew the bones were close to breaking. I tried to explain the damage but he simply ignored me and threatened to fail me. I knew if I failed, Arthur would die. My knuckles split again but the bones remained intact even as he pointed me to a rough tree trunk.

"This you will lift and carry," he said. "Twenty circuits of the arena twice daily."

I looked at the tree. Long, wide and obviously carved in such a way it would fit over my shoulders and behind my head. Fine and dandy in theory but I doubted I'd even be able to lift the bloody thing.

If I failed, Camelot failed, my Wolf Pack failed. I am the best Camelot has to offer and this jumped up prick deemed me worthless.

I allowed the thoughts to fill me with a familiar anger I used when I'd been a child and a squire before I'd met Arthur and he'd learnt to harness my temper to his advantage. Pride would force me to succeed even where my body wanted to fail. Spirit over everything that represented weakness.

The vast log sat on low wooden posts. I knelt before the centre of the trunk, then half crawled under it, setting it on my shoulders. The rough surface forced itself and the wool of my habit into the sensitive skin. I braced my arms against the floor and heaved. The stone moved off the platform and I forced one knee under me while my arms and hands braced against the wood, preventing it falling off my back. I took a breath and heaved upward. Me and the wood rose. I grunted. I walked.

Each step became a lesson in patience and endurance. The weight sought to drive me into the ground constantly, while my bones wanted to break and my muscles collapse. I discovered twenty laps of the arena meant more than one thousand steps and the more exhausted I became, the shorter the steps. Sweat poured out of me and my legs became as weak as reeds. When I finished the last step and looked at the low platforms I realised I'd need to kneel in a controlled way to ensure I'd pick up the trunk the following day. Slowly, my limbs quivering, I lowered myself to my left knee, then to all fours before releasing the weight of the wood.

I almost collapsed in a panting mess before I heard a grunt behind me, "At least you can lift heavy things, even if you are shit at everything else."

The Bastard walked off without a backward glance and left the arena. I growled and struggled out from under the stone. Shuffle appeared with a jug of water and a cup. I dismissed the cup and drank from the jug. He also handed me a rough towel.

"Thanks," I said, my voice as rough as the bark on the trunk. "He's right you know, I am too fucking old for this," I complained.

Shuffle made no comment but touched his heart and his head.

"I know, it's all about my intentions," I said. Sadness overwhelmed me and I lowered myself to the ground beside Shuffle. I sighed heavily. "And for Camelot my intentions are always the best."

We stayed in the training yard until I felt able to walk without passing out. Shuffle led me from there back to my room. Water for bathing, cold of course, and fresh clothes. A rough set of brown woollen doublet and hose as well as another habit and two shirts. Shuffle picked up the hose and began miming a fight. He looked so funny gambolling about as if he held a sword, I couldn't help but laugh. He grinned at me when I did and then pulled at the robe and mimed reading, eating, sleeping, talking.

I nodded. "Alright, I understand, the robe for everything but the fighting with Sir Bastard."

Shuffle's left eye widened in shock before he fell about laughing in silent mirth. I grinned watching him and wished he could answer the thousand questions burning inside my head. When he finished he bowed to me and mimed stuffing food in his mouth.

"I wait here for food?" I asked.

He nodded and vanished.

As I stripped, washed the shallow cut across my chest and started counting the bruises, I felt my muscles beginning to stiffen. I'd be in poor shape tomorrow and I really didn't want to face another day like today. My knuckles were bleeding slowly and my right hand hurt so much I could no longer make a fist. Trying to hold that weighted sword would be almost impossible. I slung on a clean shirt and the robe before sitting on my cot.

"I wonder what the damned farm really is like," I contemplated aloud. "Mining iron can't be worse than is going to feel by morning."

Shuffle opened the door and held a tray up. I think he

tried to appear embarrassed by his meagre offering, but to be honest his expressions were somewhat limited.

I dug at the grey mess. "A soldier fights on his stomach. This shit is going to kill me faster than her Ladyship."

Shuffle mimed me eating and I forced a mouthful down. He appeared satisfied and left me alone. I did eat the damned stuff and the bread. Then I lay on my cot and tried to think through my sorry predicament. The Lady of the Lake clearly wanted me to achieve some task, which would involve me being a better fighter than I currently appeared to be, but why? What could it benefit her to have me fighting for her rather than a thousand other fey warriors? Being half fey meant I might be stronger and faster than the average man, but I wasn't anything that special. I just worked damned hard to accomplish my goals.

"And why does the woman hate my relationship with Arthur so much?" I asked my grey stone ceiling. I thought about the terms she'd used to define me and it made my stomach clench in anger. I'd doubtless fucked more women than she'd had decent meals if her current menu was anything to go by, so branding me as some kind of pervert stung. Besides, even if I were only attracted to men, what the hell did it have to do with her?

"Maybe she just needs a good rutting herself," I mused with a sense of righteous anger. So long as she didn't want me for the job.

Knowing what I faced the next day made me tense and I missed Arthur terribly. I also missed Tancred, but I'd grown used to that ache over the months. I forced my mind to concentrate on the work Sir Bastard would expect from me the following day and eventually I slept.

The wolf raced through green fields toward a line of trees. The sun was warm on my dark fur and the wind held ten thousand smells of air and earth. My tongue lolled out of my mouth and I ran, for sheer joy, I ran.

Two strong smells hit me at once. I stopped, my claws digging to the ground and my back legs skidding up to my front so I sat with a thump. On one side I scented the white hart, my companion and the one which I'd sworn to protect.

The other side, the long missed scent of the brown wolf. True pack mate. I whined, uncertain of my path and deeply confused. Nothing else changed but the smells, each grew stronger, but the sun shone the same, and the wind blew. No clouds gathered to indicate danger, no warning sounds. I lay down in the long grass and tried to decide which direction would be best, the white hart, or the brown wolf.

A sense of urgency filled me, making it impossible to remain still. The dream wanted a decision. It wanted me to choose in which direction I truly wanted to go. I shook myself, turned to the left and raced off. I didn't think, I followed my instincts. A league, perhaps more, vanished under my racing paws. The land sloped downward and small trees began to appear. I realised I ran into a wooded dell, a sheltered dip in the landscape. Slowing, trotting now, I yipped a welcome, the scent almost overwhelming me. A brown wolf walked out of the birch trees and sat, his head cocked to one side. I approached but his lips drew back and a low growl issued from his throat. I backed off in surprise. I lay down in the grass and whined. The brown wolf stood and walked toward me. I crawled forward on my belly and rolled over. As the alpha, I shouldn't have to make such a display but his anger shocked me and I didn't want to fight him. I wanted to hunt with him, race through the warm sunshine and sleep in a bundle of warm fur.

He approached and sniffed my neck. His breath tickled my ears as it huffed out of his nose. I raised my muzzle and licked his mouth. The brown wolf whined and within moments we were play fighting, rolling around, until arms held me not paws and skin not fur rubbed against my back and belly.

Tancred lay in my surprised arms. We rolled once more and I gazed down into his deep brown eyes. He looked as perfect as the day I'd returned to Camelot and used him to find Moran, after Guinevere's rape. No scars trailed over his skin. My fingers brushed through his long rich brown hair.

Words were not exchanged. There were none in this dream world. I bent my head and we kissed. A long, lingering kiss of forbidden passion. My mouth devoured him and my tongue sought to possess him. His hands roved over my body and I realised I no longer bore my scars. We were perfectly formed in this place of dreams. I moved down his neck and he writhed under the touch of my lips and teeth. I bit the sweet spot, which always melted him and he cried out his desire. My hand trailed over his hips, down his thigh and circled back up. When I cupped his balls, his back arched pushing his engorged phallus toward me. I swiftly bent my head and licked the sensitive head. His fingers dug into my back and ribs where he held me and when I plunged over his member his body grew limp but his breath came in short pants. I sucked, licked and nibbled until my own desire drove me to the point of madness.

I crawled up my lover's body and we kissed once more. Tancred held my head and pushed me back slightly. He stared into my eyes, assessing, seeking the answers to unspoken questions. I gazed back, trying to give him the answers he needed. I was here, with him, not the white hart.

He smiled as benediction. I'd answered his questions. I'd allayed his fears. I'd convinced him that I loved him. Tancred raised his knees either side of my hips and I kissed him as our dream selves became one. I pushed into his body and bowed my back pulling my lips from his mouth. He threw his head back and I lowered mine to his neck. His hands were on my backside, his fingers digging into the muscles. He pushed up with his hips, his solid phallus trapped between our stomachs. When his fingers dug in even harder and pulled, I found myself deep inside my lover and desperate to tear myself open so I could hold all of him at once inside my own body. I loved him.

The rhythm built slowly, the desire long in the making. He remained under me, subject to me. I stayed close to him, our bodies locked tight, hardly moving in some ways, but so deeply entwined in others that just the smallest of movements made us quiver and groan. The deeper I drove into him the more I needed him to remain in my life.

His lips sought mine and we kissed with breathless passion. We moved faster, Tancred forcing his body to join with mine, faster and harder. He started to grow even more tense. His body locked under me and I felt him frantically try to use me to give him his release. I shifted my weight onto my elbow, twisted slightly, making him cry out, and grasped his torment firmly. He raised his head and bit into my shoulder. The pain drove me beyond sanity. My hand moved in time with my hips. I shuddered within heartbeats and the desire pulsed through me, through Tancred and blossomed outward into the world surrounding our dream selves. All the colours became brighter, the sun on my back warmer, the world just that bit more perfect.

I cradled Tancred in my arms and we both wept gently.

I woke, the light inside my cell only slightly darker. Night lay around me and I was alone, the mess on my belly shaming and amusing me in equal measure until loneliness and loss overwhelmed me and my aching body. I remembered every moment of the dream and how the black wolf chose Tancred over Arthur. The ache in my heart soon brought tears. This was not unusual and something I hid from my King. The few nights we'd spent together since our defeat of Aeddan didn't involve a great deal of sleeping. The tears released something just as profound as the orgasm and I slept once more.

A shift in the air near my face woke me suddenly and I reacted badly. Shuffle found himself pressed hard against the opposite wall with his feet dangling off the ground.

I dropped him. "Sorry," I said backing off from the look of terror on his face. "Sorry, you startled me. I didn't mean to hurt you."

He nodded but I saw tears in his strange eyes as he straightened his clothes. He pointed to the tray he'd placed on the floor by my bed. He'd brought more of the grey mess, more bread but also a small lump of cheese. I bent and picked it up, then sniffed it carefully. My mouth watered instantly. I love cheese.

"You stole this for me didn't you?" I asked.

He managed a half smile and a brief nod but didn't really look at me. I sat on the floor and broke the piece of cheese in half. I really needed an ally. "Here, I shouldn't think your diet is any better than mine." His company would be preferable to thinking about why the wolf chose Tancred over Arthur in my dreams.

Shuffle looked at the cheese and his good eye widened a great deal. He made some strange smacking noise with his lips as he reached out to take the offering. I broke the bread in half and handed him that too. We both ended up sat on the floor sharing my small meal. Watching him eat didn't help my appetite but it did help our relationship. When he pointed to my hose and doublet, I groaned and he patted my arm. He left for a short time, obviously wanting to give me privacy in which to change, before returning to escort me to the training arena.

Sir Bastard stood waiting for me. He said nothing but looked at me with contempt and pointed to the wooden beam. I thought about rushing him and biting out his throat. Instead I bowed my head, approached the tree trunk and realised pain is not just in the mind. When I'd been sharing my breakfast with Shuffle I'd managed to forget how much my back, legs and arms hurt. When I heaved that damned piece of tree off its pedestals, I thought I'd black out with the agony forced through my body. The first step left me gasping in shock. The hundredth actually made me puke with that burden still on my back. By my tenth trip round the arena my mind vanished in a haze reminiscent of the one I found the day I'd received my punishment almost ten years before. My only goal became survival, which meant I did not want to pass out with the heavy beam landing on my back or my head. I lost count of the steps and the circuits.

"Finish now," barked Sir Bastard, who'd spent the entire time lounging against a pillar.

The words penetrated my brain but I didn't manage to lower the wood. When I tried to kneel, my muscles gave way under the weight and I toppled forward. The trunk caught the back of my head even as I tried to compensate for the movement. The world shot to black.

CHAPTER SEVEN

I awoke with a pounding headache making me groan before the rest of my body informed me it also no longer wanted to associate with me. A cold cloth covered my brow and rough palms were rubbing my hands and arms. I opened my eyes. Shuffle sat beside my small cot and the smell of some noxious ointment hit my nose. I groaned again. He patted my bare chest and rubbed some more goo into my skin. He then raised my head off the hard mattress and placed another cloth under me. The old one he threw in the corner, where it joined others covered in blood.

He patted my cheek and lifted a cup to my lips. It contained something other than water. Brandy and some herbs. I drank it down gratefully and just let the strange little man rub the warming balm into my limbs.

I must have slept again. The next time I woke properly The Lady stood over me and Shuffle crouched in the corner with his head down.

"It seems I overestimated you," she said. Her black eyes and cold expression reminded me of something. Oh, yes, Death.

I'd had enough by now and welcomed the thought of mining iron if it'd mean I leave this place. "No, my Lady, you did not. What you failed to do is to take into account my human heritage but I have never yet met a fey who could have done what I have accomplished now and in the past," I said. I struggled upright, the room spinning so badly I groaned and fought the urge to vomit at her feet.

"You are weak," she informed me.

"No, I am not," I said, the words grinding like millstones. "I am just not able to sustain that level of training at this point. In six months, with patience, I will be able to do exactly what you want but right now, I cannot. If you want to make me the best there is then you need to find me the right trainer. One who will understand my strengths, see my weaknesses and encourage me to become the warrior you demand. There is no point to breaking me beyond repair."

"You are weak and I despise you for it. Fail me again and I will have you flogged," she said.

"That'll be a pleasant change," I muttered as she swept from the room. Shuffle cowered in the corner until the door closed. He then approached and took my right hand.

I wondered what the hell he wanted until he closed my fingers. They formed a fist. They made a fist and they didn't hurt. I experimented some more, then I moved my arm and the solid wall of agony inside my muscles now felt like a slight ache. I laughed.

"I owe you a debt of gratitude so big," I said, almost willing to kiss the ugly face. I stood and although the concussion made me unsteady, with Shuffle's help I moved well enough. "You, little man, are magic," I told my companion. He grinned up at me happily.

The rest of that day, I concentrated on easing my muscles and sleeping. I also avoided thinking about the dream, which shattered what little peace I found in sitting still. The light outside my small window never changed but Shuffle returned with more pottage and this time meat had been included.

"Your doing?" I asked.

He shook his head and pointed upward before making his hands mime someone talking.

I nodded. "Orders from above," I said and he nodded. "I guess she doesn't actually want me dead then."

Shuffle nodded and patted my arm. He disappeared before I could share my meal with him and I found the food itself more palatable. I slept well that night and did not dream.

I woke before Shuffle arrived and he looked pleased to see me up and dressed. I ate quickly and an egg size lump on the back of my head remained my only reminder of the previous day's events. We left my room and I walked with determination to conquer Sir Bastard's games. However, when we reached the training ground, I found the Bastard a somewhat different man. His pallor had been enhanced by a huge purple bruise on his cheek. He walked with a slight hitch in his step and his breathing sounded laboured.

"Today we will focus on something new," he said. I didn't speak. "Today we will work on trying to teach your stupid legs to move in the correct manner."

I followed his instructions and endured his poking at my legs and arms when I didn't move smoothly enough, all with a glad and light heart. I almost lunged for him when he smacked me across the shins for doing something wrong but then I caught sight of his bruise and my heart swelled. Clearly, her Ladyship didn't like his teaching methods and had decided to modify them in her own way. It made me happy to know I wasn't the only victim.

That day I actually found myself learning a great deal from Sir Bastard. He finally proved himself to be a good teacher now he'd lost the ego games and I demonstrated to him I could be a good student. He still moaned at me but I realised the more he bitched the better I became and the more interest he took, which meant more bitching but it did prove I wasn't the failure he assumed.

The strange days continued. The training gradually increased my core strength, my agility and further increased my speed. I began to mark the days off on the leg of my bed with a piece of stone I'd found in the yard and smuggled back to my cell. A full month passed. Then one day the route changed. At lunchtime, which I ate alone in the training ground, Shuffle appeared.

We'd been gradually building a sign language between us and he mimed our sign for The Lady, his fingers in a steeple, to indicate someone higher up the food chain than we were and then sweeping his fingers down and out to display a skirt. This meant The Lady, not Sir Bastard. I still hadn't been told any names and no one spoke to me about anything other than training. I didn't even know where I was in Albion and the damned light never changed. We also didn't have weather, just cold and slightly damp smelly air.

"I'm guessing this is important," I said, standing instantly.

Shuffle nodded and tugged on my arm. I started to walk. "I'll go ahead and meet you in my room," I said, breaking into a run. I'd not seen The Lady since the incident with the tree trunk but I knew she'd want me in the robe, so I needed to change. I began undressing even as I ran and flung my sweaty shirt onto the bed. My muscle tone had changed and the shallow cut across my chest left yet another scar, my hair had grown again and I'd begun tying it back. I'd become heavier with muscle but they were long and lean. I'd also lost my body fat. Arthur would be pleased.

Shuffle finally arrived panting and heaving just as I finished dressing. We then headed off for my appointment moving at Shuffle's pace. I'd asked him once if he actually had a true name, he shrugged which seemed a strange response. I told him how I thought about him and he nodded, smiling shyly, so Shuffle became official.

We were soon in hallways I didn't know, which made me wonder what was changing. Over the last month I'd become calmer in my spirit. When I realised I could not affect my existence through anything other than obeying my new overlords I simply relaxed. The fate of the soldier is always down to two things, their own skill and the intelligence of their leaders. Suddenly not dealing with the day to day stresses of Camelot and the Wolf Pack freed me up to become a simple knight once more, focused only on fighting. Worms in my belly informed me I didn't actually want that to change. Did I now prefer the life I'd found here rather than the one I'd sacrificed in Camelot?

I shied away from such thoughts.

Shuffle stopped in front of a large door very similar to the one leading into The Lady's main hall. The carvings were beautiful. I'd been away from works of art for weeks and somehow the images of curling, spiralling trees and flowers drew me in and left me wanting to caress the wood. My companion clearly didn't share my sentiments. He banged on the door and opened it instantly before scurrying through. I followed at a more sedate pace and found myself in a library.

The room, almost half the size of Arthur's throne room,

heaved with books and scrolls. I'd never seen so many in one place and they were all neatly shelved. Shuffle led me through two large bookcases and around a corner. The only open space in the room held a small fireplace, a table, chair and The Lady.

I followed Shuffle's example and dropped to my right knee before her, with my head bowed.

"Lancelot du Lac," her voice echoed inside my head and her contempt leaked all over me. God, she made me feel worthless. "It is time to begin your next stage in training. You are, apparently, showing progress in the arts of war." This was news to me. Only that morning Sir Bastard had smacked me so hard with his fucking stick he'd broken it over my shoulders. The Lady continued, "Now you will learn the arts of the mind. You will need to be able to think, not just kill."

"As you wish, my Lady," I said. The woman clearly had a plan for me.

"You will now study in the afternoons under my tutelage. We will examine everything from simple tactics, to how the mind works and how to take advantage of your enemies' weaknesses before they are even aware of them." She said all this while pacing in front of me. Her energy always felt restless and aggressive.

"As you wish, my Lady, but the life of a squire does involve learning a great deal from books." I didn't add that these were the bits I avoided at every opportunity. The idea of spending every afternoon locked up in the library with this woman, being forced to study, did not make me a happy boy.

A small hand whipped out and grabbed my chin. She forced my head up and I stared into her black eyes, they acted like perfect mirrors. With her small nose just a hand's width away from my own and her grip crushing my jaw she hissed, "You will learn, stupid half breed."

I tried to say 'yes' and I tried to nod, but her fingers were crushing my jaw. When she relented and let go I almost fainted with gratitude.

So began my lessons in rhetoric, literature, arithmetic,

logic, grammar, geometry, astronomy and everything else she could throw at me. Shuffle sat in the corner by the fire and merely watched as I tried to master the deeper meaning behind ancient scribes, both human and fey. The didactic aspects of our lessons involved her using every opportunity to point out my obvious weaknesses and how my feelings of love for Guinevere as a married woman, then her husband were both wrong and brought me low. How I weakened myself and the pure balance within my soul. If I rose above the cheap desires of my body, I would become a titan among men. It wasn't just sex with men she didn't like, it was sex full stop. Besides, I knew a titan, my small charge Rhea, and she didn't seem to disapprove of my love life. Nevertheless, I just allowed her opinions to rush over me and I tried hard not to allow them to steal the fragile peace I'd found in coming to terms with the strange sensations of loving a man.

When these abusive tirades against Arthur, Guinevere, or my more dissolute recreational activities became too much to bear, I retreated into memories. The longest, sustained and most peaceful relationship I'd ever managed had been with Tancred. I wrapped myself up in those memories frequently and they kept me company during long hours of sword forms and studying in my own cramped cell. She decided to give me a desk and chair in my room and every evening, after a second bout of training with Sir Bastard, I'd find work to do; either copying text, solving problems or writing my own assessment on some classical work. Shuffle would sit with me and sharpen quills, or try to help by pointing out some key passage in a text, which meant I unravelled the problems presented. He actually had a sharp mind and I often thought he'd make a much better student than me.

More weeks past with this new routine and I found myself, after nine months, becoming an even stronger version of myself. I did not allow The Lady to destroy the parts of me I'd rebuilt after my madness but I did find I could layer new thoughts and ideas onto that sound structure. I realised she wanted even more of the perfect weapon than Arthur had ever demanded. She wanted a stone hearted killer with the mind of the finest politician. A general on the field of battle and a skilled negotiator in the courtroom. I'd never bothered with politics before; that was the field of battle for Arthur and Geraint, but now I found a new taste for the cleverness of subtle manipulation. I understood why Arthur grew excited when he'd start to close some deal with the merchants in Camelot that would save his coffers while improving the lives of the poor. The joy I felt in the heat of battle, he felt in deals with foreign powers.

After nine months, however, my confinement changed forever and I once more found myself the victim of other people's desires.

CHAPTER EIGHT

I returned from training with Sir Bastard one drab, unchanging morning and found Shuffle in my room. He'd not watched my performance that day, which I regretted because I'd actually managed to knock the fatuous bastard off his feet for the first time. I stopped whistling as I saw the look of panic on my friend's face.

"What's wrong?" I asked, my recent victory gone from my mind.

Shuffle wobbled from one foot to the other and he pulled on my arm asking me to sit. I sat and tried to remain patient. Shuffle made the sign for The Lady.

"What about her?" I asked.

Shuffle made his fingers walk along my palm.

"She's leaving?" I asked. Hope lifted my heart.

Shuffle pointed to me and made the sign for her Ladyship once more.

"We are both leaving?" I asked. Shuffle nodded sadly. "Where are we going?"

He thought about how to explain something so complex. He gave up and moved to my desk. He picked up the quill and made a few scratches, I looked at the paper he held up. "Court? We are going to Court?" I asked.

He nodded and made more scratches. I rose and watched in horror as he told me everything he knew.

The words were quick and the thoughts incomplete, but we didn't need long sentences. I picked up the piece of vellum, the words drying slowly in the damp air.

I said aloud, "She is going to Court to challenge for the throne of Albion and I am her Champion, that's what she's wanted me for, that and the bloodline of Aeddan." The last part I added myself, thinking five steps ahead of Shuffle for a change. He bumped his head with the heel of his hand to say, 'Of course'. "As Champion I will have to fight," I said. "I will have to stand against the best Albion has to offer."

Shuffle nodded slowly and stroked my hand, clearly worried about my fate.

"It's alright, my friend, all this time and energy she's invested in me had to be for something other than the good of my health."

My companion nodded and set about scraping his scribbles off my vellum so neither of us would bring down her Ladyship's wrath by wasting materials. I thought about what he'd told me. The Lady of the Lake wanted to become Queen of Albion. There was an interesting slant. I didn't like my half-brother's chances if that ever happened. Compassion was not something she'd ever displayed and her intolerance of the fey capacity to enjoy themselves had become legendary in my mind. The many rants I'd endured, I now understood with great clarity. She'd been using me as an audience to help her organise her own thoughts and feelings. After all, I'd never seen anyone other than Shuffle and my tutors in all the months I'd been locked away. She'd clearly needed someone to act as an audience.

Shuffle pulled on my arm and pointed to my robe. "Alright, I'll change," I said. I guessed she'd announce the new objectives at some point. He always left hurriedly when I began stripping off my clothing, so I changed and waited for his return, forcing my mind to stillness. I had to admit I was excited at the prospect of entering the fray once more and even more excited with the possibility of seeing people, of talking to others and maybe finding some news about Arthur or even Tancred. I thought, in those few moments between Shuffle telling me my fate and us arriving at The Lady's main hall, I'd had a pretty good day.

When we reached the hall, the door stood open and no fire burned in the grate. The Lady stood in her customary place but now wore a cloak of black fur over her plain white dress. Her fine, long black hair had been caught back in a net of silver and sat in a puddle at the bottom of her shoulders. She did look beautiful. Cold, distant, but very beautiful.

I decided I needed to get laid rather badly if her Ladyship caused my neglected manhood to twitch.

"Lancelot du Lac," she said. I'd learnt she only ever used my full name when she wanted me to understand something profound. I dropped to one knee hoping to stave off one of her painful lessons, which usually had me rolling on the floor clutching my head as she stuck invisible needles into my brain.

"My Lady," I intoned gravely.

"We are leaving. We are heading for the capital. I need you to understand several points, which will be vital to your survival." I loved being right; even she'd become predictable. The Lady waved her hand and fire engulfed the hearth. It blew out into the room making me flinch and Shuffle cower. When the flames settled, I found myself looking into Arthur's private rooms. His golden head was bent over his desk and he studied some kind of paper with a glassy, bored expression. My heart plunged at the sight and tears stung my eyes instantly. I dared make no sound but every fibre in my body and soul ached to reach out and touch that familiar face.

A hand rapped me soundly across the back of my head. "Listen to me, fool," The Lady snapped. I realised she'd been speaking and I'd missed every word. I tried to focus on the here and now even as I watched Arthur rise and move slowly toward the window looking out over a wintry Camelot. He appeared tired.

"I need you to obey every order I give you when we leave here and I am not convinced of your ability to do as you are told." The Lady came to stand before me, blocking my view of Arthur. I frowned up at her and she slapped me hard across the face hard enough to send me sprawling. Shocked and hurt, I found myself lying on the stone floor looking up as she placed her small foot on my throat. "Pay attention, Lancelot du Lac, you are now under a geis. Do you understand what that means?" she asked.

I tried to nod even as she pushed her foot into my throat making me gurgle. A geis is a spell, a special one designed only for the person targeted, and it stays until a task is completed.

"I want the throne of Albion. I want to free my land of

the disgusting waste and depraved behaviour tolerated under your dissolute father. I want structure, order, the rule of law and I want morals to become the bedrock of my world. You are going to give me that throne by being the weapon I need to destroy everyone else, but I have no wish for it to be known I am using a feckless half breed bastard of Aeddan's to accomplish this task. I have no wish for your skill at stealing Aeddan's Grail to be known or your part in his death. I have no wish for your association with Arthur or Camelot to be known. You are to be anonymous. You are to be nothing but my weapon, my sword, my Excalibur." Her black eyes shone with a light I'd never seen. She appeared almost feral. "To this end I place this geis on you, Knight of Camelot. If you utter one sound, even of pain or pleasure from this moment on, your King will die and you will remain with me here forever, just like my pet over there." She pointed to Shuffle who now sat on the floor with his back to us and rocked quietly. I suddenly had a terrible thought; Shuffle was once just like me.

The Lady smiled. "I see you understand your fate, Sir Lancelot du Lac, should you fail to give me the throne as that miserable creature did once long ago…" she allowed the words to hang.

I opened my mouth and a sound of protest rose to my lips when I watched the image of Arthur waver in the fire and he clutched his chest, grabbing the wall with his free hand. I snapped my mouth closed and he took a deep breath. I saw his lips call for Merlin and confusion fill his gaze. I saw the word 'Wolf' form on his lips before he vanished, the fire gone as quickly as it appeared.

"Silence, Lancelot du Lac, silence in vast quantities and for a very long time," she whispered. Her foot released my throat but I did not move, merely watched as she drove her point home with words full of spite. "I have trained you solely for this purpose. There will be a medley between Champions, then a series of tests for the mind, body, spirit and heart. Finally you will face single combat in the arena. You will win, Lancelot du Lac. You will give me the throne of Albion and I will be Queen." She turned, sweeping from the room before I recovered.

I levered myself off the ground and rubbed my throat as Shuffle approached. The twisted body flinched when I touched his shoulder but he soon turned at my gentle tug. He flung himself into my arms and I found him hugging the life out of me. I wanted to tell him all would be well but I couldn't. I wanted to ask how he'd failed and how long he'd been her slave. I want to ask so many questions which I should have thought about before. Shuffle though pulled back and placed a twisted finger on my lips before shaking his head. Then he made talking movements with his hand. I nodded. No words would pass between us. Through a series of gestures he made me realise if I did speak she'd cut out my tongue as the next stage. Then she'd begin breaking my body.

Shuffle actually held my hand as we returned to my room. I don't know if it was for his comfort or my own. I also didn't know how to ask him if he would accompany us to Court.

When I reached my cell, I found new clothes waiting. These were beautiful. Heavy black leather hose, knee length black boots, black velvet shirt with a doublet once more in heavy black leather. The neck fastened high and the whole thing was covered in The Lady's signature motif of interwoven trees and flowers. It had been subtly embossed onto the surface. I felt like I wore a suit of armour when I finally finished dressing. There were gloves and the whole thing fit me like a second skin. I felt quite dashing by the time I tied all the laces and buckles. A long black scarf also lay on my bed but when I picked it up, I had no idea what to do with the thing. Shuffle appeared like magic at my door. His dark hair was even more of matted mess than normal. I hardly noticed his physical ugliness these days and only saw the gentle soul who still helped rub ointments into my cramping hands.

When he saw me dressed, tears rose in his eyes and he nodded approval, I smiled and opened my mouth to say thanks when a look of horror swept over his face. The brief moment deflated us both. I shrugged and tried for a rueful expression. He nodded slowly and picked up the scarf, then tugged on my arm to force me to sit. He picked up the scarf and held it firmly in front of me. I watched his mouth move. "Pay Attention," he said silently.

I nodded.

He then proceeded to wrap the long soft cloth around my head, covering my hair and most of my face. The cloth felt delicate and I found I breathed through it well enough but it held a strange quality. Off my face, it felt like any other length of silk, but when it touched my skin, it stuck to me. Not painfully and I found myself able to drag it off, but a slight resistance met my hands. It certainly helped to keep my mouth closed and my lips sealed.

So, this is how The Lady planned on keeping me anonymous.

Between the clothing and after nine months of training with Sir Bastard, I now moved slightly differently and held myself in a less solid stance. I flowed more than walked and blended with my environment. A new man indeed and one few would recognise without voice or face.

When I'd dressed to Shuffle's satisfaction he led me through the hallways of The Lady's home and I found we were going to yet another new section of the palace. We were going up.

The corridors slopped upward until we came to small door through which Shuffle vanished. I bowed low and followed. When I straightened, I saw Shuffle begin climbing a spiral stone staircase, much like the ones at home. I'd only ever been to four parts of my prison and from those I could not see the rest of The Lady's estate. However this new environment quickly grew boring. The grey stone remained the same as the walls and floor of my cell and there were no windows, only the cursed greenish blue light filtering from who knew where, and countless bloody steps. I began to feel quite giddy until I heard Shuffle's laboured breathing and realised his poor tortured body would not be enjoying the constant stepping when he only relied on one good leg most of the time. I'd have helped him but the steps were too narrow for such gestures.

Soon enough, though, we emerged and I finally found something to really make me speechless.

The strange light cast over my world for nine months now lit something I could hardly comprehend. We stood on a tall round tower, about twenty feet in diameter and two hundred feet high. It rose above the rest of The Lady's home, which spread out under the tower's watchful gaze. Crenellated walls surrounded the large compound, as if she considered a siege possible. Inside these walls were squat buildings and smaller yards like the one she'd had me use for training. I saw people moving around but I'd never met anyone else other than Shuffle during my stay here. All the buildings were of grey stone with rough slate roofs and I didn't see any trees, nor a blade of grass. The Lady's main building once more followed the same pattern of squat grey stone but long corridors joined the separate parts together. The whole structure sat on the top of a long stone hill and water surrounded it completely. What really took my breath away, though, was the sky. I finally understood where I'd been living. The sky moved, it rippled along a huge domed invisible barrier.

I touched Shuffle's shoulder and pointed up. He half smiled and nodded making wave-like movements with his hand, then holding his nose as if drowning. We were under water. The Lady of the Lake held such powerful magic she lived under water in a castle even more aggressive than Camelot. If escape had entered my head, I could not have left the safety of her magic without drowning. I also now understood the never changing atmosphere and light. She held the whole structure in a permanent stasis.

I took a deep breath and considered the implications. Not only was this woman more powerful than Aeddan appeared to be without the Grail, she'd trained me to become the best warrior I'd ever been, and I'd been good before.

Shuffle and I sat on the ground and I watched the sky. My new clothes were restrictive but I guessed the leather would soften soon enough. Gradually, equipment began to appear at the doorway to the tower's roof. I still didn't see anyone carrying it up but Shuffle pulled me and we began moving it into a pile in the centre. Heavy chests, a sack full of armour, which I wanted to examine but Shuffle slapped my hands, and all manner of furniture, books and rugs. I'd never seen anything resembling decoration while moving around the few places to which I had access, but The Lady clearly wanted to make an impression when we reached the Court.

When I began to think the stuff would tumble off the sides of the tower we stacked it so high, The Lady appeared. I wondered how many horses and carts we'd need to transport this lot and how long we'd be on the road. I had no reference for the size of Albion and the few times I'd tried to talk to Merlin about it he'd been evasive.

The Lady looked hard at me, then walked around as if inspecting a horse. "Good, you appear to be suitably imposing. You are my personal guard and champion, do not let me down."

I inclined my head in understanding.

"The only time you may utter a word is in my presence and if I snap my fingers, thus," she clicked her small fingers. "This will enable you to speak without endangering your sovereign."

"Thank you, my Lady," I said, my words already feeling strange just as they had when Tancred first appeared in my forest.

She snapped her fingers once more. "This means you cannot speak." She walked right up to me and I gazed into her shiny black eyes. Her white skin glowed almost green in the light but she was truly beautiful. Tiny hands rested on my chest. I couldn't really feel them through the thick leather clothing but whenever she came close I found myself in great pain. My heart raced in anticipation.

"You and I," she said quietly, "can achieve great things." She patted my chest and smiled, her teeth very slight sharp on the ends.

Without warning she whipped around, caught hold of Shuffle by the hair, me by my hand and the world went dark.

CHAPTER NINE

I awoke face down on cold marble. My senses rushed back quickly and my training brought me to my feet even before I focused on my surroundings. I need not have worried. The Lady stepped gently over the surface of a pool before holding out her hand toward me. The water lapped slightly against a low wall and I guessed she wanted help over the edge. I obliged, though I had no doubt she really didn't need my help. We were alone in a circular room made entirely of smooth white marble. Shuffle appeared from behind the pile of our belongings but he maintained his air of dignified terror around The Lady.

We and all our belongings were dry. The Lady approached the bag full of armour and reached inside. When she withdrew her hand, she held a sword. I'd not noticed it earlier, which made me think it may not have been there. It shone in the pale light from windows high in the walls. The scabbard was simple and black leather. The hilt was also black but the pommel and quillions were bright shining steel and perfectly plain.

"You will need this," The Lady said, handing the sword over to me. I heard a rush of footsteps behind us and drew the blade. It came from the scabbard silently and I fell in love instantly. A long broadsword, weighted perfectly, slightly narrower than the one I'd left in Camelot but double edged and I watched the light dance on watermarks left in the steel. She reminded me of Excalibur.

"The blade is called, Caliburn. See to it you do her justice," The Lady said as a dozen armed guards rushed into the room from three arched doorways.

They came with drawn blades, aiming for The Lady. I stood in front of her alone. My weight shifted onto my toes and my knees softened. Caliburn and I became one being and I became the pure weapon she demanded. The first attacker to reach me aimed for my head. I swept the blade down and blended around his body, turning toward the next man and taking his throat before he'd even begun his attack. From behind my first enemy, I reversed Caliburn and thrust backward even as I kicked out sideways to break the next man's knee. He screamed and fell, tripping another man rushing forward. Caliburn twisted inside my hand as I brought her forward and she followed the man down, cutting through the back of his neck. Blood began to make the marble slippery but it didn't stop me moving and dancing. I finally began to understand Arthur's joy when he fought with Excalibur. The blade hummed inside my mind and blended with my every thought and purpose.

"Halt this insanity," bellowed a harsh female voice. One I recognised.

"Do as she asks," came The Lady's voice inside my mind.

I obeyed instantly and retreated to my Lady's side. Shuffle handed me the scabbard and a belt to buckle around my waist. The Lady held out a cloth. I took it and wiped the blade clean of blood. She did not look at me. We both watched Nimue walk toward us. Her flaming red hair waved around her body, a living cloud of fire. She wore a dress of deepest red, which hung from a broach on one shoulder leaving the other bare.

"Cousin," she said more calmly. "We were not expecting you."

The Lady smiled. "I would have said you were, bearing in mind the reception committee."

Nimue's eyes narrowed. "My men are here only to protect the Court and its people during this difficult time of transition. If you had contacted us we would have prepared for your arrival."

"Doubtless," The Lady said. "Now, I assume my rooms are still my own and you haven't taken them as well as Aeddan's crown without asking."

Nimue's pouting mouth thinned considerably. "I have not taken the throne. I have merely held the reins while we waited for the right time before choosing a new leader. The death of my poor husband left me grief stricken but I have risen above that to serve Albion."

The Lady actually snorted. "Grief stricken," she mocked. "The only things stopping you throwing a party at his death, dear cousin, were the instant challenges to your authority from your foul children and his bastards."

I felt grateful for the cloth hiding my identity and protecting me from Nimue's machinations. I had to say time did her no harm; she still looked beautiful and unchanging.

"The important thing now," Nimue said, "is that you are here to throw away yet another lone Champion in an attempt to make us all as miserable as yourself." The spite coming from the Fey Queen shocked me. As siblings they clearly were not close. Nimue didn't bother waiting for a reply. She merely turned on her heel and left the room, taking her remaining five bodyguards with her. I'd despatched seven without a moment's hesitation.

Death surrounded me and I'd not even thought to do anything other than kill the men rushing into attack. I closed my eyes and prayed I wouldn't be forced to face these men in my dreams. I'd promised myself when I'd rejoined the Wolf Pack I would seek alternatives to the death stroke if I felt able. It seemed The Lady's training had forced that vow from my heart. Or maybe Arthur was right all those years ago when he named me his sword, maybe I would always be a stone cold killer and I just had to learn to live with the consequences.

"Come," The Lady announced, stepping over the puddles of blood and guts surrounding her as if they were piles of mud. Shuffle and I moved off after her, leaving our belongings on the floor.

The room through which we'd entered the palace proved to be a main gateway for those fey who preferred to travel by magic and water. The Lady's rooms were near this preferred porthole but for the first time in months, I saw the sky and felt the sun.

We walked through a series of open corridors, one side solid white stone, the other large archways open to green spaces beyond. Delicate filigrees of stone decorated each arch and benches made from twisted wood sat scattered through the gardens. Flowers shocked my eyes with bright colours and the sight of a large tree shading one area filled my heart until I thought it would burst. I wanted to run onto the grass and dig my fingers in the dark soil. I wanted to smell the bark of the tree and bury my face in the delicate petals of the flowers. The blue of the sky looked like Guinevere's eyes and there were clouds, big puffy white ones hovering overhead. I heard bird song and realised all those times I'd imagined being with Tancred in my wood I'd also been finding comfort in my memories of real life. Even with the forced march The Lady set, I managed to take deep breaths of life into my tired lungs and it made me smile. Even if I killed half of Albion to give this woman the throne, I would not have to kill the half that really mattered. We rounded one corner and the sun graced us. Both Shuffle and I paused for half a step to turn our faces into the light.

Pain shot through my head and Shuffle whimpered. The Lady did not want to indulge our desires. I focused, grabbed Shuffle by his shoulder and dragged him behind us.

We reached a door, pale white wood but covered in familiar carvings, and I moved to twist the latch. One of the things The Lady forced me to learn was my place in her world. I need to anticipate even the smallest event, opening doors being one of them. It was annoying. I didn't mind doing it to be polite, but if she reached it before me and then punished me for not getting there first what was the point? The damned woman was stronger than me anyway.

The door swung inward on silent hinges and she walked in followed by her entourage. Shuffle and I stood and stared. We'd been surrounded by grey stone and green filtered light for so long, I think we'd both forgotten what colour could do. Light washed in through large windows filled with glass. At last I'd be warm, I thought. The glass was clearer than anything we produced in Camelot in such quantities. The view might not have been terribly special to most people but to me it held enchantments beyond words. A stretch of thirty feet of lawn ended with a hedge in full white blossom. Hawthorn, a springtime snow. Also, covering the lawn and under the tall hedge were hundreds of yellow flowers, small pale primrose, which smiled shyly at the sky. Inside the rooms living vines covered the stonework, long green tendrils sought new paths and each plant was smothered in small white flowers. The air held the scent of jasmine. I frowned; even I knew you couldn't have jasmine, primroses and hawthorn all in bloom at the same time but I remembered from the short time we'd spent at Rafe's, such things were possible in Albion under the fey guidance.

I heard the riotous cacophony of sparrows nearby but I also heard The Lady roundly curse the birds. "Damnable noise," she muttered, flicking her small fingers at the vines. The room we'd entered was clearly meant for entertainment. Low divans in pale silks with bright cushions lined the walls, there were low chairs and tables also in pale colours. A fireplace, the mantle in dark twisting wood, acted as a centrepiece and I even noticed a lyre propped up in the corner behind the door.

Before I'd really managed to appreciate this new environment of simple design and colour it grew busy with servants and belongings. The Lady directed things like a general directing his army from a hilltop and I found myself being bullied by some officious little man with brown walnut skin who wanted to show me my own room.

We walked through a room that reminded me of Guinevere's suite but with less colour and into a small back bedroom. There were two doors, one into what would clearly be The Lady's bedchamber and a room with a garderobe. I would not be able to leave the room but through her bedchamber and I knew she'd act as an excellent guard. I did, however, have my own large glass window and jasmine plant. The rest of the room contained two large single beds and places to stow things. Shuffle came in and nodded vigorously, clearly happy with the accommodation. I watched a young woman, insanely petite and gloriously dark, try to carry in my armour. I crossed the room and lifted the pack effortlessly out of her arms. At first, her dark eyes widened in shock, then she smiled. I hoped my eyes smiled back at her, the further darkening of her cheeks implied it worked. I wondered what she tasted like; she smelt of heaven.

When I placed the large linen bag on the floor, I stood before her and bowed my thanks in a grand gesture. She giggled and bobbed a curtsy. Agony shot through my head. I tried to scream but the cloth around my mouth kept me conscious of my predicament and I bit back the cry even as I collapsed onto the floor. Shuffle moaned and scooted away from my convulsing body. The ripples of pain made me twitch and gasp trying to breath.

When I opened my eyes, I stared at two small feet in black velvet slippers. "You are not here to be distracted by the local wildlife," The Lady said, with no hint of the malice I felt inside my mind.

Once more humiliated by her strength, I forced my twitching body off the ground and onto my right knee. I bowed my head in obedience and carefully schooled the thoughts, which screamed at me to kill. Three more months and I could return to Camelot, my ever present mantra.

She walked away from me without another word and Shuffle approached. He helped me stand and move to the bed, then sat me down. I watched with dull eyes while he unpacked our belongings and found a home for everything. By the time he'd finished, the room hardly appeared to contain anything which wasn't there before our arrival.

"Champion," the summons came not to my ears but directly into my head. I winced, the headache she'd induced still pounding. After checking the scarf around my face, I rose and entered her bedchamber.

She looked at me with disdain, "We are to be present at a banquet. I want you properly armed. There is no necessity for the plate or for mail, but you will carry Caliburn and anything else you deem appropriate. I will expect you to maintain vigilance and to keep your ears open to gossip which may prove useful to our task."

I bowed my understanding and tried to squash the desire to wring her neck. When I retreated to my own room I found Shuffle with various knives laid on the bed. I picked up a long dagger and threaded it through the belt, holding the sword so they complemented each other. I then pushed two knives, which were weighted for throwing, into the top of my boots. I placed another short blade into the top of my hose at the small of my back to sit flat across by pelvis and one I threaded through a leather thong to hang under my clothing around my neck. Once done, Shuffle handed me my gloves and patted my arm in consolation. I raised a half smile.

I knocked on our door and she gave me leave to enter her room. I found her finishing her hair. No servants were present but long smooth locks of black hair wove themselves around and pins of pearl and silver held them in place against her scalp. At least half her hair now formed a complex pattern against her head. She also wore a new dress. Almost transparent, it shimmered silver with veins of deepest blue. When she rose, she pointed to a cloak of white fur.

I lifted it and placed it gently on her shoulders as she fixed the clasp. I was not permitted such personal service apparently. Her beauty made my loins stir but my heart remained cold.

We left her rooms without a word and I followed her with my hand on my sword hilt. The whole palace teamed with life and I watched those around me far more than was polite. Just as when Arthur and I first arrived here, I saw all manner of beings in all colours, shapes and temperaments. To see so much life after months of isolation left me a little giddy. Eventually, after a long walk through many hallways all decorated in live vines and complex carvings, we reached a mammoth doorway that stood open. We crossed the entrance and fortunately The Lady paused long enough for me to enjoy the view.

The place heaved with people. Most of them were tall, like Rafe or Kadien. Some were small like The Lady. All were beautiful in ways which left me hungry but somehow unsatisfied. I realised my instincts disliked their expressions. They were cold, calculating and distant. I'd seen Guinevere look like that when she used to plot against Arthur. I followed The Lady and began to see the difference between the Champions, who were men and women dressed in armour like me, and those vying for the throne who were richly dressed like The Lady. My mind began assessing my enemies.

A movement close to my left, a man coming toward us quickly and obliquely. My right hand half drew my sword and my left did draw my knife. I stepped between the movement encroaching on us and The Lady. She saw my change in stance and paused. I finally focused on the person descending on our position. I almost yelped in surprise.

CHAPTER TEN

Rafe bowed low before The Lady. Graceful, tall and immaculate as always. I merely froze because coming in behind him was Tancred, dressed in black leather clothing like myself but with Rafe's designs on his leather. He looked wonderful. When I'd last seen him, he'd softened in Rafe's company. The hard lines of muscle he'd developed with the Wolf Pack were there but not as pronounced. I now saw he'd clearly been training as hard as myself. He'd filled out and his face had thinned. He'd also grown a short beard, which didn't obscure his jaw line but did make him appear harder. I lost everything around me but Tancred's presence. He noticed me staring immediately and a vague look of confusion filled his warm brown eyes but he didn't recognise me. How could he? I didn't recognise me with the scarf covering everything but my eyes.

I dragged my eyes off Tancred and tried to concentrate on Rafe's words.

"I hear your Champion has already made an impression on my mother," Rafe said good naturedly.

"Nimue has always been a wastrel," said The Lady.

"Doubtless your hunk of manhood here will prove his worth in such contests many times over," Rafe said, eyeing me speculatively.

"Don't be disgusting, Rafe," The Lady said, but her tone contained a softness as though she were genuinely fond of her nephew. "You are going to challenge?" She nodded toward Tancred.

My heart plunged. I knew I must kill all those sent against me; the last Champion standing was the one who gained the throne. I'd have to fight Tancred. I'd have to kill him. He looked at me, assessing me in a way I didn't need to assess him. I knew he'd be equal to me, we'd trained together so many times, but kill me? Could he do that for Rafe?

I watched the confusion in his eyes as he registered my panic. I tried to school my thoughts, worried about The Lady picking up on the silent screaming, but she seemed preoccupied with Rafe's conversation. Tancred would not expect to see panic in someone who knew their own skill in combat. Warriors did not panic. I dragged my mind out of its dark, dank well of terror. I realised Tancred now stared at my left hand, where it rested on Caliburn's hilt. His eyes narrowed and shot back up to mine. He blinked several times and opened his mouth.

I very slowly shook my head and placed my left hand out from my hilt, palm down, trying to tell him to have peace.

He glanced at Rafe and The Lady, who'd moved away from us slightly. Tancred approached and placed a hand on my right biceps. His voice hardly registered and he didn't stop moving as he circled me.

"I'm right aren't I?" he asked obliquely.

His presence melted me like nothing else could have done. I looked to the ground and felt tears fill my eyes. I'd been alone for a long time in enemy territory and this time it hadn't been by choice. Not really.

I managed to nod.

"Fuck," he breathed, moving past me and back to Rafe.

The Lady shot me a look. Her black eyes pierced my fragile shell. I snapped the entrance to my heart closed and gave back my best blank stare.

Fortunately for me, at that moment a huge gong sounded and everyone in the vast hall began to move toward the edges. Servants, more of the small brown fey, filed in carrying low tables and large cushions, which were almost chairs. These were arranged in a vast circle, no head, no foot. Very diplomatic. I caught sight of Nimue and Morgana. Rafe faded from The Lady's side and I watched Tancred try to speak with him. Rafe merely brushed Tancred to one side and I saw a very pretty boy step to his side. The boy wore the same colour robe Rafe wore. Tancred's face closed down. What was going on between them? They were supposed to be in love, bonded as I was to

Arthur, but Tancred's body language spoke to me of nothing but heartache and cold misery. I forced the confusion away, I had to concentrate on the present or I'd pay the price at The Lady's hand.

I finally looked in detail at the room itself. The walls were once more white marble and stone. The vines curved upward and swept toward the centre of the ceiling to tangle together and reach out once more toward the walls, in patterns too complex to follow. Every spare inch of the walls and ceiling were carved with a form of script I'd never seen before. A part of my recent re-education had been to learn the language of the fey, as they wrote it, but this looked different, far more flowing and artistic.

When the small brown fey had finished, taller more elegant fey arrived with food and wine. My mouth instantly watered. I'd been as deprived of variations in my diet as I had colour, sound and company. I also knew I'd not be eating anything. My place was to stand behind The Lady and guard her back as she began her political manoeuvring. I removed her cloak, gave her my hand and she lowered herself elegantly onto her seat. A lovely young girl arrived to begin serving food and wine. I stepped back a sword's length. On the other side of the room stood Tancred. We were almost opposite each other. His gaze never wavered from mine. I saw Rafe raise a small pipe to his lips and inhale something. So that's why he wasn't listening to Tancred. He was stoned. He shared his pipe with the young man who shared Rafe's chair. Tancred ignored them. He really did look wonderful. He'd cut his dark brown hair very short and with the small beard he appeared far more aggressive.

The ache in my heart and loins at the sight of him finally forced me to look away. I began to study those surrounding me. There were thirty people claiming a right to the throne. I'd learnt through my lessons that the Fey King had to be dead a year before a new leading family was chosen and they were chosen through combat and cunning. An election through brute strength, skill and ruthlessness. Behind each of the figures dining in luxury stood one to three

Champions. To have more than one Champion somehow constituted weakness; it meant you didn't have the confidence in just one person and equal confidence in your own ability to train and enhance that combatant. Ego and magic as far as I could tell.

Nimue, all sinuous grace, had a huge bear of a man behind her. He stood at least eight feet tall, with a heavy brow and long thick arms, but I saw the bright intelligent eyes. Morgana surprised me; a woman stood behind her, white blonde, tall and lithe like Kadien and even quicker I guessed. Other fey had men like me. One surprised me because he didn't look anything like the other fey, far more like me, a knight. A few more had women but none as beautiful as Morgana's offering. I hesitated for a moment over one Champion, who was half my height and almost as round. Then I watched, fascinated, as he flexed his stubby body and seemed to uncurl before my eyes. He eventually became a tall willowy man, nearly nine feet high and treelike in aspect. The woman sat at his feet was just as I remembered the woodland fey I'd glimpsed when I'd been with Else. There were also three warriors who were identical. Red eyes, very short but with mean faces. I remembered my teaching; these were special men, joined together to form one unit. Kill one and the others died but killing one was not a task to take on lightly. They operated with six eyes, six ears and six arms carrying weapons.

I couldn't hear most of the conversation but I knew The Lady would want a rundown of everything I'd learnt, so I filed away many observations and opinions in case she asked for them. I did not need another one of those bloody shocks.

The meal progressed and my stomach rumbled. I grew bored and watched Tancred. He kept glancing at Rafe, my friend's face growing darker with every puff on the pipe. I shifted my weight, my legs aching from being still for so long.

A small chime from one of the people around the hall made everyone silent in an instant. Clearly no one relaxed and forgot themselves at these parties. Nimue rose and smiled graciously. "I have an idea for entertainment," she said.

Glances were exchanged. "That is not the custom," someone said.

"No," Nimue agreed. "However, I thought we might like to make our own entertainment."

I knew what kind of games Nimue liked. It made my skin prickle and the wonderful smell of food in my nose suddenly turned sour.

"Come then, what is your idea?" Rafe asked.

"Why don't we start tomorrow's games a little early? Why don't we send our Champions into the fight right here and now? If one bleeds they are out. It doesn't have to be to the death but it would be fun to watch." Her fox-like eyes glittered. She liked her blood and she liked to watch people hurt each other.

"Isn't it rather redundant if we are to fight tomorrow?" someone said.

"But there is no harm and it will give us a chance to spar without serious blood letting. Look on this as an opportunity to exchange physical barbs, not just verbal. A new way for us to test each other before the real fight," she said reasonably.

My eyes locked to Tancred's. We were to fight.

"Teams," someone said. "Two teams, one side of the hall against the other. And not to first blood, to the death. When five on each side are dead we call a halt."

Tancred nodded. We'd fight together regardless. We didn't need to face each other tonight; we could defend each other and he could speak with Rafe later. Explain to him we could never face each other as enemies.

I nodded in return.

"For our honour then," The Lady said, waving me forward.

Servants appeared and strips of cloth were tied to our arms, fifteen red, fifteen green. We filed around the circle of diners, the tables were parted and we Champions filed into centre in two lines. Tancred ended up two away from me. We glanced at each other and he looked at the man to my left, I looked to his right. The first to die would be those separating us. Those with multiple Champions chose just one. We would lose as many as a third of the contestants for the throne. Nimue had done well, felling so many so fast. It would boost her own chances greatly. I looked at her monster sized Champion. I'd not want to fight him in a hurry. I wanted to watch how he fought so I'd find a way around his style before engaging him directly. The three women in the group I also didn't want to kill. Ridiculous I know, because they wouldn't have any scruples about ending my miserable life, but I'd spent my life protecting the fairer sex. Even watching Kadien made my blood go cold when I thought she'd lose a fight and I couldn't protect her.

The tall tree man would be another to avoid until necessary. I just had to fight and survive.

"You know the rules, five dead on one team and you stop," Nimue announced. "Begin," she said calmly.

I drew Caliburn and focused on reaching Tancred. Caliburn's beautiful song filled my head and I hardly felt her weight in my hands. My skills as a warrior took over. My first opponent rushed toward me screaming, I moved as if to deflect but used his own anger to cause the deflection to become a simultaneous attack. Ducking and spinning under his sword with frightening ease, I rose and Caliburn came with me to open up the man's stomach. Blood and guts spilled everywhere and the stink of battle filled my nose. I tried to swallow the blood lust coursing through my soul. If I lost myself to battle madness I would not stop at five, I'd kill them all because I wanted to be at home and I wanted peace. If I must kill to attain that peace then fine, but I would preserve life if possible.

"First blood to the The Lady," someone yelled.

I didn't stop. I saw Tancred. He pushed the corpse of a man wearing an armband the same colour as my own, off his sword with his foot. We came together, turned our backs to each other and fought for our lives in the centre of the medley. I don't know how long it took. I cannot judge time when I am fighting. I did find three dead bodies at my feet but Tancred and I had woven through and around each other constantly, so who dealt the killing blow I didn't know. We were both breathing hard but the light in his eyes made me smile. We'd not fought together in such a way for a very long time and it felt great. We were an even better team than we'd been in Camelot. We were better than I ever remembered being with Arthur.

The fight over, we knew we'd need to separate. We nodded, very obviously on show, and I backed off toward The Lady. Rafe stood and clapped his hands happily as Tancred joined him. He hugged Tancred but my friend remained stiff in his arms. I'd seen the flow of love between them when Rafe tied me to Arthur, why had it turned bitter?

The Lady rose and walked to my side. "Are you hurt?" she asked. I shook my head. A few bruises and one shallow slice on my upper arm. "Good, but I do not approve of you fighting with Rafe's disgusting popinjay. You will not act like that again. You know the end results of disobeying me."

God, I hated that small bundle of mean disgust. I was surprised she didn't realise I knew Tancred. She'd seen him at the lake side when she'd delivered Excalibur, but maybe he didn't register; people who were not important to her plans didn't mean much. We left the banquet without further conversation and returned to our rooms.

"You will stand guard until you are relieved," she informed me. I sighed quietly. I just wanted to sit down, drink a large glass of wine and have something to eat. Some nice soft bread, still warm from the oven and some cheese with ham and an apple. I missed apples.

I bowed and took up a position in front of her door. Time passed. Servants arrived to light torches against the growing darkness and one, with a flask of water in her arms, stopped before me. Her large luminous blue grey eyes smiled up at me, offering me a drink of water. I wondered if I could remove my scarf long enough to take a drink. I certainly needed it. Would The Lady know? I decided I didn't care. I pulled the mask down and the girl blushed at my smile of gratitude. I drank the water and as she removed my cup, I felt something being pressed into my palm. I frowned hard. She winked and walked off. I glanced behind me. The door remained firmly shut. I covered my face - no point in tempting fate - and looked at the contents of my hand.

A small piece of paper. Writing, Camelot's English, *Meet me if you can by the stables.*

CHAPTER ELEVEN

That's all, no signature. My stomach lurched. I wanted to run to the stables right now. My legs shook with the need to race to Tancred's side. I just had to hope he'd wait. Time crawled and I began to fidget. The door behind me opened and I spun around, drawing my knife. Me, on edge? Never.

Shuffle opened his mouth and jumped back. He held a small plate of food, which he almost dropped. I resheathed the knife and took the food. He pushed me toward the door. My turn to rest. I resisted. For the last, I didn't know how long, I'd been trying to think about how far I'd be able to trust Shuffle. I knew he cared for me and wanted to help me but The Lady terrified him into submission and he'd never protected me from her. I couldn't ask him to, but I needed him to cover me if I vanished to the stables for a short time.

Then inspiration struck. I pushed the food into Shuffle's surprised hands and vanished into the main room of The Lady's suite. She wasn't there so I risked knocking on the door to her bedchamber. I felt her call me inside my head and realised I needed to find a way to keep her from my more frantic thoughts. I pushed Tancred out and thought only about the lie I wanted to tell.

I walked in and instantly dropped to my knee, bowing my head before her. "You have done well, Lancelot du Lac, I cannot deny this. I am pleased," she said.

I wondered how to make her give me permission to speak. Raising my eyes, I pushed my fingers toward my mouth. Not a sound had I uttered. The thought of my weakness hurting Arthur enough to make me silent during the entire day's activities. She narrowed her eyes and clicked her fingers. "If you must, speak," she snapped, already cross.

"My Lady," I croaked and tried again. "My Lady, I have just finished guard duty but I feel uneasy about going to my rest without using all the skills you have taught me. I should ensure there are no enemies or spies near our apartments, and the journey toward the pool or the stables is clear. I need to see to any places we may be weak because of the layout of the palace. I do not want to make a mistake because I have not taken due care of you."

I watched her work through this assessment. I kept my mind clear of anything other than walking the corridors to ensure her safety.

"A wise move, Knight of Camelot. I will expect you back by the first bell." Her fingers clicked and I snapped my mouth shut, covering my face once more. I had no idea how long it was until the first bell but I could move bloody quickly when necessary.

I lost no time in leaving the apartment. I touched Shuffle's shoulder, stole some bread from his hand and made myself mime horses. Stupid and humiliating.

Shuffle grinned and pointed right, counted two and then left. He held his nose, I nodded, I'd follow my nose to the stables. I raced off. The corridors were still busy with people but mostly servants. I almost tripped over the girl who had brought me the message. When she'd recovered from being pushed over by someone almost twice her size and three times her weight, I bowed and asked clumsily for the horses. She nodded understanding and actually led the way. I could have kissed her.

When we reached the stables, I bowed low over her hand as though she were Guinevere and smiled. She giggled, even though she only had my eyes to give her the smile. I am good with women. Shame I can't keep one.

I began to walk among the horses and soon realised I'd left it too late. Tancred had left. I wanted to scream in frustration. Instead I punched a wooden wall and drove a hole straight through.

"You keep doing that and you'll break a fist, again," came a soft voice I knew well.

I turned and saw a black shadow pull away from a corner beside some hay bales. We stood for a moment, just looking. Something changed and in the space between one breath and the next and we were in each other's arms, embracing tightly. I held my old lover against my body and just inhaled his scent. I loved him no less than the day I'd left him with Rafe and I knew I missed him terribly. Tancred pulled back slightly but didn't let go. He reached up and touched the scarf.

"It's magic," he said in awe. "I can feel the power, but it is part of you, not her." He tugged on it and the cloth moved from my mouth, then he pushed it back from my head and my long hair tumbled out. He smiled and I saw the love in those dark eyes. I didn't know if I were allowed to kiss his full lips but he made the decision for me. The beard felt softer than my stubble and his calloused hands were rough against my scalp under my hair. The first brush was tentative but Tancred suddenly shifted against me and a hot passion I'd never felt from him burned into me. He wanted possession and I didn't have the wit to stop him or to figure out why he felt so desperate. We kissed deeply, his tongue a weapon in my mouth, claiming my heart.

When he pulled away at last, I removed my leather glove without leaving the circle of his arms. I traced his jaw and felt the strange prickly softness of his beard. It felt so different to the smooth lines I remembered.

He smiled. "I've missed you so much." He kissed the palm of my hand.

This confession surprised me and I found myself having to actively bite back the words I wanted to give in return. I wanted to tell him how my heart wept when I thought about him too much. How I'd ached during long lonely nights for his company. I wanted to tell him how many times I turned to tell him something, only to find him absent.

Instead, I nodded and smiled sadly taking his fingers to my lips and kissing the tips.

"Talk to me, love," Tancred requested softly.

I'd been dreading this part but I'd thought of a plan. I took his hand and pulled him the way Shuffle did when he needed me somewhere else. Tancred followed but I sensed his confusion and hesitation. I pulled him toward a covering yard, the place they take stallions to cover mares. The beauty of these places is the sand they use to keep the horses safe. Moonlight graced just enough of the sand for me to kneel and begin writing. Tancred came up behind me and read the words as they appeared in the sand.

"The Lady placed a spell," I began and he read, but continued without me. "That's why you can't speak?" he asked amazed. "That's why you made no noise during the fight?"

I nodded. He knelt beside me. "You can't talk at all?" he asked.

I made a shape with my hands, fingers pinched together then pulled a part. Tancred said, "No noise at all?"

I nodded.

"How did this happen?" he asked.

I wrote a single name. "Arthur."

Tancred sighed. "Why am I not surprised."

I smiled grimly, acknowledging my own stupidity. I needed to tell him I didn't have much time. I scribbled quickly and he waited until I'd finished.

"I only have until the first bell but I don't understand what that means. If I'm not back in time she may hurt Arthur or even kill him and I don't even want to think about what she will do to me," he read, squinting at some of my bad spelling.

"It's alright, my friend, they chime bells on the hour during the night here and we haven't had number twelve yet. I'll make sure you are home in time." He stroked my arm. "I can't believe you are here. I've dreamt of you so often."

I frowned and mouthed the word, 'Why'?

Tancred rose and I watched him pace, a nervous energy about him I'd never seen before. "It's hard here. Much worse than I ever thought. After living with you, being in Camelot, the trouble I'd faced with Aeddan began to fade."

I wondered if the scars had but I sat quietly, just listening.

"When you left I could not have loved Rafe with any more depth, but fealty is not something with which he is familiar and as soon as he was sure of me, he began to find other entertainments."

I heard a world of pain in my friend's voice. I knew the kind of entertainments Rafe enjoyed.

"I also realised I'd changed in the time I'd been away from him. I'd become stronger, and giving him the long term control he desired became increasingly difficult."

Tancred has a complex relationship with sex. He'd never been interested in women for a start, but he also needed someone to take control of him sometimes. I'd learnt that when he felt vulnerable, if I forced the sex to be rough, if I hurt him until he cried out, it released something in his mind. It gave him a level of relaxation and completeness I didn't really understand. I did understand he felt vulnerable afterward and I had to maintain his safety until he came back to normality, his barriers once more in place. Tancred, like his sister, is a natural healer making him deeply empathic. It meant he could be easily hurt. I'd left him with Rafe in the belief my dear half brother would care for him more effectively than me. Especially because I'd not been able to leave Arthur alone. Apparently, I'd done wrong, again.

"I am just not what he wants. A pretty little plaything. I am part of the Wolf Pack and one day Arthur might have made me Captain or even a knight."

I had no idea that's what he wanted.

"After a few months I grew bored and restless, so I began training and becoming fitter. I thought about you constantly, trying to remember how to fight the way you do to make certain I was improving, but the more I thought about you the more I missed you and the more I changed."

Yet another strange aspect to Tancred's ability and because of his full fey heritage, he actually morphs slightly into different physical versions of himself to please the person who loves him. Rafe likes his companions young and soft. I loved the warrior in my friend, so I guess he started to manifest that aspect. It would not have pleased my brother.

"The up shot of all this is Rafe and I are…" he paused and a anguish filled his eyes for a moment. "I'm not sure what we are, you saw his latest toy. But he does want the throne and he wants me to fight for him. When I tried to tell him you were here and I wasn't going to fight you..." his voice faded again and his eyes clouded.

I rose and reached for him, recognising the look. Tancred let me hold him as he whispered, "It's not the pain, it's the cruelty I can't stand."

I saw my brother's head on the end of spear.

"We should run," he said.

I pulled back and pointed to Arthur's name in the sand, shaking my head.

"I know, you can't run, you have to save Arthur and Camelot," the words were dull and tired on his tongue. I understood his grief all too well. Camelot always comes first and had wrecked our lives more than once.

"I cannot fight you to win against you," he said pressing his forehead against mine.

'And I would rather die than fight you, my love,' I vowed silently and knew I'd see to it.

CHAPTER TWELVE

"That's a little dramatic, Wolf. I'm sure we can come up with a better option," Tancred said.

I flinched at his words, the perfect companion to my own thoughts, and backed off in shock. Tancred let go of me, clearly just as confused.

"What happened?" he asked.

I shrugged. 'I have no idea, what did you do?' I asked, only inside my head.

He didn't respond to the question. I wondered if this worked the same way the spell did with Else, through touch. I reached for his face and lightly lay my hand on his cheek.

"Can you hear me?" I asked inside my head.

"I can now," he said aloud.

We both grinned like naughty children. "How is this possible?" I asked.

Tancred shrugged. "I've learnt to enhance my skills with regard to healing and we've always been close. But it might be your natural skill. You are the child of one of the most powerful fey ever known. Aeddan passed at least some of that on to you."

"I don't care, at least I can tell you how much I've missed you," I said.

Tancred lowered his eyes. "Really?" he asked. His doubt made me angry with myself.

"Damned right."

He sighed and turned away cutting off our talk. "I don't think I can cope with this right now. You showing up is just too much of a dream."

I took a firm hold on his wrist so he'd have to listen. "Come home with me to Camelot when this over and I will prove to you how real it can become," I said and not a thought of Arthur entered my head.

I pulled him hard against my body and kissed him roughly. He struggled for just a moment before his hands began pulling at my armour. When he couldn't reach my skin he broke off the kiss, pushed me against the wooden wall, setting off a slight booming which made me flinch, and kissed me even more desperately. His strength surprised me and left me gasping.

"Tancred, slow down," I said with my hand on the back of his neck.

"I need you," he said and his teeth explored my neck. I wanted to groan, loudly.

"Wait," I said, pushing him back and taking a deep breath. "Just hold on."

The last thought he didn't hear because he broke all physical contact with me and vanished into the deeper shadows at the back of the stall. "You don't want me," his distress shocked me.

I yanked at a few laces and pulled at some buckles. The breastplate came clear even as I walked toward him. I couldn't tell him what I wanted, but I could show him. I wrenched at my gambeson and shirt. They both tumbled to the sandy floor. Tancred's dark eyes flashed and he reached for me. We came together and his hands were on my starved skin. Rough, strong fingers dug into muscles and scars. I wanted to cry out, beg for mercy, beg for more. He turned me and pushed me into the wall once more. My forehead pressed into the rough wood and my hands splayed as he kicked at my ankles.

"Spread your legs," he ordered. I couldn't argue with him, he didn't touch bare skin, so he'd be unable to hear me. I did as instructed. He bit the muscle over my shoulder and his fingers dug into my waist. He licked and kissed and bit down my naked flesh, muttering repeatedly as if he was welcoming every scar back into his world. I surrendered until he said, "don't move."

His touch vanished and I found I could breathe. When he returned though I realised he'd stripped. His naked chest pushed against my back and he laid his head on my shoulder. I tried to turn but he held me still.

"I've been so alone," he whispered and shame washed over me, even as his hands crept around my waist to hold me. He finally relaxed enough and I squirmed. I held him in a lover's embrace. Soft, no demands, just comfort. His skin felt hot and rough against my chest. We were both bigger and fitter than we'd been previously. It felt wonderful, it also make my cock ache badly. I needed more now he'd started.

I nuzzled into his neck and he sighed. "Tancred, I need you," I said. His body turned to liquid in my arms, I'd found the sweet spot on his throat and abused it something chronic, to convince him to give into my demands.

He broke off contact with me and shook his head, trying to clear his thoughts and act rationally. "Rafe will know," he said.

I wanted to ask if that mattered, but he backed out of my reach when I tried to approach. "Don't, Lancelot. I need to think and I can never think when you are touching me like that. If I allow you close enough for us to fuck, I will lose Rafe for good and there is no guarantee you will be there to pick up the pieces. And there will be pieces, because Rafe will see to it." Tancred still breathed heavily and his scent laced the air with lust.

I wanted to moan in frustration. I needed him and I wanted him but he had a point. If we made love Rafe would know sooner or later, and Arthur's spectre writhed between us as a recrimination. I realised I now had a choice to make, Arthur or Tancred. Sane, lucid, with no pressure from Tancred, I had to choose and I had to stick to my decision. No more games, no more confusion, which one of these men did I want to fight for and love?

Arthur, my King. Next to Geraint, my oldest friend. We had so much history together it often bowed my shoulders and broke my sense of peace. It had even broken my mind. He'd taken Guinevere from me, ruined my relationship with Eleanor de Clare and then destroyed Tancred's love, twice. He'd demanded more from me than anyone else I'd ever met and what had I been given in return for decades of service? Words of love, words of possession and the occasional passionate night. He confided in me and used me as his confidant. The King of Camelot trusted me with his throne, his life and his family. He needed me at his side because I gave him strength, a strength I didn't understand. I loved him but it felt so distant, so ethereal.

Tancred, he stood for everything I'd ever wanted in a loving relationship. We were equals, companions and I missed him. His calm presence, his gentle mind and utter commitment to our love. He'd left me because Arthur pushed him so hard he'd been given no choice when we'd arrived in Albion to face Aeddan. Rafe gave him the sanctuary he desired from me but Rafe couldn't make him happy; my brother didn't understand the warrior in my friend. The man who would fight and die to save others. The man who wanted to live in peace but would destroy anyone who tried to take that peace away. He'd suffered unknown agonies to save my life and then return to my side. I didn't remember Arthur sacrificing anything for me.

I should never have left him. I did not regret the ties I had with Arthur through fey magic, but I should never have left Tancred. I loved him with a simple clarity. He'd never hurt me, only ever asked for my commitment and I'd let him down constantly.

With my hands out in a gesture of peace, I approached Tancred. I reached for his hand, the wooden ring on his finger no longer present. I'd need to fix that quickly.

"If my brother learns of our desire, our love before we are finished with this game, would that be so bad?" I asked. "Or do you have so little faith in our love?"

"Love?" he asked. The word dripped with bitterness. "I don't think I understand what that is any more." He tapped his head and a twisted smile appeared on his soft mouth. An alien expression I didn't like on my friend's face.

I rubbed my thumb against his lips, wiping out the misery. "Give me a second chance, Tancred. Let me prove to you that I love you, truly love you and that what happened with Arthur will never happen again. Let me make love to you, not just a quick fuck in a stable. We are worth more than that, you are worth more than that."

He trembled against my touch and I gradually pulled him into my embrace once more. I tried very hard not to remember how it felt to bury myself inside his strength and passion.

"A second chance," he whispered and he raised his lips to mine. We kissed softly and when he pulled away he said, "you won't get a third, Lancelot. I won't survive long enough. Do you understand?"

I did understand. I didn't like being threatened but I had the feeling Tancred didn't mean it to sound demanding, just honest.

"Just give me time, love, and I will convince you I am worth the heartache I've caused," I said, running my hands over his naked back and leather clad backside.

"But first we both have to survive," he said and I felt the shift inside his mind. He closed down his heart because he needed to protect himself. I wondered how much damage Rafe had done to twist him away from me so fast.

"We can fight as a team, we know that, even if her Ladyship doesn't like it," I said. "But we are nothing compared to the power The Lady and Rafe can exert. That woman would see me dead rather than in your arms."

He nodded. "I agree. We need an ally who is more powerful than both of us. We are nothing. We need to place someone else on the throne who can protect us both," Tancred said, making the leap from lover to warrior to statesman more easily than I usually managed.

"The only two people I know capable of taking on Rafe and The Lady are Nimue and Morgana," I said. "I'm certain I want neither of them on the throne of Albion if I'm to keep Camelot safe."

"But," Tancred said, turning slowly out of my grasp, "if we consider this carefully we might actually engineer something of a coup. Morgana is strong but her desire to see women raised up in Albion has led her to choosing a Champion either of us can kill. It wouldn't be easy but it is possible. If we agree to help Morgana reach for the throne then she protects us from the others and we have a chance."

I lay my fingertips on his chest. "How? We'd both be dead by then. If The Lady discovers any of this, our lives will be forfeit and so will Arthur's," I said, imagining the pain involved in The Lady turning me into Shuffle.

Tancred smiled. "I have freedom of movement beyond you. Leave it to me to find Morgana and talk to her. She doesn't know you are here and I have the feeling she'd like to really very badly."

"Why are we automatically choosing Morgana?" I asked.

Tancred looked at me aghast, "If we put The Lady on the throne everyone not conforming to her world view will die. If we put Nimue up there, she will be just as bad as Aeddan and Rafe will be worse; that would lead to civil war. I knew I would lose, I just wanted to choose when to die and by whose hand." Again the sadness leaked through his thoughts.

"Now you fight to live," I told him.

He raised a half smile. "Now, I fight to win."

CHAPTER THIRTEEN

Time proved the enemy that night. We were not able to complete our reunion before my deadline. Something fast and furious might have been possible but I think we both wanted more. We wanted time to caress, to relearn, to nurture; we wanted something special. Tancred redressed first himself and then me with slow deliberation. He touched and kissed often but my thoughts remained silent. We kissed for a long time.

When we finally left the covering yard, having raked out our footprints and writing in the sand, we didn't do anything other than share a simple embrace but just to be with him again, to smell him, hold him, it felt so right. I loved Arthur but he couldn't give me what I wanted and I wanted Tancred.

He covered my head and mouth with the scarf but I left my hand bare so I could speak with him easily. We agreed we'd fight together the following day and do whatever was necessary to reach Morgana. I'd try to return to the stable the next night so we could talk and plan. We walked quickly through the palace and Tancred left me at the corner so Shuffle didn't see us together. The palace still heaved with people and we dare not embrace.

"Stay safe, love," he said.

I touched his hand, "And you." I wanted to say so much more, but I didn't know where to begin.

We shared a final look before turning away. I forced him from my mind as I walked toward Shuffle. A single bell tolled and Shuffle's anxiety about my disappearance showed in his rocking from one foot to the other. I smiled a welcome and his relief was palpable. The door opened on cue and The Lady's face dropped at seeing me. I swept her a low bow and waited for orders.

"Any difficulties?" she asked.

I shook my head.

"You may retire." She stepped to one side and I walked to my room.

My restless mind roved over the events of the last day as I lay in bed staring at the ceiling. Chiefly my thoughts were those concerning how Tancred and I would make a deal with Morgana. Then I wondered how things would play out between him and me. Dwelling on this didn't seem wise so I forced my thoughts back to simple relief over finding him again. I missed my friend far more than I missed a lover.

The insistent hands pulling at my clothing made me wrench myself out of the sweetest dreams. Fortunately, I didn't make a sound. Shuffle half dragged me out of bed and began throwing clothes in my direction. I'd managed to strip off my leather armour but I'd slept in my shirt. My erection died painfully. Shuffle kept his back to me and I heard his strange gurgling language of frustration at my stupidity. I washed quickly and began dressing. I heard The Lady moving around next door and hurried to tie my laces. For the first time in months, I felt genuine excitement about facing the day.

I felt the summons in my head just as I secured the last tie. I walked to the antechamber and found The Lady stood before me in a dress of finest blood red silk, the kind of red you see when the blood is fresh. I'd never seen her wear anything but white or black and she looked even more terrifying than normal. I knelt waiting for orders.

"You are to face the trials today. It has been deemed that last night's display was the medley, therefore the timetable has been moved forward," her words cut through my plans to see Tancred on the battlefield. I'd hoped he'd have news from Morgana and we'd find a way to stop this madness before it grew worse.

"Your task today is to survive the four trials you will be expected to face," she informed me.

My stomach dropped. Mind you, that could have been hunger. I dreaded these trials more than the fighting. I liked to fight and I'm good at killing people. What I'm not good with is riddles and tests of the mind. I'm a little too straightforward and relied on Geraint and Arthur for those games. However, I knew Tancred would survive and that was more important than anything else.

"Come," she said and walked off.

She led me through a series of hallways, which turned into passages, then tunnels. We seemed to be travelling deeper and deeper underground, the floor of each branch becoming steeper, the walls rougher and narrower. A tunnel, which forced me to stoop and twist sideways my shoulders were so wide, spat us out into a cave. Nothing good had ever happened to me in a cave.

I sighed and took in my surroundings. The space was barely three paces wide and maybe five long. The ceiling rose high overhead, with a deep crevasse continuing upward. Five torches spat fitfully around the walls and three braziers encircled a tall triangular stone needle in the centre of the room. A skeletal man, with jet black skin and hair and eyes like nuggets of silver stepped forward. He wore no knife or sword.

He bowed. "My Lady, you are early."

"My Champion is keen to proceed," she said. Her imperious tone annoyed me so much.

"I'm sure he is," the sarcasm didn't raise a flicker from The Lady but I'm not certain it is something she's used to from those deemed inferior.

"Step forward, Knight of Camelot," said the man.

That did get a reaction. The Lady's breath hissed dangerously. The skeletal man chuckled. "You cannot have secrets from the Throne Keepers, my Lady."

I glanced at her but stepped forward. The man, slightly taller but less than half my width, looked me in the eyes. "Hmmm, secrets indeed," he murmured, and yet I felt nothing. No intrusion or ransacking of my private thoughts, nothing like I'd experienced with fey before. He merely nodded sagely and pointed toward the needle.

"On here, is the gateway to the first test and the clues you need in order to know what you will face. Seek your path carefully Champion," he intoned grimly.

The flickering light didn't help much but I stepped up to the monolith and instantly recognised the strange carvings.

Small notches in special formations of horizontal and vertical lines covered the sides of the triangle. Ogham, the language Geraint translated in the cave under the Tor, when we'd tried to save Arthur from Nimue. I hadn't understood a word then; now I not only recognised it, I could read it and interpret the hidden meanings behind the simple expressions used.

I ran my fingers over the markings, each symbol representing a concept through its association with an object. Anything from a tree, plant or animal, to gold or even an elbow. It is a simple language on the surface but to write a complex series of instructions, the creator must rely on the mysteries and myths behind the objects described. My mind raced. On one surface, it described the history behind the Champions fighting for the throne. It prevented civil war whenever the old king or queen died. The fey didn't really believe in direct succession. Whoever was strong enough took the throne. I dismissed this tangle of argument and justification for gladiatorial stupidity.

The next side proved more interesting and more personal. It spoke of the ash tree growing strong amid a vast forest of trees, sheltered by the mighty oak. It grew strong but never reached for its own light, until one day a man came and felled the mighty oak, leaving the ash to reach for sun and become the one to shelter those who lived within the forest. I stared at this for a long time and wondered if it meant Arthur would die because of me. I finally shook my head. The fey were forever trying to convince me I would hurt Arthur. That taking his place as King of Camelot remained my birthright or some such rubbish. I would never hurt Arthur and I never wanted the throne of Camelot. They could predict a disaster all they liked, it was never happening.

I moved on. The final side described a journey.

A journey which would begin in the mind, test the body, terrify the spirit and try to break the heart. The choices made would reflect the life described. The first door to the first test asked the Champion to find the correct path which would be used to test the mind.

I understood. I needed to find the glyph for the one being tested. The story described an ash tree. I needed the mark for niun, the mark of the ash.

I stepped back and nodded.

"You know the answer?" the skeletal man asked.

I nodded.

He frowned and turned to The Lady. "I cannot test him, score him and journey fairly with him if he cannot speak. Release the geis on his soul, my Lady."

"You will promise me he will remain separate from all other Champions?" she asked.

"No one but me will know you have Lancelot du Lac in your service," he replied coldly.

I liked this skeleton. The Lady clicked her fingers and I breathed easy, no longer responsible for Arthur's life quite so dramatically.

"Give me the answer, Knight," the man said.

I cleared my throat. "The -" even after so short a time my mouth didn't like forming words. I tried again, my voice rough, "The answer is niun." I gave the Ogham name for the ash.

"The reason?"

"The reason is simple. The story describes an oak, the king of trees and the ash, his companion. When the oak is gone, the ash must take his place and do his duty." I morphed the literal translation, looking for one which didn't make Arthur a victim. "Therefore, if there is a journey of the mind, the body, the spirit and the heart, designed to test the new leader of Albion, it must be the ash, the Tree of the World, because the oak in Albion is dead." I wanted points for tact at least.

The corner of the thin black man's mouth twitched. The spin I placed on what I'd read amused him. "Well said, Sir Knight. Go to find your niun." He waved to the blank wall ahead of me.

I walked toward it and peered carefully at the rough surface. There were no carvings, so how could I find a path through to the first test? Perhaps niun did not appear as a carving. I stepped back, pleased with my reasoning and the leaps of intuitive understanding I'd begun to demonstrate. I looked at the wall as a whole, just as you'd see a forest before looking for a tree. Once that idea formulated inside my mind, my eyes found the tree. The shadows from the torches threw shapes onto the wall and one of the shapes looked like an ash leaf. I stepped forward and touched the shadow. A small click sounded somewhere and a door opened. It would admit me perfectly.

"Once you enter here there is no returning unless you complete the tasks given. You can die in this place and each task must be performed within a certain time limit. There will be different ways of winning through, but some ways will help you more than others when you are free of this place. The more efficiently and correctly you accomplish each test, the more advantages you will have when facing your enemies in the next round," intoned the skeleton sagely.

I bowed acknowledgement. I did not look back at The Lady. I merely stepped through into another world.

CHAPTER FOURTEEN

At least I assumed it was another world. Everything around me became white. I saw no walls or floor but I did not fall. I turned my head to see the cave behind me, but no door existed. I looked at the skeleton.

"Where are we?" I asked.

"We are where we need to be," he replied.

I restrained myself from the obvious reply. Instead I asked, "Do you have a name?" I'd learnt it pays to be polite.

"Yes," he seemed to consider the answer. "You will call me Lugh."

"As in the god?" I asked suddenly wary.

He smiled, his teeth very white against his black skin. "As in the god."

I wondered if I really wanted to ask the next question, which would be, 'are you the god?' How would I feel if he said yes? I decided I didn't need to know and didn't want to know. It wouldn't help me in the here and now.

I held out my hand. "It is good to meet you, Lugh, and thank you for your compassion toward me with regard to The Lady."

He looked at my hand, tilted his head as though considering the implications of what a handshake meant, then took it. His grip felt dry, strong and his fingers were thin. "It is good to meet you, Lancelot du Lac."

"So," I said with confidence, "this is the test of the mind, the first on the list."

"It might be, I cannot say," Lugh said.

"Well, the first test was described by the word uath, which is hawthorn, and that is the first tree to flower in the spring," I said confidently.

Lugh smiled. "If you like."

I grunted at his evasion. "And as this is a journey there doesn't seem much point in standing still. You never reach the end of the journey by remaining in the same place." I walked forward and there, before me, the world fell away. The optical illusion made me rock forward on my toes because my eyes saw the ground vanish under me but my feet wanted to continue; their orders had been clear. I took a deep breath and tried to calm my racing heart so I might understand what I saw more clearly. We now stood at the top of a white cliff. I still couldn't see the sides but I did see a long way below me, a board laid out on the ground. A huge board with the traditional black and white squares, I didn't need to count them, there would be sixty four. My heart sank.

"A game of chess?" I asked.

"If that is what you see," said Lugh. "Spend time in taverns do you?" he asked. The favourite place to play in Camelot, even for knights.

I shot him a look but didn't reply. The game was an old one and yes, I had learnt it in the taverns. Geraint had tried to teach me, then Arthur. I preferred cards; the complexities of chess tended to drive me mad and it would certainly do as a test for the mind.

"Am I supposed to jump down there and find the pieces?" I asked.

"Do you think you should?" Lugh replied.

"That's going to become very annoying," I informed him.

He just laughed.

As I considered my options, I watched things shift around the edge of the huge board. It appeared that the ground became soft, like quicksand, but instead of sucking people in, it pushed people out. Some wore white; others wore black. There were sixteen of each.

"The people are the pieces," I said in awe. But they weren't just people. The pawns were men and women who had their hands tied behind their backs and ropes on their legs to shackle their movements. The other pieces who represented the grander aspects of humanity were treated even more shabbily. Each had been forced into an iron cage which resembled their piece in its design. They could shuffle around from square to square but they could not escape.

"What happens if I lose?" I asked.

"You will gain no points for this round and everyone will die," he said sweeping his arm out over the board. "If you win, half will die and you gain your points. If you stalemate you will gain points but again all will die."

"And I'm on a schedule," I said.

"Yes," he replied but didn't tell me what it was.

"Best I win then," I muttered.

I didn't know which side I was meant to be on but I thought about my favoured opening. A white 'pawn' moved two squares forward in the centre of the board.

"Guess I'm white," I said.

Black answered in the traditional manner.

"Who are those people?" I asked.

"Prisoners," Lugh said.

"And they will die if I lose?" I asked again.

"It is a game of war is it not? These are prisoners of war."

"Whose war?"

"Does it matter?"

"Maybe," I replied. I would like to know who I was saving and make certain they were worth it.

"So there are conditions on your compassion as a knight?" Lugh asked.

I remembered Arthur once trying to explain why all men should have the same justice regardless of rank. He'd fought long and hard against the stupidity of his court to win that argument.

"No, there are no conditions. I would choose to save them all but if I can only save half by winning, I shall do that," I said firmly, following Arthur's code.

"I believe it is your turn," Lugh said without comment.

I made my decision quickly. Geraint always said, 'seduce and attack', when it came to chess. I made my mind see the white knight, a poor man forced into the metal shell of a horse, come forward. The other pieces shuffled slightly to accommodate him. I would play the Ruy Lopez opening.

From here things moved quickly and I found my mind able to chase pieces five or six moves into the future. I'd never been able to maintain my focus like this. As predicted, black started to threaten my bishop with a pawn. Many people would retreat at this point not wanting to lose a powerful piece but I'd been that bishop myself in times past. I forced him forward into the fray and punched a hole in the defences of the enemy by taking the black bishop's pawn. This forced the black king into the open, leaving him vulnerable to attack. It left me a piece down but the move would test the mettle of those I played against. Perhaps brave, perhaps foolish, definitely worth the risk to save lives. I had never been a coward on the field of battle and I wouldn't be cowed by a game of chess. The next event, however, shook that resolution.

I watched in amazed horror. The square in which my bishop squatted in his mitre turned into liquid and the man in the metal cage began to fight as he sank into the board itself. I couldn't hear him scream but I did see the other pieces shuffle nervously in response.

Cold gripped my heart. "I thought you said my men would survive," I said.

"He isn't dead, just returned from whence he came," Lugh replied.

"And where is that exactly?" I asked.

"You need to win this," Lugh pointed to the board. "Everything else is immaterial."

"People's lives, no matter what they have done, are not immaterial," I stated.

Lugh sighed. "They will be kept safe until their fate is decided by you."

"Can I win and save the black pieces?" I asked. "They are suffering down here already."

"You don't know what their crimes are," Lugh countered.

It was my turn to sigh. "But I should not be judge and jury when I do not know what their crimes are."

"You are not judge or jury, you are their executioner and you are running out of time," Lugh said.

Pity makes you weak in war. I'd forced Arthur to learn this eventually. I continued the game and gradually the pieces were whittled away. I played well and strongly. I made decisive moves and backed up my gambles. Black retreated but I pushed and soon enough the Queen fell.

"Checkmate," I said feeling a hollow victory. The lives of the black pieces were over. I'd added another sixteen deaths to my tally and these were for nothing more noble than a fey woman wanting a throne.

I felt a hand on my shoulder. "You have done well, Knight of Camelot," Lugh said with surprising tenderness.

I looked at him. I saw pity in his dark eyes. Unable to reply, I brushed his hand from my shoulder and asked, "What next?"

CHAPTER FIFTEEN

Next proved to be a return to the cave in which The Lady waited. Lugh and I had simply walked back through the narrow doorway, which appeared behind me.

"How was his performance?" she asked, as though I were a trained dog.

Lugh ignored her and the gleaming in her black eyes. "Find the next task, Knight of Camelot." He waved at a different wall.

I thought about how the 'mind' aspect of this ridiculous game had been played. It would not be so simple as to be an ash tree in shadow once more. This test, one for the body, would be about hard physical endurance. I considered the symbols that might represent those aspects of humanity. The wood I knew was holly, it endured in all places and climates and it kept its deeply shining leaves all year. Its wood was dense and hard to use and it did not welcome casual company. It was strong, sharp, enduring and I like it.

"Tinne," I said.

"Interesting," Lugh replied.

I didn't expect him to tell me I was right, I just stepped up to the wall and found two large stones poking out of the surface just above my head. Below my shoulders were two more, below that two more around my knees and a final one just about my ankles. If you spent as much time as I did staring at the sky finding traditional constellations, then making up your own, you recognised abstract shapes. The stones fell into the perfect symmetry of the holly leaf. A test of the body wouldn't be complete without strength. I pushed on two of the points. The wall felt like glue and my hands vanished into the rock.

"Fuck," I cursed, the coldness seeping into my bones quickly. Knowing it would mean disaster if I stepped back, I pushed on and forced myself into the wall. A small sound of horror escaped me when my face felt the sucking numbness of falling through a wall.

I didn't faint, find myself stuck forever in a seam of quartz or walk into a bottomless pit. I walked into a green wood. The shock of seeing something so normal and frankly welcoming made me chuckle. The leaves reminded me of how late summer beckoned autumn and the foliage grew so thickly overhead the ground had few plants to impede my way. Lugh walked beside me and watched as I drew in great lungfuls of clean forest air. The smell of damp, the warm kind you have in woods, made me smile wider. I let my fingers brush the trunks of the trees and feel the waxy strength of the late season leaves.

"Just in this moment I feel really glad to be alive," I said aloud.

"Just in this moment?" Lugh asked.

"As a warrior you need to take simple pleasures were you can find them and I've learnt to enjoy the simplest, but I never take them for granted. I've learnt the hard way to push the fears and pressures of life to one side occasionally, so I can remember what it is to be free and that gives my soul a healing balm which is hard to find anywhere else," I said surprising myself with my articulate statement.

Lugh nodded but made no comment. We walked on for a time in silence until I became aware of a shift around me. Nothing I could determine changed but I felt the world alter subtly. A threat came through the trees. I reached for the pommel of my sword and modified the way I moved, becoming silent on the soft ground. The earth around me grew harder and the trees appeared warped and damaged. Many now looked as though they'd been burnt, their blackened branches reached out to snag the unwary.

"This isn't going to be fun," I muttered, wishing we had more cover.

Heat, waves of great heat made me begin to sweat inside the leather doublet and hose. A huge boulder appeared beside the path, its surface just as blackened as the trees. Sat on top of this rock was a dwarf. A man of small stature and foul temper. His hair stuck out at all angles and looked like sparks of fire, his eyes were vivid green and he threw small stones at us as we approached. They didn't hit anything because he stamped and cursed and bounced too much. His displeasure at our company was in no doubt.

I stopped out of stone's throw distance. "Sir dwarf," I said politely. "Perhaps you can spare a moment of your valuable time to help me?"

He lobbed a larger rock in my direction. It fell short by a long stretch. "No," he barked in a high voice. "You are here to be crowned and I hate you."

I blinked and glanced at Lugh, who shrugged. I cleared my throat, "Sir dwarf," I tried again to maintain civility. I could rush up there and cut the little bastard's throat in a dozen heartbeats, but I'd try for nice first. "I only ask for your help because your counsel will doubtless be wise and just."

The dwarf stopped bouncing. "You will be king," he sang and pointed. "It will be funny to watch you suffer this and so much more for you to win your prize."

I frowned. "Sir, I will be king of nothing." Another reference to Nimue's dreams of putting me on the throne of Camelot? When were the fey going to let that one go? "I am just a man who is in search of a test of the body. I must pass this test or those I love will pay a terrible price. Please, help me."

The dwarf promptly sat down. "You want to save others?" he asked.

"I love my friends very much," I said. "I would not see them suffer because of my lack of courage to face or even find a test I must endure."

His head cocked to one side. "Alright, here is a simple riddle but the answer will lead to the harshest of trials. You face two bridges and two knights. If I tell you one will always answer you with a lie and one will always answer you with the truth, you know the rules of the game. Before you are two bridges. One is safe to cross and will give you the victory you seek to protect those you love. The other appears the same but will lead you into your future friendless and hopeless. Neither path will be easy and to be king you must prevail in the right way."

"I have no wish to be king but I will unravel your riddle and cross the bridges to save my friends," I told the dwarf. "Thank you for your kindness and patience."

The dwarf vanished.

"Great, riddles," I moaned, as we walked on through the barren forest.

"Do you know the answer?" asked Lugh.

"As it happens I do," I said.

"Good," he said.

I proceeded to qualify my answer. "I will ask one of the knights, if you were the other knight, which bridge would you say was safe to cross? Then whichever answer is given I choose the other one. Do I need to explain any more than that?"

Lugh smiled. "No, not if you don't want to."

I sighed. "Good, because I can't be bothered..." My sentence trailed off to nothing. I became focused on the bizarre scene in front of me.

I realised why the land appeared to be blasted by fire. We'd approached two bridges, but they spanned twenty feet of moving fire. I'd never seen anything like it, the heat blasting off the surface of the moving river of glowing liquid coals made me gasp. I watched as chunks of black, which I assumed were rocks, drowned in a tumbling morass of red heat.

"What is that?" I asked in awe, looking down but not approaching the edge of the hellish gorge.

"That is the centre of world made real on the surface," said Lugh.

I looked at the bridges. They were metal, gleaming and shiny but I could see the heat haze surrounding them and I knew they'd be a torment to touch. The bridges were also blade edge thin and I mean blade edge. The haze might shimmer but it did not conceal the sharpness of a fine sword. There were no handholds to help and the bridges were too far apart to use both, aiding a possible balancing act. On the other side were the knights, one in red, one in black, sat on horses.

"Am I expected to cross, then fight them?" I asked.

Lugh shrugged. "You are expected to make the right decisions and live."

"Ever helpful," I bitched.

Fighting two fully armoured knights on horseback, even with my newly acquired skills would be insane. I did not want to fight and I did not want to cross the bridge.

I considered my options. Going back meant losing and losing threatened Arthur and Tancred. Not really a serious consideration. Going forward would be hard but I might find a way to stop a fight.

"Sir Knight of the Red Armour, could you please tell me which bridge the Black Knight will say it is safe to cross?" I asked aloud when I'd planned my strategy.

"This bridge, Sir Knight," came the strangely hollow answer.

"Many thanks, Sir Knight, then I shall choose the other bridge," I said and approached the blade. I had no idea how I would survive my mad plan but one problem at a time.

I considered asking if I had to fight one or both of the knights, but working out which would be telling the truth to this question would be complicated. I just had to assume I'd need to fight and be prepared. To be honest I did not want to leave my sword behind, Caliburn already gave me comfort. The thought of crossing that river of fire, then battling two fully armed mounted warriors didn't fill me with confidence. "This is not going to go well," I muttered. "I feel like a fish on a hook, completely fucked."

"It seems a fair summation of your situation," agreed Lugh.

I glared at him and he smiled. I was melting already inside my leather armour and to cross the blade safely I'd need all my skills of balance as a swordsman. I'd also need my blades.

"This is going to hurt," I said. I thought about Tancred. Was he facing similar trials? Would he be suffering physical torment? Would he survive and would I see him later? The thought of not seeing him because I'd failed and plunged to a fiery death didn't feel like an option. "May God guard my steps," I begged.

I began stripping my clothing. One of the things I knew for certain, if I tried crossing fully dressed I'd melt or slip because I couldn't feel the surfaces well enough. Once on the other side, my clothing would be irrelevant against two armoured knights. If they caught me with a strike from their weapons, the leather would not be enough to save me from losing a limb regardless of its thickness. I stripped completely naked, then grabbed my shirt and ripped it into bandages. Dignity be damned.

I tied these strips around the palms of my hands and the centre of my feet. I left the fingers and toes bare so they would help with gripping any surfaces I might find. I then took my sword belt and tied all my knives onto it, before fastening it across my back. I wanted my hands and feet free to move in case I overbalanced.

"Different," Lugh said mildly as I stood up, naked but for wraps.

"I don't need to be dressed to fight," I stated.

"Clearly," he replied.

I scowled and approached the bridge I'd chosen. There appeared, on the surface, to be no difference between this one and other but I had to trust in the game. The heat from the molten river made me feel sick and my skin prickled with sweat. I stepped onto the bridge with my left foot and tested the heat and balance. Even in that one movement I realised I'd never make it across the bridge in one piece if I tried to stay upright. The time it would take to hold my balance on each small shuffle forward or even step if I felt brave, would leave me slowly cooking like a pig roast turning on a spit.

"You are right, Lancelot," I told myself firmly. "Dignity be damned. I need to save the fucking day, not look pretty while doing it."

I crouched before the blades and placed my hands on the sword's edge. It felt sharp but not so sharp I'd slice myself open so long as I moved carefully. The heat though did cause my skin to inform my brain this was not a good idea. I'd soon have blisters on my palms, that would make holding my blade hard, but I'd had blisters before and they healed eventually. I'd endured great pain and won in the past. I'd do it again. I created an image of Tancred as I'd seen him the previous night, the moonlight softening the edges of his face. He'd changed and grown hard in the two years we'd been apart. I wanted to explore those changes and find some peace in his arms once more. I'd never been more broken but strangely happy than when I'd been in his embrace. These thoughts saw me take three carefully crawling steps forward. I didn't have my knees covered so I used a strange tilted walk forward on hands and feet. I kept my appendages as far to right angles as possible to my limbs so I didn't cut into my toes and fingers but used the palm of both my hands and feet. I'd have to quicken the pace if I wanted to reach the other side. Sweat now ran off my face and dripped down my flanks to run off my belly. I caught sight of the liquid hissing at it evaporated in the heat before ever reaching the river. I decided looking any further down than the blade would not help my courage. The rags covering my hands began to fray and smoke with the heat off the blades. My feet were screaming at me and I felt certain not all the liquid dripping off my body was sweat.

"Half way," I muttered. I felt sick, dizzy and disorientated. I still had miles to go, a league at least. I wanted pass out. "Come on, Wolf." I tried to summon Arthur but I couldn't feel him near me. I started to weep in pain, the blades now slicing into my hands, which had known nothing but abuse for decades. I heard the laughter of the dead, finally certain of their quarry, and I realised I'd picked the wrong damned bridge. The other would have been the safe one. I knew nothing. I was not strong enough, fast enough or clever enough to defeat these fey traps. I was just a man. A broken bitter man who loved the wrong people.

"And I do love you, Tancred," I said. I did, I did love him and I'd be damned if that were wrong. I wanted to spend time with him and I did not want to die in this godforsaken fey game for a throne I didn't give a fuck about. I'd found my lover once more and I was going to take him from my damned brother, bugger the consequences. I loved Arthur but I wanted a home and I could have that with Tancred. I wanted our dream. It all rushed back to me; the long descriptions he'd created on the side of Sister River's banks, laying together in dappled sunshine, listening the water and the birds. He'd stroke my hair and talk of gardens that I could tend or chickens and dogs we'd raise.

I clenched my jaw and forced my body, convinced my skin was turning into crackling, forward. I didn't slip, I didn't fall, I hurt, I burned and I bled but I didn't vanish into the burning heat of hell. When my hand touched terra firma, I lunged forward hitting dirt. I rolled instantly, hoping to avoid being an easy target for the knights. I made it to my knees and dragged my sword from its scabbard over my shoulder. Caliburn didn't feel as she had before. The heat in the blade made her song discordant and flat. I hoped she'd survive this fight and not shatter on impact.

The knights were not present. Lugh approached. "Put up your sword, Knight of Camelot, you have survived the test of the body." He actually held out his hand to raise me up.

I let him. My feet and hands wept with blood but the pain had yet to really register passed my relief.

"You have great courage and resourcefulness," the skeleton informed me.

I tried to smile but my throat was parched. I did ask one question. "Can you tell me how my friend is?"

Lugh's dark eyes softened. "His journey is not yours, have as much faith in him as he does in you. That will keep you both on course, I feel certain of it."

I nodded thanks for the answer and found the world dissolving around me.

CHAPTER SIXTEEN

The cooling effect of the cave in which The Lady and the pyramid needle waited caused me to collapse. Lugh knelt beside me and held a cup of water to my lips.

"You have earned the right, brave knight," Lugh said.

"He's naked," The Lady said. Her disgust almost made me laugh.

"He has faced a great trial and won," Lugh replied. "The test of the body can in many ways be the hardest and he has found the strength necessary to go forward with his talisman."

I didn't like the sound of that; talisman sounded like more torment. I stayed silent though and watched The Lady warily in case she chose to hurt me for being naked. I could see she felt tempted.

"He cannot face the other trials in that state," she said waving her hand but not looking at me.

"He clearly doesn't mind," Lugh countered.

"That's because he is an animal."

"He is a brave and noble man," Lugh said sharply.

"He is a man that we can agree on."

I sighed, bored with being torn apart by a vindictive bitch who needed a good fuck. I heard Lugh choke beside me, clearly swallowing a laugh. Could he read my thoughts?

"I am ready for the test of spirit," I croaked. Blood pooled near my hands and feet but not so much as I'd miss it. I did feel wonderfully comfortable without my leather armour.

"Then seek the door, Challenger," Lugh said, once more formal.

I considered the implications of spirit; there were many. If you travel far enough into the complexities of a symbol, you find the essence of the universe, the piece of pure spirit, which all objects hold. Willow, for instance, bends and blends with the world around it, just as the spirit should to learn from life and continue to grow strong and true. Apple bears the fruit of the summer and represents the world with the seeds of rebirth inside and let's not forget the symbols around the star in the centre of the fruit. Ivy? That goes everywhere, but it is invasive without giving rewards. Vine perhaps, because of its ability to travel, and yet it does give rewards when cared for properly.

The thought of spirit made me think of Sister River. She'd been the essence of spirit and through her I had found my home. A part of my heart still lived in that place. The wood in which I'd lived for one brief summer with Tancred.

There were reeds on that river. Reeds grew strong, repairing themselves whenever possible and were completely innocuous yet vital for the comfort of a good home. A fine home nurtured the heart and the spirit. A home is what I lacked. What my own soul cried out for and craved.

"Reed, getal," I said, using its true name. I approached the last wall without the steps through which we'd entered a lifetime ago. "The spirit lives in the body but needs to blend with the wind of life to survive. I don't bend well. I am strong, stubborn and often arrogant. The reed is humble but essential to the river which supports it and gives so much life. It is a home to many, a food stuff, a refuge. My spirit needs to learn from such a plant." Well, that was profound. It seemed at least some of what I'd learnt from The Lady had sunk into my battered brain.

I silently hoped I'd find something as simple as a carving of the actual Ogham. I lacked all inspiration and found nothing, no matter how long I stared at the walls. A sense of despair began to overwhelm me and when The Lady began tapping her foot, the pressure of time made me want to scream.

I placed my still bleeding hands on the wall and thought of Sister River and my lover. If I failed and remained in this room I'd see a fate worse than the one Shuffle represented, of that I felt certain.

"Think, fool," I said and a tear slid down my cheek to land on my hand, still pressed against the rock. Blood and tears, spirit and heart, reeds never lived without water. A soft sound alerted me half a breath before the wall vanished and I hit the floor once more. Lugh appeared as I stood and brushed myself off. Dust covered me and I turned full circle. We were in Tintagel. The sun beat down on my bare skin and I heard the sea behind me.

"What the hell?" I asked no one in particular. Nothing had changed from the memories I held of my adolescence. I watched two young men, Arthur and Geraint, race toward the castle over the bridge and onto the promontory of land. They were truly young again. Arthur rode the big bay stallion who'd sired Willow. Geraint rode his brother's dun mare, a fine horse. I heard them shout challenge to each other.

I turned, wondering how this had happened. The horses came charging back out of the castle, something we were not allowed to do unless battle orders were given. Geraint's mare stumbled. I'd never seen what happened next, I'd only ever heard about it. The mare slipped and fell into the stallion. Arthur tipped in the saddle not concentrating. The stallion lost his balance, fought for control on the slippery surface of the bridge and crashed to his knees. He'd been lame for weeks afterward. Arthur flew forward and fell. He reached for the edge of the bridge. Geraint screamed his name and lunged making a grab for our young prince, almost falling off his own horse and plunging to his death. Arthur missed the edge.

"No!" I bellowed and raced toward the bridge. I'd never reach him in time and I didn't. Arthur fell and hit the rocks below. The tide was in and I saw a wave crash over his broken body. He did not move and the wave washed back stained with his life's blood.

The image faded and I now stood in a simple chapel of heavy stone with vivid paintings covering the walls of birds and animals talking to some saint. A young strong man stood next to a beautiful girl with long golden hair. Geraint stood to the right.

"Guinevere?" I whispered, walking forward. A strong hand clamped down on mine.

"No, Lancelot, you cannot approach or be seen," Lugh said.

"What's going on? Arthur didn't die that day and I never married Guinevere." The pain of my confusion softened the guide.

"Ever wondered what your life would be like without Arthur and Camelot to love?" he asked.

I watched as a young man, God was I ever that young, kissed his blushing bride. She really did love me, I could see it in her eyes and I was the proudest man, but I felt the shadow of sadness. Arthur should have been there with me. The young version of me, a version that never existed, swept Guinevere up and carried her laughing through the small church.

The image faded and I ducked a blow to my head. We were in the middle of a battle, some city somewhere and I bellowed orders. I looked older, harder but no less the man I am now. I heard the other Lancelot snap at someone to his left, "If we don't win this I'm going to be broke. I need this to pay for the rest of Guinevere's damned home." I was fighting for her, to give her the life I felt she deserved, the one I couldn't give her through inheritance.

Another picture overlaid the last. Guinevere with children surrounding her and another in her belly. She laughed as a tall, dark haired child of about eight tried to teach his young sister to play a whistle. She looked tired but happy. Gone were the fine clothes but she did wear a pretty necklace and the place she lived in looked comfortable enough, if not as grand as Camelot. I watched a version of me, about ten years younger, walk through the door. My son called to me and raced into my arms. He'd be ready to become a page soon, leaving his mother and starting his journey toward being a knight. I held my son in one arm and swept my daughter up with the other. She giggled and kissed my cheek. I looked so happy, my eyes and my smile were softer. I kissed Guinevere with real affection.

I turned to Lugh. "What does this mean?"

"What do you think?"

I growled in frustration. "This is what would have happened if Arthur had not married Guinevere, I get it, but what does it matter? He did, I lost, simple as that," I snapped. I really didn't appreciate this ideal life being laid before my exhausted mind and body.

"Perhaps this will help," Lugh said and I found myself in a plain white room once more facing two mirrors. They were set inside golden frames and stood as tall as I did.

My naked reflection faded and an image shimmered into view on the mirror's surface. Arthur. He sat in a window seat looking out over Camelot. He held the amulet I'd given him in his right hand and rubbed his fingers over it unconsciously. The images were the same in both pictures.

He was the right age. This was a mirror into my own world. I did not move, I knew I'd not be allowed through. I just watched. Guinevere came in from her private suite. She walked to him and took the amulet out of his hand.

"It won't help to sit here and waste a day brooding," she said firmly. "You have things you need to do."

Arthur sighed. "I know, I just miss him." At least that's what happened in one. In the other something else entirely occurred.

Arthur brushed Guinevere's touch away and rose in anger, making his movements sharp. "It is not your place to tell me what I can and cannot think about," he said.

The scene continued, I watched in horror as Guinevere's eyes filled with tears. "I know you love him but you have a family who need you here with us," she begged.

"And I have my heart out there, not here with your demands and pathetic whinges," he snapped.

Both pictures froze.

"I don't understand," I said. I realised being confused wouldn't help but I genuinely didn't get it.

"Which is the real Arthur?" Lugh asked. "If you choose right then your life will not change and he will live."

"But if I choose wrongly?" I asked, thinking I already knew the answer and didn't dare consider the implications.

"If you choose the other option," Lugh said carefully, "you will have your life back and you will be able continue on the path without Arthur's interference."

My mouth opened and I felt real terror for the first time. I could free myself of a love I'd never really understood if Arthur died on that bridge. I'd sworn myself to him by then but I'd never confessed how deeply I truly loved him. We were young men experimenting and we were meeting as equals for the only time in our young lives.

"I can have it all back?" I whispered.

"All of it," Lugh said. "It is the one thing you appear to want the most."

I sat down. I wanted Guinevere the most? I shook my head, I didn't believe that. I wanted my life back and she was the beginning of the end of my peace of mind.

Arthur gone and I'd never really miss him. I'd have a son and daughter of my own. I'd never have to tangle with the fey and I wouldn't be driven to become the best knight of Camelot so I could forget my pain. I'd been fighting all my life to rid myself of that ache.

"Guinevere," I said and reached out to touch the image in which she displayed her frozen hurt.

Arthur was capable of both versions represented in the mirrors. He could react with great kindness to her gentle remonstration or he'd verbally snap her head off to make some point or another. I'd seen him do both.

The version I'd believed in and loved was, of course, the kinder version, but the honest version was perhaps the harsher man. He'd apologise within moments and hold her hands, kissing the palms, saying he was sorry, he just missed me and it made everything a bit too hard sometimes.

I knew which picture I should choose. I knew which picture I wanted to choose.

"This is unfair," I said.

"It isn't designed to be fair, just honest," Lugh said.

I thought about that perfect family, with my golden haired goddess. There would be no punishment, no fighting for her virtue, no mad quests. "And no Tancred," I finished aloud.

I would never turn to the arms of a man for comfort because I'd never need that comfort. I wouldn't have to live with the complications or the heartache. I'd also never know the incredible gifts that came with such love. Not least of which was a true companion for someone who did love the life they led most of the time. I'd never met a woman, even Else, who could live with the way I am deep inside my heart.

Tancred understood me but would he be there when I left this hell and returned to the fray of the battle for the throne? Would he really leave Rafe? Would I really surrender Arthur to keep Tancred happy? How badly did I want normal and safe? Guinevere could keep me happy, but would I know the peace I felt with Tancred or Arthur? I knew in their arms I felt something a woman had never given me, an indefinable completeness.

I remembered Lugh's words about trusting Tancred loved me as much as I loved him. Had he used me to help him through his versions of these trials, as I'd used him?

"A chance to play the game of life from the start is a tempting offer," I said, remembering how beautiful my children looked. "But, the life I lead now is the one I want. For all my heartache and suffering, I have known great love from more than one person and the world needs Arthur Pendragon." I rose and touched the mirror, just where Arthur's angry mouth had frozen in response to Guinevere's pleading. "This is the true face of the man I love," I said with certainty.

Lugh smiled. "I never doubted you would choose correctly, Knight of Camelot."

CHAPTER SEVENTEEN

The world around me faded and I found myself sat on the floor of the cave. I lay back and stared at the ceiling, which vanished far into the darkness overhead. I felt wrung out. Choosing the image of Arthur stole from me a life I'd craved since I'd first laid eyes on Guinevere. I'd rejected that image and made my decision. This life, with Tancred, is the one I'd live.

"Lancelot, you must rise and we must continue," Lugh said.

I continued to lie on the floor, cool and comfortable. The Lady approached. "Get up, do your job. Find the heart."

I looked up at her and wondered if she understood the irony of that statement. "Well, my Lady, at least one of us has a heart," I said. I'd never spoken to her so far out of turn. Her breath hissed and her eyes flashed. I closed my eyes, ready for the agony to begin.

"My Lady," Lugh's voice interrupted. "I suggest in the strongest terms you leave your Champion for a moment. If he dies, you have nothing left." He remained calm and almost toneless. Something more must have passed between them, because I heard The Lady's slippers pad quietly away.

I opened my eyes and saw Lugh standing before me acting as protector and guard. I liked this strange man.

"Right," I said to the ceiling. "The heart." I lay and considered the options of what image might be chosen. I ran through the choices. Many of the runes used in this challenge could be taken to represent the heart. Again I considered apple; it gave so much it could heal the wounds of the heart. Hawthorn represents the heart and all the sentiments of love, friendship and spiritual growth. Hazel transforming dreams into reality, and my mind circled back to Arthur. The oak and the ash. The two mightiest of trees.

I needed thorns to protect myself from Arthur, always had done. If the ash could have chosen a companion, it would have chosen something beautiful, useful and a plant to heal or harm. I backtracked. What would I want to grow around me to protect my heart, what plant would grow thorns designed to protect delicate fruits and flowers? What plant aided the heart's blood when a man was weak? And what plant offered love and friendship in the first bloom of spring?

I sat up. "Huath, hawthorn. The heart, love, friendship, used for releasing blocked energy and for spiritual growth. All of which I sadly lack most of the time. What better way to test my heart."

"And where will you find the symbol?" Lugh asked, obviously aware of my increasingly delicate state.

I sighed and looked up at the black stone needle. The rune for Huath sat on the base near my hand. Far too easy. I rubbed my hands over my smoky face and wondered why I was doing this to myself. Oh, yes, Tancred.

I touched the symbol with my fingertips and the world gradually dissolved around me. Everything faded with a gentle caress. The Lady's mouth moved but no sound reached me. The cold stone floor, the dark walls and the braziers all vanished. The only thing which came with me was Lugh. He remained at my side while stone turned to dirt under my naked backside.

My head hung down. "I don't want to do this," I said. "I don't want to be here and I don't want to tarnish these memories."

Lugh crouched beside me and placed a cool dry hand on my shoulder. "Lancelot, this is your final test and the test of the heart doesn't have to be bad," he said softly.

"But anything involving my heart always goes bad. I don't want this tainted," I said and stood up, anger stirring me to action at last.

"Lancelot," Tancred's voice rippled through the forest we'd used as our home for that wonderful summer. The trees shivered in the light warm breeze and Lugh backed slowly away into the wood. "What have you been doing?"

my lover asked looking me up and down. "You are covered in soot and -" his eyes widened in shock, "blood."

"I'm fine," I said, confused by my ability to interact with the past suddenly.

"You don't look fine," he said. He picked up my hands and looked at the damage on the palms. Blisters, cuts and blackened sooty marks. "It looks as if you've been playing with the fire." He sounded so cross with me and exasperated that I laughed.

"I am sorry," I said. He frowned at me, so I bent slightly and kissed his mouth. His lips were warm and soft, his skin clean of his beard and his hair long once more. I didn't question where I might really be in this world, I just held the version of Tancred I remembered from two years ago and loved him.

What kind of test was this? What kind of torture for my heart? What was I learning?

Tancred pulled back from the kiss and looked at me with a slightly quizzical expression. "Are you sure you are alright?" he asked.

"I am when I'm with you," I said.

He smiled. "We are meant to be leaving, not standing here naked playing with fires," he said.

I looked around me and realised it was not high summer but the beginning of autumn. The horses were ready with our meagre belongings. Today was the day we would leave for Camelot and Arthur would soon stand between us like the titan he is in my life.

This was the test. I glanced behind me and caught a Lugh shaped shadow. No, this couldn't be the test, the decision was the same as the one I'd faced over Guinevere. I'd chosen Arthur before; I would choose him again because it meant I saved him and Camelot. If I had to sacrifice Tancred for another two years I would, if it protected the Fitzwilliam and Pendragon families.

"Tancred, is something wrong? Is there something I should know?" I asked trying to figure out what I needed to accomplish.

He frowned, confused by my question. "Nothing is

wrong, love, except you aren't dressed and I have wounds to clean," he said. I watched him walk to Willow to retrieve something to use on my hands.

The only thorn which stood between us, known and unseen were the secrets Tancred kept from me about my brother. That and my feelings for Arthur, which flourished when we returned to Camelot.

He returned and began wiping my palms. "Your feet are filthy," he complained.

"They are burnt and cut like my hands," I said and watched the top of his bowed head.

"Why? What were you doing?" he asked.

I didn't know how to challenge him about this without scaring him and I knew we were on a schedule. I needed to be clever and force Tancred to open up in a way he'd never done for me when we'd lived together. I turned my hands in his and took hold of his fingers. "We need to talk about something," I said.

"We don't have time," Tancred said. His impatience made him harsh with me.

"We have time for this, I promise," I said. "It won't take long." I took hold of his hand and led him to the cold fire pit and our logs. I knelt before him and kissed his wrists which always made him shiver with pleasure. "I have to confess something," I began. If I told him about the amulet and how hard I'd find it letting Arthur back into my life, he might tell me about Rafe. "Camelot is looming large in our lives once more," I said.

"I told you I'd protect you," he said. "There is nothing to fear while I stand at your side."

"I know, my love, and you have no idea how true that sentiment is, but I really need to tell you something." I had to deal with this correctly or I'd lose these games. I wished the rules were as clear as those for chess or as simple as a straight fight.

"When we return to Camelot, Arthur isn't going to be able to cope with how deeply damaged I am and he is not going to cope with how much his presence harms me," I said, focusing on Tancred's hands not his face.

"You don't know that, Lancelot," he said.

"Yes, actually I do, but I don't have time to explain, so just listen," I said. "His pain is going to draw me to him, because if I don't help him I will cause his grief to send him to his death."

Tancred grabbed my face and raised my eyes to his. "What are you talking about?"

"Please, just let me speak," I said calmly. "I will force myself to become his friend once more because I want to save Camelot. In the process, I will see the man I fell in love with and he will fight you for me. Literally. His is a force of nature, Tancred, and you will leave me because you will consider it impossible to stand against his obsession. I will let you. I will let you because in my heart I cannot reject Arthur's power."

Tancred's eyes filled with tears. "Why are you saying this?" he whispered.

I continued, "I will give him a gift, meant to show friendship, but he will know it actually represents our love and it will destroy you. It will drive you into the arms of another person."

Tancred gasped and drew back, away from me. I watched his eyes close down. "What witchcraft is this? Have you been speaking with fey without me knowing?" he asked. He grew hard and brittle.

"I have spoken with no one, love," I said. I remained passive, careful and quiet. "I just needed to be honest and I need you to be honest in return." I felt bad I couldn't explain our current twisted reality. I guessed I'd not be affecting my past or Lugh wouldn't allow me to interact; this was all an illusion.

"Honest about what? I don't love anyone else but you," he said. Illusion or not, Tancred's suffering felt very real.

I remained on the ground, sat back on my heels and just looked at him. His face became mutinous. "You know nothing," he said. "You can't."

I stayed quiet. He paced back and forth for sometime. I watched his chest heave and he swiped angrily at his face to brush away the escaping tears. His hand flexed on the pommel of his sword. His distress cut through me but I didn't go to his side, I waited him out. Sometimes love is about watching your partner suffer in order to clean a festering wound. Sticking a poultice on the wound merely causes more problems down the line. My relationship with Tancred proved that point with unerring effectiveness.

"There was someone," he finally spat out. "In Albion. Happy now? Can we leave?" His short sentences gave further evidence of his misery.

"Tell me, please," I said without moving and remaining gentle.

"There is nothing to tell. Besides," he rounded on me and actually shouted for the first time since we'd been reunited in the wood, "you have confessed to still loving Arthur. How am I supposed to feel about that?"

"I don't know," I said. I didn't blink or turn away from his anger. I just let him yell.

"Do you know what it's like? How my stomach aches when I think about taking you back and knowing you will see Arthur. I fear losing you and if I make you strong, I know I will, but that is my job. I am a healer. You will become strong through me and then you will leave and I will have nothing," his grief broke. The rage and fear made him speechless.

I rose from the ground and finally wrapped my arms around his trembling body.

"Tell me who he is, love."

"You will never forgive me," Tancred clutched my naked body with desperation.

"Tell me."

"I promised a fey lord I would return to him. But when I came back to Camelot, all I thought about was you and I couldn't leave. When Arthur told me I could search for you, I grabbed the chance and I didn't even think about the consequences. I love you and always have. He was just a safety net during a year of my life in which I suffered more misery than any soul should have to bear." He spoke into my chest, unable to look at me.

I forced his head up. "What was his name?" I asked.

Tancred's lips quivered and his body hummed with tension. "Rafe. He is your half brother through Aeddan," he said and I watched his fear of losing me writhe in his eyes. As secrets went this wasn't a serious one, not like others in my life. Anything with Tancred was always easier for me, kinder, more gentle. His soul brushed against mine, it never dominated or hurt. This was not much of a test.

I bent my head and kissed his lips softly. A chaste kiss. "Nothing will ever turn me from you. I just needed to see into your heart and you needed to know mine. Leaving this place is a pivot point in both our lives. Now we have no secrets and the future can unfold fairly."

"I don't understand." His gentle brown eyes were full of his confusion. "What is happening?" he asked.

"Nothing bad, my love. Nothing bad." I held him tightly, my fingers in his long hair, and wished I could save us both from the next two years of our lives.

CHAPTER EIGHTEEN

The world around me dissolved. My arms grew empty and cold but I did not return to the cave room. I found myself somewhere much worse.

A white carpet made the grass sparkle and my leather clad knee soaked up the thawing frost. I wore fine riding leathers and Guinevere lay at my feet.

"Oh, God, no," I said. "Anything but this." I closed my eyes for a moment and when I opened them, I looked through the trees and Lugh stood among the shadows. His head was bowed.

"Lancelot," Guinevere's voice wavered and I watched her mare trot back toward us looking very confused. The Queen's perfection pulled at my heart. Her smooth skin, uncreased by time and unblemished by heartache, allowed me to time this incident perfectly.

Our first kiss after her marriage to Arthur. The beginning of the end.

Before this moment I'd been denying her advances for months but the gradual increase in flirtation eventually wore me down. She'd begun with shy smiles, her large ice blue eyes glancing up at me coyly. Then the teasing whenever we were alone, or with Arthur and his mood allowed the subtle suggestions. After that casual caresses and whispered words. These began to pull me into her orbit, holding me fast because of her personal gravity. I wanted this woman for my wife. I wanted to watch her belly grow with my babies and I wanted her to smile up at me after we made love, not imagine her with Arthur.

I gently slipped my arm around her shoulders and raised her up, then knelt completely and pulled her into my lap. She felt so light in comparison to a man's weight.

"My Queen, are you hurt?" I asked. I knew the answer. I'd known the answer then. Of course she wasn't hurt. She'd raced far enough ahead of me to fall carefully from her poor mare, without me ever actually seeing the accident.

"Lancelot," her eyes fluttered and she swooned against my chest. I ached in response to her presence. I stroked a stray golden hair away from her face.

What was I meant to do now? Kiss her as I had done and cause our lives to run along the same punishing channel? Or was I meant to reject that kiss and explain to Guinevere that her marriage to Arthur would not be damaged by my infidelity? How should I manipulate this situation like I had the one with Tancred?

"I don't really need to ask," I muttered.

Guinevere's eyes opened. "Excuse me?" she asked, her swoon dropping away from her surprisingly quickly.

I smiled down at her and thought about the images I'd seen of our children. This trip down memory lane to force me to face the torments of my heart and soul was cruel but not unbearable.

"Are you hurt, my Queen?" I asked with tenderness in my voice and in my arms.

"I think I've knocked my head," she said and struggled against me, moving closer.

"Then I will go to fetch the King, my Lady. He will need to return to Camelot with you and have your physician check your wounds," I moved to hook my arm under her knees.

Guinevere had other ideas. In my memories, I'd kissed her. I'd held her and in her delicate state, so vulnerable in my arms, she became my prey. A victim to my desire. A willing victim to my lust.

This time she'd obviously sensed she'd lost her control over me and as she shifted against me because of my own movements, she turned her head and kissed me.

I froze. One knee raised, the other tucked under me.

"No," I said and I placed her back on the ground. I untangled myself from the sublime body and stepped back. "No, Guinevere, not again. You aren't doing this to me. You aren't doing this to yourself or Arthur. He deserves our loyalty."

"Arthur stole me from you, don't you want to do

something about that?" she immediately challenged. "How can you allow this? I know you love me, Lancelot."

"Don't, Guinevere. I am not the man you think I am and I have learnt many lessons since I first met you. Not least of which is my desire not to make our lives miserable. Why are you doing this to yourself? Why are you intent on this grand seduction? Is life with Arthur so terribly dull?" I actually allowed myself to show her an anger I'd always kept hidden for fear of hurting her. However, by denying that anger I always became vulnerable. My anger protected me and smothering it meant I always caved into her demands.

"What are you talking about?" she asked, scrambling to her feet.

I backed off further. "Tell me why you love me. It shouldn't be difficult. Or is it Arthur you are angry with and want to hurt?" Just as with Tancred earlier, I used prior knowledge to act as perceived intuition.

Her eyes narrowed and I realised something. What had happened here in this wood changed Guinevere forever. She became increasingly bitter and angry, more manipulative and less joyful. It took Stephen de Clare to shock her out of her vindictive habits.

"Just talk to me, Guinevere. We were once friends, good friends," I said and tried to convey compassion.

She studied me for a long time and I wished I could work out how her devious mind wanted to play this game.

"We were never friends, Lancelot. I was to be your wife and you let him take me from you," she said and her eyes filled with defiant tears.

I opened my mouth and snapped it shut. Then managed a confused, "But you wanted him, he is the King. You loved him."

"No, I loved you. He took me from you because you wouldn't stand against him and why wouldn't you challenge his right to me? Why wouldn't you fight him the way you fight for everything else?" she asked her tears now scoring lines down her face.

Pain began to gather in my chest and slowly leaked out

to fill my legs with draining weakness. I stumbled back and sat as my history, all of it, rippled around me.

"You wanted me to fight him," I said to my boots. Then I looked up into her eyes with utter horror, "You couldn't say no to him and needed me to do it. You loved me, you wanted me."

"I'm the daughter of an insignificant noble. When Arthur showed interest in me, my father forbade me from continuing with you and begging for you help. Remember, Lancelot? Remember how Arthur did everything he could to ensure we were never alone again? I couldn't speak to you, I couldn't ask for your help. I didn't know how. The moment Arthur returned to Tintagel you just gave up and stopped loving me. You let them sell me off to Arthur. I thought I could bear it, at least I would be near you, but I can't. I can't live like this," her voice broke and she sobbed into her gloved hands, her body bowing under the pressure.

I watched her shoulders jerk with each tormented breath. I'd never thought about it from Guinevere's perspective. I'd never considered her actions were not her own, but she was so young when we met and her father owned her. She didn't choose the King, he did, and why not? I was nothing. I realised I wept, silently and with great sadness. If I'd chosen the other image in that damned mirror I'd be married with children because that's what Guinevere truly wanted.

She hadn't ruined our love, I had done it because I wouldn't stand against Arthur's desire.

"I know you love him," she said, her voice soft. "I know he desires you over me. I've seen him, when he thinks no one is watching and his eyes change. He never looks at me like that."

"Guinevere, don't, not now. You aren't meant to know. It's nothing." How could I be lying to her? It was everything. It always had been everything.

"How can I not know? You love him more than me, you must do because you let me go and I know how he feels about you." She threw her head back and I watched her try to gather herself back into the form of the Queen of Camelot. "I love you, Lancelot du Lac. I know I will never be enough for you, or for him. I know that is my burden, my grief to carry, but you..." whatever determined thoughts drove her to this, suddenly abandoned her and she sank to her knees in silence.

I twisted and crawled her side. I gently pulled her into my chest and she clung to me. "I didn't know," I said. "I didn't know you loved me that much. I thought I was just a game piece for you to play with and discard when you had the prize."

"You are my heart, Lancelot," she said more calmly than before. "You always will be and I can never let you go. I am so sorry. So very sorry, love."

I kissed her golden hair. She lifted her face to mine and I kissed her lips. The kiss grew steadily, with far more passion and depth than the original one had all those years ago. When I pulled back, she lay in my arms and smiled.

"Thank you," she said. "At least I know you still care."

"I will always love you, Guinevere. Always. I am sorry I didn't fight for you and give you the life we both wanted, but we must live with this one and eventually you will know that it is right and good. I do love Arthur. I will always love him and I'm sorry about that as well, but this isn't right or healthy." I stroked her cheek, her skin so soft I feared I would mark her with my rough hands. "I will always love you both but there is someone out there for me. A man." Her eyes widened in shock. I continued, "a man with warm brown eyes and soft brown hair. He will be my salvation, my future. I cannot change the past and neither can you, but we can live in peace with the present because it's not that bad and we can at least be friends."

"You won't be my lover?" she asked in a little girl voice.

I smiled with such a mighty weight in my heart I was surprised it continued to beat. "No, Guinevere. I will not be your lover."

CHAPTER NINETEEN

The world around me dissolved once more and I wondered what fresh hell I'd be forced to endure. My arms ached. I'd never considered Guinevere's inability to say no to Arthur because of her duty to her father. So many small things she'd done and said at the time finally made sense, but I had no time to consider them.

I stood, bloody and torn, in Stephen de Clare's castle. A sword, Excalibur, pressed tight against my neck and a hand held me by my hair. My heart rate soared and I tensed, ready to fight.

Lugh appeared for the first time. "Rest easy, you cannot change what happened here," he said.

"This is an evil game you are playing, my friend," I said, my voice strained by the rush of memories.

"Yes, it is, but you have done well, Knight of Camelot, so it is not as bad as it could be." Lugh's black eyes were sad as he looked around at the death I'd caused that terrible day. "No wonder you are a haunted man," he said. He seemed to collect himself. "You can move away from Aeddan by the way, he won't move."

I pulled my hair free and slid out of Excalibur's deadly embrace. "I don't understand what can be learnt by making me relive these parts of my life," I said. My eyes were drawn to Tancred, lying on the floor, his legs broken and his hand smashed. He'd heal well in body but I knew how damaged he'd be in his mind. He didn't move as I walked toward him. I wanted to touch him, lift him up and carry him from this terrible place.

"What am I doing here?" I asked. Anger made me bitter and tense.

Lugh sighed. "You must bare your soul to those who would know the man challenging for the right to be King of Albion. It is not a game I would choose to play. You have proved yourself to me," he said.

I frowned. "But I'm not going to be king. When are you people going to understand? I don't want to be king of anywhere. I have to do this for The Lady or Arthur will die. Champions don't become kings."

"You are a good man, Lancelot du Lac. You deserve to be free of these memories and sometimes the only way to be free is to understand." Lugh waved a hand and the frozen tableau released Arthur.

"Fuck," I muttered.

"Wolf, what's happened?" he asked, utterly mystified by the frozen scene around him.

I gathered myself together. After the shock of Guinevere's revelation, I wondered what Arthur would dump on my shoulders. "Arthur, if I just asked you not to worry about this," I waved a hand around me vaguely, "strangeness, would you let it go and allow me to speak with you?"

Something inside the magic of this insanity evidently helped Arthur concede to my request. He approached me and his fingers reached for my face. This place had lived in my nightmares and for six long years held me inside the thrall of madness. I jerked away from Arthur, unable to allow him to touch me.

His eyes tracked to Tancred, lying silent and broken in Merla's arms. "You are turning from me," he said and his sadness rendered me mute. "Loving you has cost me so much, Lancelot."

Here we go, I thought, now I have the unsurprising revelation that actually all this crap is my fault.

"But I fear it has cost you more and will continue to do so." Arthur's eyes left Tancred and he looked at me. His cold determination snaked around my calves, thighs and torso. Those dark blue eyes of his bored into my soul. Arthur would have his Wolf.

I felt cast adrift in the confusion of this situation. I understood my relationship with Tancred when we'd been alone in that wood, that conversation had been easy compared to this insanity. But being with Tancred was always easy. I even understood Guinevere, her desperate manipulation and my capitulation to her demands. But this? Why was I here? Of all the memories to choose between Arthur and I, why this one? The lowest point in so many ways. Lower even than when he found himself forced to condemn me for adultery with his wife. And a situation I'd never really found peace with or forgiveness for my own actions, never mind his.

I glanced at Aeddan. Had he made his demand? Had he given Arthur the ultimatum? Me and the damned sword or Merla and Tancred? I'd been on my knees when Aeddan struck his bargain, so no, Arthur didn't know the terms. Was I supposed to make him take a different path?

It was something I wished for constantly. Every time I saw Tancred's scars, it came to my mind. The guilt of the survivor.

I took a breath and felt the pain of broken ribs, weird. "Arthur, you have chosen fatherhood and Guinevere. You wish to cast me aside for them," I held my hand to force him to silence, "which is fine. I understand and I want you to do that but you can't have both. You can't cast me aside and then expect me to remain faithful to a memory of us in blissful union. It isn't real, it's never been real."

I watched the muscles in Arthur's jaw jump as he controlled his temper. "You chose him," he used the stolen sword to point at the bundle of misery on the filthy stone floor, "over me?"

Fuck it. I was tired of this game. "Yes." I couldn't change the past. This never really happened. I wouldn't wake up from this dream and discover Tancred healed and well. There would always be nights when he woke screaming or crying, sometimes both, because of Aeddan's torture.

"Save my friend, Arthur. Save Tancred so I can have a life with him," I begged.

"He is nothing," Arthur said, clearly bemused by my choice.

"He is everything to me. He will be everything. Please, Arthur, let me go. For once, just let me go," I pleaded.

He stared at Tancred for a long time and I knew I would

not be able to shift him. He'd not give me up. Why? Why couldn't I get him to surrender his control over me?

Because I didn't want him to, came the answer from deep within my heart.

"Alright," I muttered. "I'll play the game. Why don't I want to give him up?"

"What are you talking about?" Arthur asked.

I limped toward him and lifted my bloodied hand to his neck, grasping him firmly. "Why don't I want to give you up? What do you have that I need? Why do I keep surrendering Tancred to be with you? Am I going to do it again or will I actually stay in Albion for him rather than return to your side?" I asked the illusion of my King.

"You belong to me, Wolf. You always have and you always will," he said, without knowing the awful cost of that possession. I would eventually stand in a river and Rafe would bind our souls together for all time, but it wouldn't make me happy. Tancred made me happy and I wanted my freedom from Arthur. I still wanted to stop fighting.

He was right, even locked in misery we were unable to survive without each other. Like any drug, my mind informed me. Drug. I'd never been addicted to anything in my life, unless you counted training to be the best of knights, but that wasn't a bad thing.

I looked at the slaughter in the room around us and realised that in my berserker rage I'd killed dozens of men. My training let me do that, my desire to protect Arthur and Tancred. I'd do anything for Arthur.

I'd trained in warfare my whole life, even as a child. I'd never been soft and adorable. I'd never been pampered. I'd been born and bred a warrior. I was addicted to a life of death because I believed it would lead me to peace in the end. Sooner or later I believed I would run out of people to kill. Arthur fed my addiction because he needed it; he needed me to be that part of him so he could be the soft one, the loved one, the one that didn't make the final cut, just gave the order. I was the dark corner of his conscience. He was my justification.

I still had not come to terms with the terrible chaos of war that I craved but wanted to surrender.

I thought that my madness and then the acceptance of Arthur in my life allowed me to understand, but it just meant I'd given up on fighting for what I really wanted because it was too damned hard to sever my ties to Arthur. He gave my life validation.

I let my hand drop from his neck. I needed to fight for freedom, like I'd never fought for Tancred, or Guinevere. The only person who could rescue me was me. Arthur would never understand. It wasn't his place to surrender me because he just gave me what I wanted and until I changed he could no more release me than yield Excalibur to Aeddan.

I looked at my father. Strong, wilful, arrogant, darkly beautiful and capable of hurting a man like Tancred with unimaginable agony. The apple never fell far from the tree. In the old religion the apple was a symbol of abundance, generosity and ability to heal the heart. In the new religion of Camelot, temptation, sin, greed and knowledge of the world. I was of the new world, a creation of my father's greed and sin for my mother, who became the sweet temptress.

Lugh walked from the shadows and Arthur froze. "You understand?" he asked.

I nodded. "I must not become my father. I must not be used by others because I seek validation for my actions. I must find the beauty of love, not the pain, and I cannot do that while I fight without acknowledging my responsibility to those I kill. Only I can protect me. Not Arthur, Guinevere or Tancred. Only me. There is only me." The sweeping loneliness of that statement hurt but brought with it a profound easing of a burden I'd carried my whole life.

I gazed at Arthur. "It's over," I said.

Lugh took my hand. "Perhaps," he said. "You will have to find the strength and the words to sever the ties. Your dependence on each other runs so deep it's frankly surprising one of you can take a breath without the other feeling it."

I smiled at his incredulous tone. "Sometimes we can't," I said, but continued with my lesson. "I must change my reason for living. I must stop thinking death will give me peace and actually find it within myself. Once I have it inside me, I can give it to the world surrounding me. Then I can stop," I said. The understanding still felt so ephemeral, I worried I'd forget the lesson and return to well worn paths of behaviour. After all, I'd tried to stop fighting on more than one occasion and not managed.

Lugh looked at me slightly alarmed. "You don't have to break your sword and never fight again, Lancelot. You must simply find a different perspective which will give you back your heart and therefore your peace," he said.

I chuckled. "Anyone would think you had plans for me," I said.

Lugh merely smiled and the world of Stephen de Clare once more started to return to my memory, dissolving slowly to live behind a door I would never open again if the old gods and the new agreed on leaving me alone.

My companion on this journey said to me, "I wish you well and know you have proved yourself worthy of the title, Greatest of Knights. You will make a fine King." He bowed and everything vanished.

CHAPTER TWENTY

The cave was empty when I woke. I was naked and I heard a scratching shuffle on the passageway. My sword lay trapped under me. I rolled, rose and wobbled as blood shifted unnervingly from my brain.

The scratching shuffle proved to be my friend trying to carry new clothes down the passageway toward me. I laughed as I saw him and walked to help. He jumped and turned away, avoiding looking at me naked.

"Shuffle, you loon, it's just skin," I said, and remembered Else's reaction to me being naked when I'd thought her a boy. "You aren't a girl are you?" I checked for the first time.

Shuffle's eyes widened and he made his strange hissing laugh. He patted my arm and forced his embarrassment to one side. By the time we were finished I was dressed just the same as before but I now had ointment and bandages on my hands and feet.

"I won, Shuffle," I said tiredly. He patted my arm and held my hand to pull me out of the cave. I glanced back at the needle, wondering about its references to kingship and the constant nagging of the tests. Was I missing something? Did The Lady want me for something other than Champion? My blood ran cold with the thought and I covered my mouth with my scarf. I realised I'd spoken aloud without thought, could she punish me for that infraction?

We returned to our suite of rooms without further adventures, the day now dark. I'd been in the cave from dawn to dusk. When I reached the main room, The Lady waited. I bowed. She lifted her hand, looked me in the eye and snapped her fingers.

"Just because you succeeded at these tests do not think you will conquer me, mortal half breed," she said, her voice sneering and cold.

I bowed once more and hoped she planned on feeding me. I realised I'd hardly eaten for two days.

"Go to your room, I have no wish to watch you eat. Then perform the patrol you did last night before returning to your room. I will be elsewhere tonight and this thing can be on guard." She kicked out toward Shuffle.

I bowed and left for my room. Food lay everywhere and I saw Shuffle's attention to detail. He'd found, or stolen, every fine piece of food I'd missed and talked of during the last nine months. Pheasant, peacock, ham, fine bread, cheese, fruit of all kinds and bowls of buttery vegetables. A flask of wine sat on the side and I spent an hour gorging. Who knew when I'd next eat? My thoughts were filled with the need to reach the stables and to find out if Tancred had survived. I carefully avoided all thoughts about Guinevere and Arthur.

I heard The Lady leave and decided I'd eaten enough to satisfy one of those elephants I'd read about; they still made me smile. I found Shuffle outside, sporting a new bruise on his jaw. I frowned and knelt beside my friend. I touched his face and wished I could say, "When I leave here, you are coming with me."

His eyes widened in shock and he tapped his head. "You can hear me?" I asked, maintaining contact.

He nodded and grinned.

"Don't tell her," I warned.

"Promise," came back the reply inside my mind. The first word I'd heard from my friend.

I dropped a kiss to his scruffy crown, buckled on my sword and tried not to limp as I walked toward the stables.

Exhaustion did pull at me but my desire pulled harder. I found the yard, quiet and abandoned. No Tancred. My heart dropped. I sat on the hay bales and let fear race through my blood. If he'd lost and I'd given up the chance to turn the years back I'd never forgive myself. The eyes of those children would haunt me forever.

"Lancelot?" came a soft and pain filled voice.

I rose from the shadows pulled around me and found Tancred leaning against a wall. His eyes were surrounded by dark circles. His skin looked pinched and sallow. He held himself badly and I heard his breathing hitch. He'd been hurt.

He almost fell into my arms. I'd taken a glove off and I touched the skin at the back of his neck. "What happened?" I asked.

"I cannot speak of it and I shall not," he replied. "Just hold me for a moment and take the hurt away."

I didn't press the issue. He'd tell me when and if he felt ready. I didn't want to speak of my trials or the decisions I'd made through the day and how he'd held me true to my ideals. I didn't want to frighten him off; he'd understand exactly what it meant to surrender Guinevere.

"Are you physically hurt?" I asked eventually.

"Broken ribs I think," he muttered. "Broken pride. I thought Rafe was going to kill me, never mind the fucking tests. I'm cut up a bit but nothing serious. At least I lived, which is more than can be said for some."

"Rafe hurt you?" I asked.

Tancred smiled grimly. "Don't, Wolf, I don't need you fighting my battles for me. That one I have to face alone."

We kissed, more for reassurance than for passion. I think we were both exhausted and felt alone in a strange world where the rules were different to the place we knew the best.

"You are hurt," he said, holding my bandaged palm up. My fingers were raw and blisters poked through Shuffle's bandages. Some of the lacerations were also obvious.

"It's nothing," I said, as he bent his head to kiss the wounds. The thrill of his touch electrified me.

"What happened to you? I know that every decision and action I took in there, you were at my side," he said quietly.

I revelled in his words, feeling more secure every moment. Above all else I feared his love for Rafe overpowering what we shared. "You helped me stay true to my course," I confessed.

He smiled, the smile I remembered from before, a smile which seemed to come rarely these days. One unaffected by pain. "We need to go to see Morgana." He sounded and felt regretful, as though he'd far rather spend the night here in the stables.

"You managed to visit her?" I asked amazed.

"I think that's why I'm so exhausted," he confessed. "I spent all last night talking to her."

"What did you sort out?" I asked, wondering why I felt a shiver of fear run through his mind. It was strange sharing my thoughts with him rather than actual words. I sensed his changes of mood and I knew when he wanted to hide things from me.

"You should speak with Morgana, she has a plan and although I can agree to my part, I cannot speak for you," he said.

I didn't like this, he felt full of trepidation and confusion but I knew he'd never confess why and we didn't have all night to argue. I pulled my glove back on, cutting off communication. He nodded silent consent and we left the safety of the empty stables. We wove through a long series of corridors, Tancred clearly comfortable with the complications of the palace. The artwork slowly began to grow and become more complex. Colour enhanced the carvings, which interspersed the more dramatic vines. Clearly, The Lady's apartment was the simplest and least decorated. Here the scents, the colours, the visual feast started to become an assault. Tancred jumped over a low wall into one of the gardens and I followed. I hadn't walked on grass in nine months. I couldn't help but crouch down and dig my fingers into the soil.

"Lancelot, we don't have time," Tancred hissed. "If we are caught out here, this close to another contender's home, we will be killed." He pulled me upright. We came to a darkly shadowed garden, full of large trees, through which the moonlight couldn't penetrate. We both moved silently and Tancred took us to a window. He placed his ear against the glass. I could hardly see him, with the room beyond concealed by heavy curtains. He tapped lightly. A chink of light appeared but I didn't see who lay beyond. A simple latch opened on silent hinges and Tancred scrambled through. I heard his grunt of pain.

"I was beginning to think you'd both died." Morgana stood before us.

She looked pale and tired. Her beautiful crystal blue eyes were surrounded by dark circles. Her mouth appeared pinched and her cheeks hollow. I noticed a fine tremor in her hand as she brushed back a lock of long black hair. Tall, dressed in dark green, her figure enhanced by the simple silver rope draped over the round swell of her hips, which matched the swell of her full breasts, made her incredibly appealing.

Both Tancred and I bowed low.

We also drew swords at the sound of a wail from the next room. I didn't think, I just stepped in front of Morgana. She stood unarmed and my training made me want to protect her, despite the fact the bitch had stabbed me in the back, literally.

"Stand down, boys," she said tiredly. "It's not what you think. My Champion..." I heard a choke in her words and turned to look at her. "My Champion..." Her eyes filled with tears.

The woman, the warrior woman I'd seen the night we'd arrived, fighting for her mistress. Morgana swayed. I caught her by the elbow and she leaned into me. Tancred grabbed a chair. She smelt of honey and incense. A warm, rich scent.

Morgana rubbed her face with her hands and made an exasperated sound. "To business," she said, then looked at me. "So, Lancelot du Lac is really here."

I pulled down the scarf covering my face and inclined my head in acknowledgement.

Her mouth twitched in a strange half smile. "I'll be damned, The Lady did well choosing you. I'm told she holds you under a spell, threatening your precious bloody King."

I inclined my head once more.

"And now you want a deal?" she asked.

"We want to help you get what you want," Tancred said, sitting down slowly and holding his side. "Morgana, we went through all this last night."

"Listen, puppy," she snapped, pointing a manicured

finger at my friend. "You are Rafe's lapdog, so forgive me if I want to discuss this with the grownups."

I grabbed her finger in my bare hand. "You speak to him like that again and we won't be making any deal. If I fight to the death for The Lady, your Champion in there will die." I pushed the words into her mind. A wall of resistance met me and I felt her trying to force me out. I just pushed harder. I was tired, pissed off and angry. I wanted to take Tancred and leave Albion. I wanted to go home but if I did any of those things, Arthur would die.

She snatched her hand back, her eyes wide. "You are your father's son," she whispered.

I scowled. I hated it when the fey told me things like that. My father was the worst kind of man.

"Alright, Lancelot, have it your way," she said. I watched her lean back in the chair and she assessed me, her teeth chewing the inside of her mouth while she considered her words. "You might want to sit down for this," she said. "You aren't going to like it if what I've learnt about you is true."

I frowned and just stood my ground. Another wail came from next door. We all flinched.

"I never wanted this," Morgana muttered. She looked up at me. "My Champion, Enora, is not strong enough. She never was. I knew it but I allowed her to talk me into it. She can fight, she'd give you a run for your money." Morgana waved a limp hand at me. "But I knew her heart was not strong enough to face the tests. I can deny her nothing," she said. I heard a world of pain and loss. Morgana it seemed held Enora close. "I wanted the throne. Aeddan..." she glanced at me, "before you killed him, grew to appreciate my skills and even started listening to me about his excesses. Nimue fought me but I found myself enjoying the challenge. When Aeddan sent me to de Clare, I became even more powerful at Court. Losing to you and Merlin didn't help," she said darkly. "But I grew strong again."

I walked to Tancred and touched his neck. "This is all very well," he said aloud for me, "but what's the point?"

"The point," she said, irritated by our interruption. "The

point is this, I am the best person for this fucking job, but I am not strong enough to gain the throne and keep it. I cannot win against Nimue, Rafe or The Lady. Not now. I need a spectacular trick and you are going to be that trick." She rose and I saw the power grow inside her.

"Lancelot du Lac, if you want to save Arthur Pendragon, yourself and your brother's bed warmer, you are going to get me the throne and you are going to help me keep it by marrying me."

CHAPTER TWENTY ONE

My hand slipped off Tancred's neck and I think I stumbled. Regardless, I found him gripping my upper arms as he lowered me to a divan. I opened my mouth to speak but he covered it and turned my face toward his, where he knelt.

"Just listen to her, Lancelot," he said. The desperation in his eyes was very real. "It is a good plan."

I grabbed him by the throat. "You knew?" I asked.

My words were harsh and he groaned with the power of my projection.

I gathered myself, not wanting to cause him pain. "You knew about this?" I asked again.

"You are Aeddan's son, an acknowledged bastard. You killed him and destroyed his power. You are whispered about in circles of power as something to truly fear. Do you know the uproar it will cause when you win the throne for The Lady and everyone realises it's you that managed it? And what plans do you think she has for you? You are tied to her for a year and a day, she will force you to marry her or she will hurt Arthur. At least this way you can be Morgana's equal." His words tumbled over each other. He'd really thought this through.

I glanced at Morgana. She said, "I'm not happy about it either but I will do almost anything to protect Albion from the more extreme aspects of fey obsessions. I am the least corrupt of a corrupt family."

"Tancred," his name leaked through our connection on a river of confusion, fear and anger.

"I know but just wait and think," he said. "Listen to Morgana, she isn't all bad."

"Thanks for that," muttered the object of my confusion.

"I want to go home," I pushed into Tancred.

"I know you do," he said.

"Do what?" asked Morgana.

Tancred looked over his shoulder. "He wants to return to Camelot. It's all that keeps him focused. It is all he wants, all he ever wants." My friend's tone darkened and I knew he was thinking about Arthur.

"It's not all I want but it is home," I said to him.

"Why?" Tancred asked. "Why is Camelot home?"

I stared at him as though he'd lost him mind, "You want to return as well."

"No," Tancred said. "I want to be with you."

"And that is the beauty of this arrangement," Morgana interrupted, understanding Tancred's side of the conversation. "This is how it will work. You will marry me now, tonight. Tancred knows how to seal the union between us so others can feel the truth of our words when we reveal the status quo. We make a deal, you become my husband, you become King of Albion and you give me a child. So long as I am with child within the year, you are then free to leave. I will dissolve the union and you can take your plaything back to Camelot. In the meantime, if you must, we will bring Arthur into Albion to visit so at least you won't pine to death."

She spoke with the passion of a visionary but also the bitterness of a woman who is having to compromise herself for her ideals.

Tancred spoke words I placed inside his head, "How do you know I am good for breeding?"

"I don't, I'm trusting you are. If I tie myself to Aeddan's family line I have more chance of holding onto the throne even if you are gone by giving the Court a grandson of the same line."

"But the fey do not inherit the throne," Tancred said for me.

"No, but it helps if you can continue the line which came before," she said.

Politics, madness incarnate as far as I could tell.

"You really want me as King of the Fey?" we asked.

"No, not ideally, but you are most impressive of Aeddan's sons and I know you have honour. I have watched you, Lancelot. I have watched Arthur. I know the kind of man you are and I want that. If I'd known you'd sold yourself to The Lady I'd have intervened earlier." Morgana paced.

"How will this actually work, how will you save your Enora and Tancred?" I asked.

"This is the bit where you have to trust me," she said. "The only way we can stop Tancred fighting you or Enora tomorrow is for him to die."

Tancred pulled out of my grasp with my wail of anguish at the thought. "Whoa, love, stop. Slow down. It's fine. Morgana has talked me through it. I take something to kill me but hold me, you ensure I come here and she can revive me. She dealt with the Grail and created the golem, she understands more about life and death than you do."

I doubted that somehow. I looked up at Morgana. She continued, "Once I have him here I can revive him but he and Rafe will be out of contest. You will then need to kill everyone left. I can bribe enough people to stop Enora having to face anyone but the last Champion standing. That will be you. The truly clever bit is this - you can't fight against me if we are married. That's how I save you and the contest ends. I win because you cannot face my Champion but The Lady cannot hurt you or Arthur. Your marriage to me takes priority even over her magic. She is more powerful than I am but she is not able to play the game anywhere near as well."

I disagreed on that point, they just played the game differently.

"I don't want to be king," I stated. "I am not designed to be a king. I can't do it. Make me a consort or something."

"I can't," Morgana said, and I heard her regret. "I can't make you a consort or I'd have suggested that. Do you think I want you to outrank me?"

"I'm a half breed, there must be rules," I said, flopping like a fish on a hook.

She shook her head. "You are Aeddan's son. Almost every Champion that you have killed or will kill belongs to Aeddan's line. You have as much right to the throne as Nimue or Rafe. If he hadn't acknowledged you it would be very different."

I sat back on the divan. Another year in Albion but the goal posts had changed. I now had Tancred and did Camelot really need me back? Once Arthur knew I was safe we'd be able to build a union between the countries which would keep Camelot safe but I'd remain in Albion.

I touched Tancred, "I'll need a Wolf Pack."

He grinned, "You'll have one."

"Have what?" Morgana asked.

Tancred rose. "A Wolf Pack."

"He's agreed?" she asked.

I stood and approached her. Her crystal blue eyes watched me warily and I wondered if she'd been as much a victim of my father's excesses as Merla and Tancred. I touched her cheek very gently and held her hand.

"I will agree to become your husband and I will give you a child but I want my freedom after a year. You agree that for the time of your reign and that of any offspring we produce, England is safe and left alone. You agree to keeping Tancred safe from Rafe and you allow Arthur Pendragon free access to Albion so long as he does not bring an army at his back." I learnt about how to negotiate a good deal.

"Deal," she said.

"Then I will get you the throne," I said. My stomach lurched and my hand shook. King? I was going to be a king?

Morgana smiled. "Thank you." She actually looked a little shy.

"Just don't stab me in the back again," I said.

She laughed, a rich rolling sound. "I won't, I promise."

As far as fey women in my life were concerned, Morgana had at least always been honest and straightforward with me. Despite the knifing, she'd actually hurt me less than any of the others, including Else or Guinevere.

I wondered briefly what Arthur would think. He'd be bloody angry I wasn't going home easily and he'd be really pissed off I'd married without his consent. He'd also be hurt by my love for Tancred. I wondered if I could write him a letter somehow; at least that way I wouldn't have to deal with the anger directly.

"Give me both hands, Lancelot," Morgana said, interrupting my racing thoughts.

I gave her both hands. Tancred approached.

"Kneel," he said, pushing on the back of my neck and holding me so we could talk. Morgana and I both knelt and I felt a surge of power come through Tancred's hand.

"Who are you?" I asked him suddenly.

He smiled and winked. "I am the Morrigan's little brother."

"Rafe bit off more than he could chew didn't he?" I asked.

"Perhaps, or perhaps I am meant to love another after a few adventures of my own."

I glanced at Morgana. "How can you cope with marrying me if I love him?"

She said gently, "Marriage isn't about love. Marriage is about survival. You will help me survive."

"I wanted to marry for love," I said.

"You might, you have in a way." She glanced up at Tancred. "And Arthur moves through you. I can feel him."

"And you have Enora," I stated.

Morgana shrugged. "Perhaps."

"I need quiet," Tancred muttered. He closed his eyes and I watched a slow corona of light begin at the crown of his head. It spread downward, over his face and when it hit his shoulders, it rushed down his arms and into Morgana and I. We both flinched slightly. The light coursed into me but it felt very different to my binding with Arthur. It was softer, lighter and when it opened my mind up there were no memories to call my soul into Morgana's. It were as though Tancred wanted to pull me into Morgana but only with the briefest of touches. We were not soul mates, we were not lovers, we were going to be married in the fey way, but we were not bound together.

He intoned words I didn't understand.

His breathing grew shallow and I felt his arm tremble on my shoulder. Where his fingers touched my neck, so we could speak, I felt small shocks of power flicker into me.

"Something is wrong," he said. His eyes were closed and the colour drained from his face. "It's his binding to Arthur. I can't pull him into you, Morgana. There isn't anything to pull."

"But he loves you," she said and heard strain in her voice.

"That isn't the same thing. His soul is bound to Arthur even if his heart is mine," Tancred confessed.

"I don't understand," I said still feeling nothing of the pain the others appeared to suffer.

Morgana's eyes glowed passionately. "This is going to be unpleasant."

I tried to ask, 'what' and I tried to say 'stop'. Instead I felt a screaming agony inside my body and mind. So bad, I couldn't have cried out if I wanted to. My whole sense of self became blood red and black. Every wound I had ever suffered came back to me tenfold and I caught a flash of Arthur doubled over in his conference room screaming in agony. Geraint and Yvain caught him as he fell and Gawain ran for Merlin. For one moment his eyes looked straight into mine. "Wolf," he choked.

The world went dark.

CHAPTER TWENTY TWO

This time I woke on a soft bed with my doublet and shirt gone. Tancred sat beside me. "He's awake," he said to someone else.

I touched his hand and felt him grip my fingers. Damn me, I had fingers and toes. I wanted to groan but remembered I dare not. He brushed hair out of my face. "Sorry, love, we couldn't make it happen gently. We didn't have time. You'd need to fall in love with Morgana and that's not overly likely. It seems Rafe did a very good job of binding your soul to Arthur's, which is why he still lives. The Lady used it to heal Arthur in the first place. If I'd understood a bit more..." he let the sentence trail off.

Morgana came into the room. "We don't have much time," she said.

She'd changed. A light white gown of damask silk, embroidered with white vines and flowers, hung from her shoulders and hinted to the curves underneath.

"Leave us," she ordered.

"I think I ought -" Tancred said.

"No, you leave now." Morgana's eyes were haunted but determined. I wondered what the hell was going on.

Tancred glanced at me. "Enjoy, my friend, and we'll talk later."

I opened my mouth and clutched at his fingers as he vanished from my side and left the room. I struggled from the bed intending to go after him but Morgana stood in my way.

"Drink this, it will help," Morgana said, thrusting a cup into my hand. She hardly looked at me.

I put the cup down, and reached for her hand. "What's going on? What happened?" I asked.

"We are married but we need to fuck to make it real," she said. Her brutality shocked me far more than the essence of what she'd said.

"Morgana, I don't understand?"

"I know you prefer men and I'm sorry I can't allow you to fuck me up my - "

"Don't," I snapped into her mind and she flinched. "Don't cheapen what I desire and don't presume to know what I prefer." I paused. "Now, just calm down. I'm not going to jump on you or hurt you." I would have made a joke but now didn't seem the time.

She stared at me with her jaw thrust out and her full dark lips pouting. I brushed my hand up her neck. She had fine white skin and her hair felt so heavy when I lifted it slightly off her shoulders. She was a beautiful woman.

"Were you lovers with Aeddan?" I asked, maintaining eye contact.

"None of your damned business," she snapped and tried to pull away.

I held her firmly but gently. "It is if he hurt you even half as much as he hurt Merla."

Her eyes flicked to mine in surprise. I had my answer. I leaned forward slightly and kissed her brow. "Morgana, listen carefully. I am not my father. I have never taken a woman by coercion or force and I will not begin now." Her eyes suddenly swam with tears. "Tell me," I said gently, "what I can do to make this easier? What is the minimum we need to do to make this a real union when The Lady screams the place down tomorrow?"

Morgana relaxed slightly, "Really?"

I nodded.

"When was the last time you laid with a woman?" she asked.

I shrugged. "It's been a few years but I've had a lot of practice. I'm fairly certain I won't forget where everything is."

She smiled slightly at the joke. My fingers found her pulse and it began to calm. She was terrified of me. I bent only a little to kiss her neck and my left hand encircled her waist but I didn't hold her tight to my body. She felt very stiff and her breathing changed but it wasn't desire, unless you count the need to run.

I pulled back. "You really need to tell me what you can handle. I can't see how to do this quickly without causing you hurt and I don't want to that." Her distress upset me badly.

"Just get it over with," Morgana said, pulling me toward the bed. "It won't be first time I've done this to gain want I want."

"I can imagine, knowing fey as I do," I said, resisting her tug and lacing my words with contempt for their methods. "But it is not how I do things."

She stamped her foot. "I don't need you to make love to me."

"Well, tough, because that's what I do with women, including the lovely ladies I pay," I announced.

She blinked at that. "Really?"

"Yes, really," I said.

She returned to my body and ran her hand over my chest, her fingers brushing my newest scar. "Where is the one I gave you?" she asked. I found her soft curiosity slightly disturbing.

I turned and pointed to the one just beside my spine in my lower back. "You almost killed me. If it hadn't been for Merla I'd have died."

"Interfering old woman," Morgana cursed.

I smiled but didn't comment; there didn't seem much point. Morgana bent and kissed the scar, she then ran her hands over the others. Some had almost vanished now, but others were still rough. I remained still, just watching her exploring me. When she returned to stand in front of me, she looked down at my erection.

"Hmm," she said with a small frown.

"You are a beautiful woman and you are touching lonely skin," I explained.

"You have a romantic streak in you a league wide."

I shrugged. "The last time you lay with a man, was it a bed or the floor?" I asked.

"Bed," she said and her shoulders stiffened.

I led her toward the softest rug I could see. The skin of several sheep. "Lie down," I instructed.

"You have to place your seed inside me," she said in a small voice.

"Alright, but we do this gently and when you want to, we stop," I said. I wondered how Arthur managed to do this with Guinevere after Stephen raped her.

I lay on the rug and just waited. Morgana took a deep breath and almost dropped beside me.

"What would be better for you?" I asked by touching her hand.

"I don't understand."

"What position, Morgana?" She wasn't making this easy but I guessed I wouldn't in her place. I frowned and sat up. I sensed ants running over my skin because of her power escaping through her fear. I didn't like this, it felt wrong. If she ever came to my bed, it would need to be completely on her terms. "You really can't do this can you?" I asked, my ardour fading.

"I can do anything. I'm going to be Queen of Albion." She set her jaw in a stubborn thrust. I had the feeling I'd learn to dread that look.

Her hand gripped my cock through my hose. I grabbed her wrist. "Wait." She paused. "Get Tancred back in here," I said.

She blinked. "What? Why?" Her voice rose.

"You just need my seed inside you right?" I asked.

"Technically, yes."

"Then get him in here and I'll make love to him which is actually what we both want. All you need is something to smear in places you don't want me right now."

"You can pleasure yourself, you don't need him," she said.

"Listen, woman, this is my wedding night and I'd like to spend it with someone who actually wants me," I snapped, finally running out of patience.

She had the good grace to blush but she did scramble upright and head for the door. I heard a hurried and confused conversation before Tancred appeared.

"What the hell is going on?" he asked.

I'd had enough of waiting. Nine months of celibacy

suddenly pressed hard and my balls ached. I didn't bother to play nice. I slammed the door shut, grabbed Tancred and kissed him deeply. He groaned. I found words even as we kissed.

"I need you," I said inside his mind.

His groin pressed into mine and his hands pulled me into his body. He devoured my mouth, my neck, my shoulder and licked my chest. "New scar," he muttered, fever quick.

I wanted to give voice to my desire. I wanted to howl the palace down. I tangled my hand in his short hair and pulled. He rose up my body and we kissed once more. I tugged at his doublet and we broke apart long enough to strip. A huge purple and yellow bruise on Tancred's ribs reminded me he was badly hurt, but I'd also never seen him look stronger. His skin, the scars still harsh, remained hairless and muscles rippled. I wouldn't want to try to wrestle him to the ground. We were a match in strength. Anything he gave, he gave willingly.

We half stumbled, half fell on the bed.

His hand took hold of me. "She said she needs your seed?" he asked, confused.

"I can't come inside you," I said.

"Can I come inside you?" he asked.

I cocked my head. "That's not what you usually want."

"I do now," he stated. I remembered his demanding presence the night before, kicking my legs a part and keeping me pinned against the wall. The only thing that had controlled him previously seemed to be his emotional vulnerability and my lack of time.

"Is it a deal breaker?" I asked. I preferred the dominant role.

"Never, but it is what I need," he said, and something in his eyes told me to be careful.

"Alright." I'd consent to anything right then just to feel him touching me.

He smiled and suddenly I found him everywhere at once. His mouth delved into mine. His fingers explored and he forced my knees up. He pulled a small vial of oil out of his clothing and licked up my cock.

"I wish I could hear you cry out my name," he whispered even as his fingers pushed into my body.

I bit back a cry of desperation. He pulled himself up my body, with his fingers still probing me. "Your ribs," I managed to think.

"What ribs?" he asked.

He'd never been so strong or so insistent. When I tried to help, he slapped my hand away and bit my neck, hard. I quivered in desperation. He growled, "This is for leaving me, Wolf."

And he was there, pushing against me. I wanted to say he'd left me but now was not the time and I didn't care. I tilted my hips up and tried to relax. He groaned, bowing his head. I licked his ear and his neck. He thrust hard and I clamped down on his shoulder, smothering a groan behind my wheezing breath. He pushed deeper. I couldn't take it.

"Yes, you fucking can," he said, pushing harder.

I felt the orgasm grow, the spiralling power turning into the perfect vortex of energy. Tancred thrust and withdrew with precision and perfect timing. I felt something wet land on my chest and pulled his face up to mine. His eyes were full of tears. "I love you," he said and shuddered.

The vortex spun out of my control and shot out of my body, both through the top of my head in the form of perfect shining love and desire over my belly. The muscles in Tancred's arms trembled as he held himself over me, panting and weeping quietly.

I pushed him out of me, my body a mess of sensations, and helped him curl up beside me, his head on my chest, his body inside the crock of my arm. I kissed his head and held his fingers between mine. I felt my desire cooling on my belly.

There were no words, just peace for a moment.

It didn't last long.

The door opened and Morgana walked in. She didn't comment but approached me, saw what was necessary and scraped a knife blade along my flat stomach. I grabbed her wrist.

"You could have waited," I said bitterly, somehow feeling I was being robbed.

"No, I couldn't, and neither can you. You both need to return to your places." She pulled out of my grasp and vanished.

CHAPTER TWENTY THREE

Tancred and I argued as we dressed, which proved complicated because I needed to touch him to talk to him.

"Lancelot, I will be perfectly safe," he insisted.

I yanked my shirt over my head, then slid my hand up his back, while he pulled on his hose. "No, you won't. You will be dead, how is that safe? Even with Morgana's magic holding you to this word, your soul will have left your body. Why can't you just stay here and hide?" I reached for my doublet.

"I can't, Rafe will find me. Please, trust me and let's just get this day done. It's hard enough knowing I can't be there to help you fight," he said. His bitterness made it obvious he wanted to stand at my shoulder and help me win this throne.

I grabbed the back of his neck as he laced his boots. "And I will fight more efficiently if I know you are safe," I said trying to help.

Tancred twisted away, knocking my hand off his neck. He was properly angry by the time he turned to face me. "Is this what I can expect? Fucking hell, Lancelot, I'm a grown man and I am more than able to make my own fucking decisions. This isn't about you, it's about Rafe. I have to find a way out from under him and Morgana has given me a way out."

A horrible idea occurred to me. I snatched at his hand before he could move back. "You've made a deal with her."

"Just leave it alone," Tancred said.

"What's the deal?" I asked.

His brown eyes were harsh, like garnets full of dark flame. "The death will untangle me from Rafe. But I need her to put me back together. I am bound into Rafe, like you are to Arthur, but you don't want to escape. If I leave Albion, or Rafe, he can hunt me down. I cannot be what I want to be and have myself tied to him. I want to be your equal, not his slave. In return, I never get in her way. My job will be to facilitate your relationship with her until it stops."

I stood and just stared at him dumbly. He was right. I did treat him like a child who needed looking after. I didn't understand his relationship with Rafe and I didn't respect his ability to care for himself. Tancred needed to fix his life his way and I just had to trust him. With regard to him helping Morgana handle me, that worked both ways. I was just grateful it wasn't anything worse.

"Sorry," I mouthed silently.

He paused, nodded and before I knew it we were kissing. "Just make certain I am here when I need to be, Wolf," he said.

"I will, I promise, and the first thing I am doing when this is over is to make you King's Champion."

He chuckled. "That would be a fun twist on an old motif."

We left our room. We moved as a unit, profoundly attached to each other but we were definitely separate men of power and intent. It felt odd; good, but odd. As though, because of our time apart, we now knew how to live as dominant men in our own right. Maybe confidence is the correct term, we were confident in our own abilities and each other.

Morgana sat near a fireplace I'd missed completely, with all the confusion and drama. We looked at each other. She now wore a housecoat full of the colours of gold and yellow. She was very beautiful, the hardness in her face softened by the grief in her eyes.

"How is Enora?" I asked gently, by crouching beside her chair and touching her fingers.

"She will live." Morgana looked tired. I realised it must be very late at night after a profoundly long day.

I felt like I should offer comfort but Morgana didn't seem like the kind of woman to accept emotional aid lightly. I just said, "Good." I rose and returned to Tancred.

"Leave now, you both have your instructions for

tomorrow." She turned in the chair slightly, giving us her back.

Tancred and I bowed. I honestly had no idea how to deal with a woman I didn't know and would have said I hated less than half a day ago, but who now declared herself my wife. I walked in silence next to Tancred, weaving my way through the complex palace hallways. If everything went to plan, I'd be King here by tomorrow night. The idea felt so alien and ridiculous I almost laughed.

We made it to The Lady's hallway. I pulled Tancred to a stop.

"Listen," I said, hooking my fingers through his. "What you plan for tomorrow scares me. But I will accept your choices. Just be careful. Although I know I can live without you, I'd rather not." I tried to inject some humour into the thought.

Tancred smiled. "I love you," he said. He laid a brief kiss on my cheek and simply left me there in the hallway. I stared after his retreating back. He really had changed.

Shuffle sat in front of the door looking miserable. When I came around the corner, he hurried toward me and threw his arms around my waist, pressing his poor deformed body against my legs and his head into my ribs.

I touched his face. "What's wrong?" I asked.

"Lady back," he howled. His fear at the horror to be inflicted on me made me very sorry I'd taken so long.

"It will be alright, Shuffle," I said. "I'll find a way out of this."

He'd become so unused to speaking, I didn't receive clear thoughts and messages like I had from the others. I just received blurred emotions and concepts, which made my head pound. With gentle hands, I pulled him off me and prepared myself to meet my real enemy. I had the feeling this would happen so I had my cover story ready if she asked.

I didn't bother to knock. I did, however, bow toward the small figure spitting rage in the darkness.

Her black eyes shone from the shadows. "Give me," she

hissed, "one good reason I shouldn't cut your heart out and feed it to you."

I could think of a great many reasons, but I didn't say anything.

The pain hit me and I toppled like a felled tree. It was so inevitable I almost welcomed it. I retreated, diving inside to escape, but this time she followed. Wave after wave smacked into my mind. My body jack-knifed with the agony none could see. She stripped away Tancred, Arthur, Morgana, everything. I had no defence before her and my exhaustion left me weak.

In desperation and feeling as though she might actually kill me this time, I forced myself to think of a wall, a stone wall around the core of my being. Just as I'd learnt with my new form of talking and through the experiences I'd had learning to control my magical addiction to Else, I pushed that wall out. I let the pain in but forced it around the wall and I gradually expanded the sensation. I didn't think about the sweaty, gasping mess on the floor of our suite. I just concentrated on not allowing this fucking woman to steal my mind.

I'd gone through hell today because of her. I'd been slogging my guts out for months on her orders and I'd never even had a thank you. Chivalry works both ways. Women want my fucking protection and service then they have to at least say thank you.

My own anger made the wall big and it shot up quickly. It spun out of control and tore from my mind, an independent rock of raw power. The agony torturing my body ceased and at the same moment, The Lady screamed. I watched her crumple, my breath wheezing and twisting inside me. The door opened and Shuffle stood there. He opened his mouth but nothing came out.

I pulled myself off the floor, feeling sick and dizzy. I approached The Lady, as though she were a snake about to strike me. Had I killed her? Shuffle came toward us, collecting a lamp and striking it. The light filtered through the darkness and gradually revealed the small figure. She looked like a child with her eyes closed and her defences down. Shuffle clearly didn't want to breach her physical presence, so I knelt and reached forward.

My hand shook slightly, reaching for a pulse. I'd often wondered if she had a heart, now I'd know. The essence of what had just happened baffled me. How had I caused this? How had I created a weapon from the pain and panic inside my head? What the hell was I turning into?

My hand stopped a finger's width from her neck. Her black eyes snapped open. Shuffle yelped and hid behind me.

"Don't touch me, you animal," she said. Her voice conveyed her loathing, perfectly.

I snatched my hand back and stood, pushing away from her quickly. She rose far more slowly and her legs clearly didn't want to know.

"Get out," she snapped, her voice thin and reedy. "Get out of my sight, both of you."

Shuffle pulled on my doublet trying to make me move. I bowed my head and we left, returning to our own room. I threw myself on the bed and lay back, covering my face with my arm. Images flashed through my mind, Tancred with his muscles straining laying over me, his heat and passion overwhelming. Morgana, her fear and anger alongside her resolve making me respect not just her beauty but also her integrity. The series of tests I'd faced, which now seemed a lifetime ago. Arthur, Guinevere, and the choices I'd made which I'd blamed on others.

Arthur. Was The Lady now going to kill him for my rebellion? I'd not even thought about Arthur when she'd been hurting me. All I'd wanted to accomplish was survival. I wanted to survive so I could save Tancred.

Despite my assumptions that I would always choose Arthur, when I'd been faced with the terrible pain The Lady inflicted, my subconscious had chosen Tancred. I had no way of knowing if Arthur lived. I just had to trust she wanted to use him to goad me into winning the gladiatorial contests tomorrow.

I felt Shuffle banging my hand against his head. He wanted to talk. I sighed and turned my head to look at him.

His eyes asked clearly enough. I said gently, "I don't know what happened. She was killing me and I have to survive."

Shuffle dropped my hand and twisted his ugly broken face into a frown. He didn't want to know any more, so I rolled onto my side and closed my eyes completely, welcoming the darkness lurking in the background.

CHAPTER TWENTY FOUR

A door slamming open woke me completely and suddenly. I shot to my feet and found myself heading for the antechamber before I registered my surroundings.

"Where is he?" I heard Rafe scream.

I walked into chaos. Rafe stood in the doorway, his long red hair in disarray around his shoulders. The Lady stood before him and they were yelling. When Rafe caught sight of me, he fairly flew across the room. I turned slightly and reached for him even as his hands sought my throat. My half brother's face twisted in hate and grief. Unfortunately, he didn't have my skills, so I ended up pushing him to the wall to hold him still, rather than the other way around.

"You bastard," Rafe screamed into my face. "You killed him. He's dead because of you." He waved a note in my face. The first part of the plan and something to provoke Rafe into telling me instantly what had happened.

Tancred. Shit. I glanced outside the window and realised the sun graced the horizon bathing the sky in that beautiful azure blanket. He'd taken the potion.

I dropped Rafe and headed for the exit. The Lady stood before me. Her black eyes emanated hate. "How do they know who you are?" she asked, her anger dancing around her.

How could I explain to this woman of spite and hate my heart lay dead in Rafe's suite? I couldn't, so I continued to play her game within my rules, not hers. For my own reasons I now wanted the other fey to be ignorant of my identity, so I covered my face with the scarf she'd insisted I wear and simply left. Whatever she did to Arthur, I'd deal with separately. I had to reach Tancred and I had to ensure he reached Morgana and she would protect Arthur from The Lady. I raced through the twisted corridors, trying desperately to remember the way, and I prayed I'd save Tancred while leaving Arthur whole.

Chaos reigned outside Rafe's rooms. A young man sobbed in the doorway. I pushed him aside and strode into Rafe's apartments. It looked almost identical to his villa in the countryside, tasteful but far too decorative for my tastes.

Tancred, still dressed as a Champion, lay on his bed, in a separate room to Rafe's grand bedroom. He didn't move as I entered. His eyes didn't open, his head lay off the edge of his bed and his limbs were contorted. A grimace spoiled his face and I realised the poison hurt him. I should have found another way to untangle him from Rafe - and what the hell had my brother done to him to make him want to die this badly?

I lifted Tancred's chest to mine and hooked my arms under his knees. Blue lips remained still as I lifted, but his eyelids opened. The soft brown of his eyes now contained a film of white. My heart quailed. I'd left it too late.

I heard Rafe screaming his grief. I hugged Tancred close to my chest, then shifted position. I'd need my sword. I threw my friend over my shoulder and drew Caliburn. My half brother appeared in the doorway.

"What did you do?" he snarled. "And put him down, he belongs to me."

I said nothing. I simply lifted Caliburn toward my brother's chest with surprising calm. Tancred had made me promise I would not harm Rafe.

"He died for you. To save you, because I wouldn't withdraw and he knew he'd beat you in a fair fight. " Rafe's voice cracked. His grief moved me. My brother truly loved Tancred. It was a shame he manifested it in a way Tancred couldn't handle.

I shook my head. I dare not speak if this geis still lay on my soul and touched Arthur.

The tears in Rafe's eyes glittered dangerously. "You planned this!" His finger jabbed toward my chest. "You planned this between you. You made him do this."

I raised Caliburn to his throat.

"Never. You will never take him from me." Rafe lunged forward. I tried to deflect him using the back of my sword but, hampered by Tancred's considerable weight and general lack of space, I twisted badly. Caliburn caught Rafe in the shoulder. It glided through him and out the other side, separating his arm almost completely at the joint.

His forward momentum stopped. His eyes opened wide in shock and his mouth formed a comical 'oh' of surprise. He dropped. Caliburn sang in my hand as I watched in horror the blood of my brother spread over the floor.

I shook myself. I stepped over Rafe's body and raced out of the chaos erupting around my hasty departure.

Fortunately for me, Morgana's suite lay only a short distance away. I rounded two corners at a full run and almost collided with her in the corridor.

"Where in all the darkest pits have you been?" she snapped. "I can feel him slipping away."

I didn't bother to try to explain. She hurried me into her rooms and I lay Tancred on the bed we'd used that night.

"I need his chest bare," Morgana began trying to undo his laces. I batted her hands away, drew my knife and cut through the leather armour. I cut through his gambeson, then attacked his shirt.

When Morgana saw the river of scars over Tancred's chest her breath hissed. "I had no idea it was this bad," she whispered running her hand down his stomach.

I grabbed her hand. "You knew about this?" My guts twisted. Of course she knew about it, she was Aeddan's right hand.

"I..." her blue eyes looked up at me and I saw a world of confusion.

"Just bring him back," I said swallowing the bile.

She nodded once, placed her hands on his chest and I staggered under the weight of power she summoned instantly. Words, older than any I knew, flowed in a guttural torrent. Her shoulders hunched and sweat formed on her brow and lip. She didn't stop speaking but I watched her climb onto Tancred's hips and push harder onto his chest. I thought her hands would vanish into the muscles that stayed horribly still.

Tears began to flow down Morgana's face and her voice became a weapon of grief and pleading. I stood back and tried to figure out if there was anything I could do to help her.

Morgana suddenly flattened over Tancred and she kissed him, deeply. She held his head between her hands and plundered his mouth. I remembered kissing Else to stop her slipping into death. It had been a great deal softer than this vision of lust before me.

"Come back, for Albion's sake return," Morgana muttered when she broke away. "For Camelot, for your Wolf's sake, whatever it takes, Tancred, just come back because I need you to live for him."

I didn't really understand what she was saying because all I heard were words which meant she was giving up on my Cub.

Tancred's chest heaved and he bucked under Morgana. She flinched and squeaked as his arms wrapped around her body. He pulled her against him as if he could steal the warmth of her body.

She turned to me. "He'll live." Her eyes were wild, the power pulsed through her trembling form. "Leave now and win, the fighting will start soon. Fight for us, Lancelot."

I glanced at Tancred but he didn't seem to see me. I bowed to Morgana and left, feeling disoriented and exhausted. Fighting. I began to focus on fighting. That I could do and I understood. Gladiatorial battles to the death were a great deal easier than confusing magic and emotional drama.

The months I'd been subservient to The Lady fell away. Something inside me had been released, unplugged. Through her training and treatment of me, I'd become different. I felt a consuming fire in my belly that gave me great purpose. If I won today, I would become King of Albion. Still an absurd idea, but one which gave me a focus beyond myself. When I defeated my enemies, Arthur would be safe, and Tancred. So would everyone else I loved. If I took control, Albion would cease to be a threat.

Feeling the pressure of time, I broke into a loping run, holding Caliburn tight. It felt good to have an objective. I rounded a corner and found Shuffle in the hallway. He beckoned and I approached with half an eye on the door, waiting for The Lady to appear. Shuffle grabbed my hand and pulled it to gain my attention.

"She gone to watch the fight. She thinks Lord Rafe was the one you wanted to stop because of the boy," Shuffle screwed his eyes shut trying to think clearly enough for me to hear him. "She wrong though."

Shuffle's perception disturbed me and I found it hard to control the images of Morgana flying through my head, or Rafe's bloody body collapsed on the floor of his apartment. I still didn't know if I could trust him during my betrayal. I knelt before him and held his crooked head in my hands.

"Trust me, please. I need you to help me dress and then I need to fight. I promise to tell you everything but I can't yet. Our lives depend on me winning because I don't think either of us will survive The Lady's anger if I don't win."

"How did you hurt her?" Shuffle asked. "Who is Tancred?"

"I don't know how I hurt her. I am Aeddan's son and I'm beginning to feel like that might not be such a bad thing. She has taught me a great deal more than she intended." I paused when I thought about his next question. I admitted, "Tancred is my lover. We are both vassals of King Arthur."

"I had a lover once," Shuffle said. A wave of sadness engulfed me and the image of a lovely young woman with bright red hair and freckles rose to the surface of his mind.

I wanted to wrap him in my arms and protect him from any more loss. "I have to fight," I thought instead and he nodded, blinking back tears.

"I have not said thank you for your friendship," he managed. "Whatever happens next, I want you to know how much it has meant to me."

"You are the only thing which has made life bearable, Shuffle, and I will never forget that," I touched his broken face tenderly.

He smiled his lopsided smile and nodded briefly, acknowledging my affection. He then shook himself and said, "Fighting." He ended the connection between us by walking away.

I dressed quickly, the armour perfect, a second metal skin encasing me tightly but not restricting my movements. The smiths of Camelot couldn't have done a better job. Still tightening the odd strap, Shuffle led me to where I would fight. After moving quickly through a long series of tunnels, I heard the roar of a crowd. I finally realised our destination would be the same arena where I'd faced Aeddan and he'd died. The whole damned city would be watching me destroy all those that stood between me and the throne of Albion.

Nothing but the fight filled my head as we approached. I saw the warriors who remained. Nimue's giant man remained, with the slow voice but sharp mind and fast body. The pack of small soldiers who moved as one unit but were actually three, fixed their bright red eyes on me balefully and they growled their hate in my direction. Another set of eyes looked at me from a deep shadow; Enora stepped forward. She looked terrible. I stepped toward her, pulled by her obvious pain. Her white skin looked slick with sweat and her breathing came in shallow gasps.

With my hands encased in metal, I couldn't touch her, but she raised her hand to the only piece of skin showing on my face, just under my eyes. "Win for her. She has healed me as well as she can considering she had to save your friend, but you need to win." Enora's eyes were almost white. I nodded my promise.

There were others under the arena floor with me. A man who dressed and moved like a knight. He bowed to me and I returned the honour. He would fight in a traditional style much like myself. The strange tree man appeared in his small form and I watched him warily. How I'd fight something like that I had no idea. I'd expected more of us to survive the recent trials but we were all that remained of those proud men and women who attended the banquet. I suddenly wished I had Tancred beside me and we were fighting as a team.

"We have drawn lots," came the snarling voice of a man more scars than skin. He carried a long black single tailed whip and a short sword at his hip. He stood shoulder height but his muscles far outweighed mine. He pointed a short finger at me, "You and you," he pointed at the tree man. "You are to fight first. Only one of you gets to walk back in here."

The tree man grinned at me. His teeth were very sharp. Trees with sharp teeth? And I thought I would know how to become a king of these people?

Shuffle pulled on my hand and as I knelt before him, he touched my face. "Every enemy has a weakness. His will be his balance. Get him down and you can hack him up."

Easier said than done, I imagined. Those that survived the tests of yesterday would not be easy to defeat. I lowered my visor and followed the man in charge of this madness up a short corridor to a large gate. The smoke from torches and heat made me desperate to uncover my face but I knew I'd lose the sallet at some point, I always did, that would make me vulnerable to unpredictable enemies. I also couldn't afford for my cover to be blown just yet.

I focused as a vast iron gate swung open before us and we walked into the arena.

CHAPTER TWENTY FIVE

The noise, when you are fighting a personal battle with a crowd present, is overwhelming. Whenever I took part in a joust at home, I'd never managed to control my despair at the crowd's blood lust. Here it smothered me tenfold. Engulfed in wave after wave of noise I just watched the spectacle of hundreds, perhaps thousands of people crowing for death. The stands swept up from the ground, the large branches of some tree controlled by fey magic forming the walls and floor. Overhead the sky remained clear and blue, the heat punishing me for wearing full armour. The faces around me blurred and I turned, looking for one which might stand out in the crowd. I finally found the main area for the candidates. The Lady sat, dressed in white, perfect and isolated from the others. Nimue sat beside her cousin, her flame red hair enhancing the beauty of her features and blending with a dress of the same colour, making her look almost naked and yet clothed all at once. Weird. Her expression appeared bored but I saw the tension in those elegant shoulders. Several men surrounded her and I wondered if they were also contenders or acolytes. On the other side of the platform sat Morgana. My breath caught. She rose as our eyes met. She wore a plain gown of green and raven black hair cascaded over one shoulder. I'd never seen her look so fragile or so beautiful. If she wanted to manipulate me into fighting for her, she'd picked exactly the right image to portray.

Tancred was not there, neither was Rafe.

An announcement dragged my mind back to the present. I bowed to the platform, hoping both women would think I bowed for them.

On the ritual words, "let the fight begin," I moved back toward the centre of the arena. I thought about attacking the tree man while he remained small, but he unravelled so fast he blurred and came at me in the same instant.

I drew Caliburn and dived to my right to avoid my head being instantly smashed by an arm the size of a ship's mast. I hit the ground, rolled, rose and turned, sweeping Caliburn up and out. I made contact with shocking effect. The sword juddered in my hand and I felt her wail in my head. We were not fighting something she understood. It was like trying to grapple fish while riding Ash. The sword, once a comfort, now hindered my mind and filled me with confusion.

The tree man laughed, clearly aware whatever magic he held damaged me. Another swift movement of his arms and thick branches with fingers like jagged twigs lashed out at me and knocked me clean across the arena. I hit the barrier protecting the jeering crowd with my back and shoulder. Pain coalesced inside my head and as predicted, I tugged at my helmet. It came away as the tree man waved his arms in celebration. Fucking stupid thing to do. Never celebrate a victory until you have your enemy's head on a spear.

Rage filled me. The rage I knew when those I loved were threatened. If this tree man won against me, I'd die and so would everyone I loved. I stood up and regained my breath. I sheathed Caliburn and ran. Shuffle said his balance was his weakness. I knew how to take a man's balance. A tree wouldn't be any different. With a knife now in each hand, I ran inside his long reach and once more tucked and rolled, imitating him when he was in his small mode. I pushed myself up and lashed out with my knives. Two shallow wounds opened cleanly on his long legs. He howled his unhappiness. I continued to move past him and under him. He turned to keep me in view but couldn't reach me with his long arms quickly enough. I twisted and thrust once more toward his legs. The wounds opened and strange milky liquid began pouring out. He stamped at me and I lost ground by dancing back. His hands caught me and I found myself once more spinning through the air. I hit the barrier again, but this time I felt my head smack back against the wooden wall. My vision faded and blood filled my mouth. I'd bitten my tongue. Hands once more grabbed me and I lashed out blindly. I was hurt.

Instinct made me slash at the right places. I dropped a long way and landed badly. My right knee buckled and twisted. I needed to scream in agony and frustration. I was better than this but with everything I'd endured and experienced over the last few days, I'd grown far more exhausted than even I could handle.

I stumbled upright and spat blood onto the arena floor. I also felt blood down the back of my neck and down my face. Joy.

The tree man came at me again. I danced back, stooped down and picked up a handful of sand. It trickled through my fingers but I threw it toward the gnashing teeth in front of me. He reeled and I rushed forward, throwing my knives down. I grabbed his right arm, the one with most damage and made contact. I slammed the side of my left hand into where his biceps would be and felt something akin to a muscle flinch badly. My left hand dropped to the place his elbow sat and my right hand controlled his forearm. I pushed toward and past him. I aimed for a spot behind him, where his third leg would be if he were a three legged stool. He cursed and began to lean back impossibly far. I just maintained my focus on that one point and angled him into it while keeping control of his arm. Just as when the wind spends too long punishing a tree, no matter how deep the roots, the tree will topple before the larger power. He collapsed with a strange sound. I didn't stop to think, I just acted. As he fell, I moved his arm to bring the elbow joint over my knee and I snapped the branch. He screamed.

I continued on and dropped both knees onto the place resembling his ribs. They cracked and gave far more easily than a man's. I landed a punch in that strange mouth and watched milky liquid fill it, only to bubble out and slip into the sand. The tree man sighed and closed his eyes.

I'd won.

I stood up and swayed slightly, feeling sick. When would I ever be able to stop fighting?

Morgana still stood, when I finally managed to face the platform, fear and relief warred over her face. The Lady smiled smugly. A man cursed and stomped off the platform in rage. Nimue laughed. A shadow moved behind Morgana. She held out her hand. A man stood beside her, his face covered just like mine but he wore soft black clothing, not leather armour. It didn't stop me from recognising Tancred. He moved slowly. His eyes were shadowed and I saw the pain of his death and resurrection haunted him but he nodded toward me. I smiled in relief and nodded in return. The Lady's head shot sideways as she watched the exchange.

I shook my muddled head. Let Morgana deal with the politics, I had more people to kill.

How I made it back to the now cool tunnel under the arena, I wasn't quite certain. My right knee hollered the entire time and my back moaned. Blood flowed down my neck and my tongue started to throb. I felt way too old for all this shit. Shuffle appeared and I leaned on him; so did Enora, which surprised me. They half carried me into a small cell off the main corridor. Shuffle began stripping me of the armour covering my limbs and I heard the crowd cheering the new contestants. I just surrendered to his care and Enora's. Her hands were quick and light. I felt her hold a cup to my lips and I drank water with gratitude.

"You fought well," she said. Her accent sounded strange and I needed to concentrate. The vowels were very round as if she found the language alien. "The Orction are a difficult race to fight," she assured me.

I touched her arm. "They are not so difficult."

She smiled at my obvious lie, then chuckled. "Morgana will be relieved, she is worried for you."

"She is more worried about you," I pointed out.

Enora's smile faded. "I let her down."

"No, that's not what she feels. And if you hadn't done this she wouldn't be able to save my miserable arse," I said.

"If this is saving your," she paused, "arse," she said slowly, "then I am glad I never had to face you in battle, your Majesty."

Shuffle grabbed my free hand and almost knocked himself out he bashed it against his head so hard, "What?" he screamed inside my head.

I flinched. "Calm, my friend, please."

"What is she talking about? And what's all this about Morgana and why is she helping me care for you?" Shuffle demanded.

"Any chance I could explain later?" I pleaded.

Shuffle scowled at me. I sighed and tried to explain our plan. I ended with, "Part of the deal is getting you out from under The Lady."

"You married Morgana?" he'd repeated this thought several times.

"It seemed the best option," I told him.

Enora had spent the time we'd been in silent communication examining me. "You have bruised ribs. Your armour is bent so badly we'll never get it back on you and your right knee is badly damaged. You have a bad head wound and I suspect concussion. But you can hold a sword so you can go on."

Shuffle smacked her hands and pushed her away. He stood before me. "You married the woman who killed my girl and handed me to The Lady in the first place."

The news took long laboured breaths to make sense. "If it helps," I finally thought, "she tried to kill me by stabbing me in the back."

"No, it doesn't help." Shuffle's wail ground through my mind.

"Alright, I'm sorry," I pleaded, "but sometimes we just have to live with the way things are. Please, you have to understand. I couldn't face Tancred in there and I will not allow The Lady to take the throne."

"She is better than Aeddan's puppet and murderess!" Shuffle screamed.

I stood up slowly and towered over Shuffle. He looked up at me. Now no longer in physical contact we shared no words, but we knew each other well. I saw the hurt and betrayal in his eyes. He witnessed my determination in that I'd chosen the right path. He dropped his gaze first. I knew he would and I felt dirty making him do it. We were no longer equals suddenly. I wanted to say to him, we'd find the time to sort this out, but I didn't know how to breach his shell.

Enora vanished but Shuffle stayed. He stitched the head wound, none too gently, and strapped my knee. He helped me redress in the bits of detached armour, banging it and twisting it in his strong hands with some passion, so it would fit me again. I watched in silence and wondered about the consequences of my actions. We left the small cell and I realised the other knight must be fighting the three small men with the red eyes.

The giant walked toward me. I looked up at nine foot of solid wall. "We are to fight," he announced. "I thought I would fight the woman, but you have been chosen again."

Great, I thought.

"Just so you know," he said in a rumble, "I don't want to kill you but I will. It is the only way." He ambled off and I shook my head. I looked for Shuffle but he'd vanished.

Something awful dawned on me. What if he'd gone to find The Lady and to inform on us? I should not have allowed Enora anywhere near me, but I'd been so disorientated I'd not realised what was happening around me and I'd not deflected her words.

Fuck.

I grabbed Caliburn's hilt and ran back up the long corridor, hoping to catch up with my friend and stop him. My head pounded and my vision wavered but I recognised a miserable bundle crouched in a dark shadow between two smoky torches.

"Shuffle?" I asked, stroking his head.

"Morgana killed so many, you don't understand," he wailed, with tears staining his dirty face.

I knelt beside him. "I know. She killed men I knew and cared for. She tried to kill Arthur and she helped hurt Tancred. I know what she did under Aeddan."

"No you don't," Shuffle exploded the thought in my head.

I tried to make him understand my perspective. "Please, Shuffle, I need you. Don't do this now. I will find out what happened and I will -"

"You will what?" he interrupted. "You will kill her? That's what I vowed to do if I ever escaped."

I stroked his miserable face. "We will sort this out, right now I have no idea how, but I needed her help."

I heard a commotion behind me. The knight had won and I needed to face the giant.

"Please, my friend, please, I need to know you will be here to help me when I return."

Shuffle's misery burned my conscience. He nodded. "She will make a bad queen," he announced.

"But I might make a good king with the right guidance," I said.

He harrumphed but took my hand and we walked back to the fight.

CHAPTER TWENTY SIX

The huge war axe actually whistled as it missed my head by a hand's width and only because I yanked my hips round to avoid being cleaved in two. Caliburn sang with joy in my hand but my body felt every damned wound. The giant moved too fast and I was too tired. My knee hampered me badly and my vision wouldn't clear. The mighty war axe circled and I saw an opening. Caliburn raised her point and I thrust forward. She sank into the giant's side, carving a narrow slit between his ribs. Unfortunately, it didn't stop the axe. It hit my unprotected left side, the shield I'd carried with me long gone. Fortunately, the back of the axe hit me, not the sharp edge. I'd already tasted that, the blood oozing from a slice across my stomach. My left arm died and I fell to my right trying to absorb the impact and needing to save my shoulder.

I blinked dust and sand from my eyes. The giant crumbled to his knees. "I should have won," he ground out and collapsed. I hadn't wanted to kill him but I was losing control of my actions and Caliburn seemed to be taking up the slack. She only understood death. How the hell had Arthur learnt to control Excalibur?

I realised I lay in the sand staring up at the blue sky. I hadn't seen the sun all day and I wondered what time I might be allowed to stop.

Something, someone, tugged hard on my mind. The Lady sent the order to rise. I wanted to groan. I wanted to curl up around the pain and fade away. I had one more fight and I didn't even know how to stand up. The tug once more, this time with a barb in there to goad me. I used my anger at her relentless ambition and rolled onto all fours, my right knee and left arm were livid with me. I rose and the fucking crowd screamed its approval. The scarred man walked toward me and I found my hand in his being raised over my head. I didn't see Tancred in the crowd but Morgana looked ashen with fear.

I limped toward the tunnel entrance and men rushed past me to clear the giant's body away. A part of me wanted to acknowledge his prowess as a warrior but I didn't have the energy or strength.

Shuffle hurried in his ambling gait but another figure reached me first. Strong arms wrapped around me and took my weight. I almost whimpered in relief.

"Hush, Wolf, you are safe now," Tancred said for me only.

"You lived," I confirmed, but he couldn't hear my thought.

My deformed friend stopped and stared at the man whose face remained hidden, just like my own. His mind leapt from one point to the next and he made the right connections. I lunged for him before he could run away.

"Wait," I yelled into his mind. But we weren't connected. I fought to free my hand of my glove but nothing worked well enough and the movements, along with my fear, desperation and confusion made it all too much. I collapsed.

Cold water trickled into my mouth. "Easy, Lancelot, easy." Tancred's face floated into view. "Welcome back."

I tried to smile but the swelling in my face prevented it. He placed his palm to mine. It hurt, my right hand hurt, again. "Shuffle," I managed to think.

"He's fetching something to help you. I tried to explain but I don't know how much he understands," Tancred said.

"Morgana killed the love of his life," the thought whispered out of me.

The implications were not lost on Tancred. "Well, if he is going to betray us, it is too late. The Lady cannot stop this fight and you are already married."

"She can kill me or Arthur out of spite until I win and don't think she won't," I said.

"Does Shuffle know this?" Tancred asked, his concern clear.

I nodded and wished I hadn't. In silence, Tancred cleaned everything he could without undressing me. We both knew the drill, take off a man's armour when he's as badly broken as I felt and you'd never get him back in it. I knew I had to find the strength for the last match. I had to face the knight.

I reached for his hand. "What do we know of my final opponent?"

Tancred sighed. "He's good. Really good, but he is traditional. Honourable to the point of stupidity. He fights like you do when you're trying to win in a tournament rather than on the battlefield."

I knew what he meant, different styles for different places. However, I'd spent nine months studying under Sir Bastard, so I'd become altogether a more effective fighter, surprising even myself with my improvement.

"Tancred," I said. "I am doing the right thing, aren't I?"

He looked at me, startled. "You are fighting for our lives, for Albion."

"I know, but it is worth it, isn't it?" I asked in all seriousness. I'd become so tired of all this and now I had to face Shuffle over Morgana.

Tancred paused and gently held my bruised face. "I died today to be free of Rafe but I lived to be able to love you. Or it would be my blood out there covering the sand. You have given me a reason to live, just as you did when I found myself Aeddan's prisoner."

"I need you to love me," I confessed. "I need a reason to keep fighting. The throne of Albion means nothing. Morgana means nothing. Even Arthur," I paused. Did I really mean this? "Even Arthur means nothing right now. I just want to stop."

"If you stop, The Lady will take you from my side and turn you into something like Shuffle. If you stop we will never find peace together, and that is what I want." His warm brown eyes bored into mine. The wolf, lying in a bloody heap of fur and damaged limbs, raised his head and scented his pack mate. He struggled to stand on all four paws and limped toward the source of the scent.

"You swear you will be here when I finish," I said, feeling the wolf fill me with his endless strength and desire for a pack.

Tancred placed his lips gently on my swollen mouth and I heard his thought. "I will always be here, my dearest love. You really are the only reason I go on."

His hot breath caressed my lips and they began to tingle. A warmth spread from his mouth into mine and it whispered down my throat into my chest where it sat for a moment before expanding slowly to fill my heart with courage, my limbs with strength and my mind with a clarity sadly lacking for some time.

I looked into his eyes. They shone garnet bright. He smiled. "A gift to help," he said.

"Time to fight," came a gruff voice. Tancred covered his mouth and mine with black scarves. Mine instantly adhered to my skin. I stood up alone and walked on a leg which actually seemed to work.

I strode toward the gate and stood next to the knight who still wore his plate armour just as shiny as the day it was forged. I remained in my battered, blood stained, armour. He carried his great helmet under his arm but did not carry a shield, only a small buckler. I wished I knew his name. His hair, sticking out from under the coif, resembled dark honey and his eyes were smoky grey. We were the same height.

"This isn't fair. You've fought enough today," he said. "I should be facing the woman."

I placed a hand on his arm and he looked at me startled. I shook my head.

"You are dumb?" he asked.

I nodded; it seemed simpler than explaining a spell. I didn't have time to uncover my hands so I could speak to him, besides I doubted it would work. He didn't feel like fey. My intuition surprised me but it became yet another thing to consider if I lived through the rest of the afternoon.

He frowned. "You are a man of honour if you offered to take her place."

I nodded. I had taken her place and I really didn't want to kill this man. I wondered for whom he killed.

He saved me the bother. "One of us will die today and I at least can tell you who I am." He straightened. "I am Sir Bors, stolen from the land of men to fight for the fey when I should be at King Arthur's court in Camelot. I allowed myself to be distracted by a beautiful woman and thus I am enslaved and punished for my crimes of lust."

Oh, shit.

"I only wish I knew the man I faced, as his courage and honour surely supplants my own," Bors continued. His young handsome face looked so bloody earnest. I had no idea to which family he belonged but if he travelled to Camelot, I knew I needed to protect him.

I touched his hand and slowly pulled down my scarf. He looked confused, his brain trying to track a face he recognised but seemed too far out of context.

"Sir Lancelot?" he finally managed.

I covered my face once more. He processed the information after I nodded confirmation.

The gates swung open.

"I cannot fight you, my Lord," he claimed instantly.

I grabbed his elbow and almost pulled him after me. We were going to fight and we were going to make a bloody good show of it and I thanked whatever God wanted to see me win for this final scrap.

When I faced the platform, Morgana nodded and managed a faint smile, her relief plain. The Lady now stood, her black eyes focused on me and her face twisted into a snarl. Shuffle stood next to her. He'd betrayed us. He did not look at me but The Lady reached out with a small hand and stroked his matted hair. His head hung down.

I glanced back at Morgana in panic and wondered if Tancred would reach her and keep her safe. She nodded very slowly, aware of her danger but unable to do anything in the open. Unless The Lady actually called us on the full betrayal, we continued to play our hand as planned. I wondered if Arthur still lived, or if The Lady had crushed his heart already and I fought for nothing more than my freedom with Tancred. To be honest, brutally honest, I knew it would make no difference. I was so desperate to know some peace and quiet in Tancred's arms I'd just fight and worry about the consequences later.

Bors bowed toward a man sat between the women. He

resembled Aeddan, but an effeminate version and very overweight. He'd only managed to reach this point in the hideous game because he held something over Sir Bors.

We turned as one unit and walked back to the centre of the arena. "I cannot fight you, Sir Lancelot," Bors said. He spoke quietly. The crowd were almost silent, thinking this the penultimate battle.

I nodded at him, trying to say he didn't have any choice. I drew Caliburn and her song filled my head. This wouldn't help me maintain focus. Sir Bors stood there and didn't draw his own sword. The crowd grew restless and jeering began. Calls of 'coward' made Bors flinch. I dropped Caliburn's point to the sand.

"Fight, please, Arthur," I scribbled almost illegibly.

Bors reached for his hilt. "King Arthur wishes for me to fight?" he asked.

Close enough, I thought, and nodded.

"Am I to win?" he asked.

I wanted to laugh, instead I shook my head and turned to the crowd with my arms raised, forcing them into a frenzy.

"I am to make a show?" he asked when I turned back.

I nodded.

He grinned. "I am to fight the greatest Knight of Camelot at last."

I might well be the greatest but I still felt like crap. Only Tancred's magic kept me upright. I wondered how long it would last. Bors finally lowered his visor and we prepared for a fight.

The swords clashed. I caught Bors' clean overhead strike on the flat of my blade and his weapon slid off mine while I was already moving in for my own attack. We began the dance and I found a worthy opponent. Sir Bors fought well and with confidence. He flowed and blended with each of my attacks. My breathing slowly grew laboured and I knew I needed to finish this dance in a way we'd both live. With him dressed in full armour, knocking him out would be hard. I must find a way to take his sallet off. I twisted from a thrust, my right leg taking my weight and the pain up my leg made my vision blur. I stumbled and my leg folded. I looked in panic at the platform. Tancred stood next to Morgana. He stared at me, demanding I stand and fight. I stayed on my backside and swept toward Bors's legs.

"My Lord, we must stop," Bors panted and raised his visor.

I shook my head and pushed upward on my left leg but my left arm began to go numb and blood started to flow from my head wound. Whatever magic Tancred had put in me started to fade. I looked at the platform. Morgana stared at The Lady, who now grinned with sheer malevolence. She'd unpicked the spell from a distance. I was dying. Blood flowed quickly.

I lifted Caliburn and she felt heavy, her song silent. I dropped the sword, useless now The Lady had stolen her joy at the fight. Bors frowned. "What devilry is this?" he asked in shock as I began to bleed and sway before him. "You can't keep going. This is madness, Sir Lancelot."

Fuck it, I thought, if I can't win fairly I'll cheat. I just hoped Bors would forgive me. I beckoned him close and bless his heart, he dropped the point of his sword and he approached. Arthur once caught me like this when I'd been on the point of beating him during a competition between the squires. I bent and placed my arm around Sir Bors shoulders, he bent to join me. My right hand held the hilt of a knife but the blade pointed to the ground. I placed my left hand on the back of his head. The stink of sweat and blood filled my nose.

"What is it, my Lord? I am yours to command," Bors said.

I wanted to tell him to lie down and fake death. Instead, I punched upward into his open face.

Bors jerked back and had nowhere to go. I followed through with my arm encircling his neck from the front and my left hand pulling on the back of his backplate. For added effect, I swept his leg out from under him and toppled him backward. Not as dramatic as the tree man, but almost as loud.

Air rushed out of his lungs. I dropped over his armoured chest and pinned him down, then sliced through the leather holding his sallet in place. I pulled it off his stunned head, wriggled around behind him and placed a simple choke hold on his neck. Bors passed out quickly without a murmur. The crowd bayed in celebration. Many would think I snapped his neck and that suited me. Give Bors some time and he'd be up but sporting a newly broken nose. I held him against my chest ensuring the poor bastard didn't drown in his own blood. My own wounds continued to weep copiously.

CHAPTER TWENTY SEVEN

The scarred man approached. He said, "You have to stand." He could have said fly to the moon, it would have meant the same to me at that moment. He knelt beside me and looked at Bors. "The man isn't dead," he said quietly under the noise of the crowd. "And you have to stand."

Shouts from behind me caused my body to move in panic, the threat implicit. I tried to pull Bors with me, while I turned on my arse to face the attack, knife in trembling hand. A vision in black raced across the hot sand. The knife wavered and was gone.

"Get up," the instruction rough. "Are you a knight of the realm or a fucking animal? I gave you an order. Get up, soldier." It sounded like my old drill sergeant. What was his name? I panicked, unable to remember. No, wait, Moran, my sergeant was Moran, now my captain and I was the King's Champion. Moran was not a man you wanted to disappoint.

I dropped Bors gently onto his side, tucked my left leg under me and used my right arm to lever myself upright. I managed to stand, sort of, leaning heavily to the left, but I was up. The crowd screamed their approval. The scarred man raised my arm.

"We have a winner for the next round," he bellowed.

"We have nothing," came an imperious and enhanced voice. The crowd fell silent instantly. Nothing, no sound. Weird. I wobbled uncertainly. A strong shoulder filled the space I wanted to fall into, so I fell against that instead.

"Just stay conscious," Tancred muttered, holding a cloth to the wound in my belly.

The Lady stood on the platform and pointed toward me. I watched her fade in and out of focus. "This man is cheating," she said.

"And how is he cheating?" asked Tancred when the

scarred man didn't reply. "He is your Champion, my Lady. And I believe you are currently emptying him of life."

The red splodge I could see, which I assumed to be Nimue, rose. "What is happening here? Why are you on the floor and who is he?" she pointed at me.

Tancred reached up and pulled down his own mask. Cries from near the platform informed me Rafe lived. Damn it. My companion reached up to my scarf.

"If you reveal his face his King will die," came The Lady's voice.

"No, he will not," came another voice I really did know all too well. "Merlin, Tancred, bring my Wolf to me."

Another figure, this time in a black robe, walked across the sand as if it were an orchard in spring. "Well, this should be interesting," Merlin said happily as he took up the slack. "We are almost there, Wolf. It's taken a long time to train you but I think you are now ready to face the last part of your destiny."

I blinked several times, his words confusing me. I assumed he meant the throne of Albion but how he knew of our plan was a mystery. I saw Arthur standing before the platform with Excalibur gleaming wickedly in the light and concentrated on him, not the mage. Tancred freed my fingers from my gloves and touched my skin.

"Please stay awake, I can't deal with him alone," Tancred sent to me silently.

"I'll try, just don't let him take me back to Camelot without you," I managed before everything went dark again.

****

Noise filtered through my pounding head as I slowly became aware of my new surroundings. Raised voices. Vomit burned in the back of my throat and before I'd managed to try to control it, I was sick. Fortunately, someone held me upright and I found a bowl in my lap. A soft voice cooed and a cool cloth sat against my brow. I remained upright and temperate breezes tickled my face. It made me breathe deeply once the bowl vanished.

"He's awake," the soft voice informed the loud ones.

"Lancelot," a firm hand grasped mine.

"Leave him alone," barked another.

"Tancred," I thought.

"It's safe to speak, if you can," he said.

"Tancred," the name came out blurred and my jaw ached horribly.

"At last, I hear your voice," he said and kissed my brow.

"Wolf," came another voice.

"Arthur?" I managed, but did not release Tancred's hand.

"I'm here and we are leaving," he said. It was not a request.

"No," I contradicted.

"Yes," he shot back.

"No."

"If you think you are staying here with this witch." He gestured to Morgana.

I finally raised my eyes and realised the soft voice came from my wife. I tried to smile.

"Don't do that, husband, it's quite terrifying at the moment," she informed me, but I heard her fondness.

"Don't call him that," Arthur barked.

"Wife," I managed. "Married to Morgana. She is now Queen, right?" I asked Tancred, I think.

He grinned. "Technically, you are now our King but they are having something of a row about it."

Arthur sat on the floor beside me. White marble, bet it was cool. "You are married?" he whispered. "Really? To her? They aren't lying?"

"Really married," I said in a slightly singsong way.

"Now," Morgana said, stepping close once more, "can you please let me near enough to heal him and at least stop the bleeding before he dies?"

Arthur's presence beside me vanished to be replaced by my beautiful wife. I kind of liked the sound of that even if we didn't love each other. Words were rapidly exchanged between her and Tancred. Apparently, Arthur had prevented either of them coming near me to do anything but the very basic of health care.

"He doesn't trust me," Morgana said. "You are going to have to take point on this."

"Neither of us has the strength left to perform a full healing," Tancred muttered unhappily.

"Just do it," Morgana said.

Tancred shifted, knelt between my legs and I found myself staring into his warm brown eyes. I instantly relaxed and handed myself over to him. He smiled, sensing my willingness to trust him. He held my face in one hand and Morgana's in the other. She closed her eyes and sank onto the floor. Warmth began to flow from both fey. Tancred's soft light, a gentle silver, wove into and out of Morgana's energy. She felt and looked deep red, almost ochre. It felt good, soft; invasive but not bad.

The wolf finally raised his muzzle and his pack mate licked his mouth, lying down over the larger black paws. I lay over the brown wolf's back and closed my eyes, happy and home. A short sharp bark made me raise my head and a small black she-wolf approached. Her eyes were blue. She approached slowly. Neither of us moved, both male wolves felt she was already our pack. She lay down beside me, her nose tucked into the brown wolf's coat and her scent filling my nose as much as his. She smelt good.

When I focused, Morgana sat, leaning against Tancred. My hands touched both their heads and I bent to kiss each crown.

We were a fragile family and it touched a lonely place in my soul, which I craved to fill.

Tancred roused first. We were all under a spell, not one of magic, one of simple desire.

"Let me look at you," Tancred said, pushing Morgana upright. She'd grown pale and she moved very slowly, almost languid. Tancred straightened me in the chair and I allowed him to start poking certain areas in his quest to find out if their healing magic worked. I winced several times.

"Hmm, we have stopped the bleeding and reduced the worst of the damage to the fractured bones but I don't think we've done enough and that knee is as bad as it's ever been." He'd helped me the first time I'd damaged it when we lived together in the forest.

Voices filtered through a door. "We need to sort this mess out," I said, or rather croaked.

"They are saying we are not married," Morgana said, handing me a cup of water. "They say there is no law which covers our situation. The strictest interpretation makes it clear but The Lady, Nimue and Rafe have ganged up. Arthur appearing has confused matters because he announced you cannot be a part of this world. You swore your loyalty to Camelot, not Albion."

I grunted, knowing she was right but unable to think of a way around this chaos. "How did he get here?" I asked.

"Desperation," Tancred said, and his own reflected in his voice. "Merlin forced a way through after you married Morgana. There is just the two of them, but he is a force of nature."

I grabbed Tancred's hand and said, "I am not going to leave with him. I have made my choice."

Tancred pulled his hand away. "You've said that before." He turned his back and I recognised the set of his shoulders. He waited for me to break him again. I sighed and found Morgana watching us.

"What?" I asked.

"Nothing," she said.

"Just tell me."

Her mouth twitched and I waited. She finally said, "I've never found my animal."

I blinked, completely baffled.

She qualified, "It is something all fey have. The powerful ones can manifest certain aspects." I thought about the bite marks my wolf left in the real world. "I've never found mine. I can force animals." I'd seen Merla do this when necessary. "But I've never found one which just happened. I am wolf."

I smiled at her confusion. "We are a pack, at least for now."

Her mouth managed a half smile in response and she nodded. "It feels good." She sounded surprised.

"It does, which is why I'm not leaving," I said pointedly

to Tancred. "Now, help me up, King's Champion, and we will win the throne from these buggers."

Morgana and Tancred lifted me up and held me still while the world wobbled uncertainly. I am going to sleep for a month after this, I promised myself. I hobbled to the door and Morgana opened it. A small private antechamber decorated in subtle colours and plain furniture. I didn't think it belonged to any of those in the room. Nimue sat elegantly in the corner, watching her son, Rafe, arguing with Arthur. The Lady stood with Shuffle beside her and conferred with a woman in a brown robe. My friend did not look at me as I walked in and I wondered what he thought about all this. The baleful look he shot at Morgana gave me a hint.

Nimue sashayed over, elegant as always. "It really is interesting to see you again, Lancelot," she said, with eyes full of humour.

"Always a pleasure, Nimue," I said. I didn't want to take my eyes off such a dangerous opponent.

Rafe stepped forward and he looked terrible. Ashen, thin, his arm heavily bandaged. He must have used a healer of his own to be standing after all the damage I'd done. He pointed a long elegant finger at me. "I want him dead."

Tancred instantly drew his sword and stepped in front of me. Arthur matched him. Morgana propped me against a chair. Humiliating.

"You stand against your Master?" Rafe hissed unpleasantly at Tancred.

"I think we have more important things to think about than what your catamite is doing with my Champion," The Lady said, also stepping forward.

"He is not your Champion, he is mine," Arthur announced.

I realised Merlin stood in the dark corner watching all this with interest. A faint smile played over his lips and his words from earlier came back to me – was this the destiny he wanted? Was he yanking my life around like so many others had or was he up to something else? His machinations were played so far into the future not even Geraint could anticipate his game. Morgana remained passive at my side, which surprised me. Nimue grew closer to Arthur, his sword moved toward her and I felt the atmosphere grow even more violent.

"Stop," I spoke quietly. "I will have no more bloodshed and we will discuss this without trying to kill each other."

"You have no voice," The Lady snapped.

"I do, and I should never have allowed you to rob me of it." I managed to stand and move to Tancred's side. We did not touch, but his heat warmed me. "Put up your swords and sit."

No one moved.

"If you people don't sit, I will have Tancred start the fighting and he will finish it. Can we really afford to destroy each other or can we not find a path through your unhappiness?" This, my first attempt at diplomacy.

Nimue sat the smile still on her lips. Merlin remained in the shadows but Arthur, still with Excalibur in his hand, sat with his back to a wall. Rafe sat but I think he collapsed more than made a willing effort. I knew how he felt. Morgana lowered herself onto a chair with Merlin behind her, clearly the only person she'd trust in the room, strangely enough. The Lady sat but I sensed her violence. I lowered myself slowly. Tancred stood at my shoulder, just as I would have done for Arthur in Camelot. It made my brain ache.

"Good, and thank you," I said. "You all want to know what I've done and how I've done it. Well, honesty is something I value so I will start at the beginning and once you have all the facts you can begin arguing among yourselves." I looked at Rafe. "Tancred has made a decision, brother, he chooses to work with me and I am afraid that is not going to change. Not again."

"If you think this is the final word you are wrong. You tried to kill me," Rafe choked out, genuinely heartbroken. I glanced up at Tancred, worried he would react badly to this claim. His expression didn't change, he merely placed a hand on my shoulder.

"You ran onto Caliburn while I tried to save his life. You live and by fey standards I'd say I barely nicked you," I said. "And that's the point of this mess. Over the years, I've suffered from endless fey manipulations and cruelties. I believe we have a chance to make a new start and I'm enough of an optimist to believe you might want the same."

Feeling utterly exhausted I then explained how I'd come under The Lady's control, how she'd trained me for this competition, and why I'd married Morgana.

"I have a claim to this throne," I finished. "You all know it, or you wouldn't be willing to listen to me now and I'd be dead already. Some of you are curious as to my next move, some of you want to control me so badly I have no choice but to react. Albion has great potential but she is a rudderless ship and civil war lurks in the darkness waiting to strike. If you value your hold on this place, you will not cause the contest to begin again."

"What do you mean?" Nimue asked, leaning forward.

I delivered my only weapon, "With a claim to the throne, if you don't acknowledge my marriage and the fact that my wife controls my victory in the arena, you will have to hold this contest again. Next time I will join the race and my Champion will fight once more." I touched Tancred's hand.

Nimue sat back, a small smile on her lips. "Well, I always wanted you on the throne. Of course it was Camelot's and I was to be your wife, but we have time for that game."

Morgana stiffened but remained silent.

"I don't give a damn about anything," Rafe declared. "I have lost the only thing that ever mattered."

"Perhaps you should play more gently with your toys," Tancred said mildly.

I looked at Arthur. He said nothing and gave me back his best blank face. Merlin appeared amused. I stared at The Lady.

"You are an animal. I thought I'd managed to beat your father's disgusting habits out of you." By that she doubtless meant my fornication.

I looked at the only other member of the room. The old woman in the brown robe. "I take it you are some kind of law keeper?" I asked.

She stepped forward. "Yes, I am Albion's Ritual Keeper."

"My wife tells me you are uncertain as to the outcome of this situation," I said politely.

"The Lady Morgana has made some interesting leaps of logic, it is true," said the woman. "As her husband you cannot fight her Champion. As her husband you cannot win for The Lady," here she made a small bow to the Bitch. "You did not complete the fighting but you suffered under a magical attack while you were fighting." No one looked at The Lady. "The only opponent left is Morgana's Champion, who did not fight during the final battles; therefore you won the contest."

"But he is my Champion! You heard him, I trained him," The Lady snapped. "And he cannot be married to that," she waved a dismissive hand at Morgana. "She is little more than Aeddan's lap dog."

Morgana stiffened and finally spoke. "Whatever I was or whatever I did because of Aeddan is over and is irrelevant here."

I glanced at Shuffle. His twisted body rocked from side to side. His distress worried me but I had to concentrate.

"Let your Ritual Keeper speak," I said.

The woman bowed toward me before continuing, "You are married to one of the contestants, therefore you won for her, not for the one who trained you. The Lady Morgana has won the throne and you as her husband are now our King. It has never happened before but this is a ritual that should be played out on many levels. You out-manoeuvred your fellows. I can find no reason to stop this."

"They are not married, he prefers fucking men," The Lady shot to her feet and actually shouted.

Morgana rose. "You may test the validity of our marriage." She sounded so fragile I wondered what form this test would take.

"No," I said and forced my body out of the chair. I took Morgana's hand. "No, I will not have you abused or hurt. You are my wife and I will not have them hurt you." I didn't want The Lady to touch Morgana. I knew what the sadistic bitch could do with a single touch.

"Calm down, noble knight," Nimue said. "I'll do it and it won't hurt."

Morgana's face flushed and her lips pressed tightly together. The other woman approached her with a gleam of sheer mischief in her eyes.

"Nimue," I said with warning.

She looked at me, the strange elongated irises dilated, while her hand brushed Morgana's neck. My wife stiffened and I watched a small jolt cause her breath to hitch. Nimue smiled. "Lucky girl."

"So, you agree we are fully married?" Morgana asked.

"I do." She sounded surprised. "I don't know how you did it, but you win, Morgana. You have Lancelot du Lac as husband and Champion."

"She wins because the worse she's ever done to me is stab me in the back. The rest of you are nuts," I muttered. Tancred grunted trying hard not to laugh.

"We are all agreed then? We have a new royal couple," the Ritual Keeper announced.

"I am satisfied," Nimue said. "It will make the game even more interesting watching you two trying to live together."

"I have no grounds to dispute this?" The Lady asked.

"I am afraid not, my Lady," said the older woman.

Rafe did not speak. I looked at his defeated body language and realised I might actually have to apologise. A movement flashed at the side of my vision. Shuffle rushed forward with a wicked looking blade.

"No!" I bellowed and tried to lunge at him, wanting to prevent the inevitable.

Tancred hit my shoulder and with my dilapidated state, I actually fell, hitting the floor hard. I missed the movement which meant Shuffle ended up facing me on the ground with a sword piercing his twisted chest and blood pouring out of his ruined mouth.

"No," I whimpered. I pulled myself toward him in vain hope.

Tancred's sword rose from my friend's chest.

CHAPTER TWENTY EIGHT

"No, please, no," I reached Shuffle.

I heard voices, explanations, Morgana's shock, but I only focused on my dying friend. I sat up and half pulled him onto my lap.

"Shuffle, please." I pressed my fingers to his face and forced the thought into his mind. "Why?"

Shuffle raised his hand weakly and grasped mine. "Promised she must die. All that kept me alive. Vengeance. Knew you wouldn't let it happen but I had to try."

"Who are you really?" I asked. The tears fell into his blood. Arthur knelt beside me.

"I am Shuffle." He began to fade.

"Please don't," I cried out brokenly.

"Had to try, your job to stop me, you did well, thank you for the peace, I can now go home, you are a good friend." Shuffle thought I'd killed him to save Morgana and he forgave me.

Air made the blood bubble out of his mouth, his body jerked just once, his hand grabbed mine and then the light died in his eyes. He died. In my arms. Arthur pulled the sword from his chest and I curled over his body. The tears came hot and the pain felt more real than any of the agonies I'd suffered so far in my life. Arthur quietly ordered everyone out.

The grief lasted a long time. In the end, I didn't know if I cried for Shuffle, for losing Camelot by staying in Albion or just for my miserable existence. I merely held my friend and wept. His body slowly cooled.

"Lancelot, you need to let him go." Arthur's voice finally penetrated my beleaguered mind.

"You don't know what he did for me," I said, the words broken and harsh.

"No, but I know he was important to you, which makes him important to me. I will listen if you want to tell me what he meant." Arthur finally touched me. Blood covered everything. "I think we need to talk," he said quietly.

I nodded and allowed him to pull Shuffle out of my arms. He tried to help me stand but my body no longer showed any interest in standing. So we sat, facing each other. Me in a drying puddle of blood and Arthur on the cleanest area he could find. I told him everything I remembered about Shuffle, which meant I went into a great deal more detail than I'd done when explaining to the others why I should be king of Albion. Arthur just sat and listened patiently. He laughed with me sometimes and let me cry at others. My friend listened.

"What actually happened?" I asked.

"Shuffle rushed toward Morgana, you and Tancred saw the blade in the same moment. Tancred threw himself in front of Morgana and shouldered you out of the way. You were unarmed and would have been stabbed if Shuffle had reached you. He has a nasty wound himself but managed to stop Shuffle before he did any more damage. By the sounds of things Shuffle didn't want to live anymore and this way he left on his own terms, not those of The Lady," Arthur said, his grief at the waste plain.

"Tancred's hurt?" I asked, my concern very hot and real.

"He is, but he'll be alright."

"We need to talk about what you are doing here," I said.

Arthur sighed. "I thought I'd be able to save you for a change but once more you've saved yourself without my help."

"Tancred and I –"

Arthur held up his hand. "I know. I can't pretend it doesn't hurt like hell but you seem to have made some life changing decisions without me and there isn't much I can do. I can't stay here with you and I know you'll never let him go. We can never be more than something riddled with grief and guilt. You need so much more than I can give. Perhaps here with Tancred and Morgana," here his voice became incredulous; I laughed, "you might find happiness."

"You don't sound convinced." Was he really letting me

go this easily? Did he really understand my commitment to Tancred?

"Morgana?" he asked.

"The best of a crazy bunch of women, my friend," I said. I held out my hand. "I think I can move now."

"Crazy is the word. This place," he heaved and I finally moved, "is deeply fucked up."

I laughed. "That's my kingdom you're talking about."

"I'm glad it's yours and not mine. Makes Camelot look spectacularly normal by comparison."

I grunted. "Just help me find Tancred and let's see to Shuffle's body."

Limping badly but moving, I left the small stateroom we'd been using. Tancred stood in the corridor. He took one look at me and dropped to his left knee. "Forgive me, Sire," he said. "I will pay any price you see fit."

My shaking fingers touched his bent head. "I hear you saved my life and the life of your Queen."

"I should have done something else. He did not need to die," Tancred's voice broke. His empathy as a healer would be causing him great distress over his actions and my own suffering.

"Perhaps, but ultimately you did the right thing." His head shot up at my words. "Tancred, being King's Champion is not easy. You saved lives today. Never forget your duty is to the throne of Albion." It hurt to say; I wanted to be angry but Tancred shouldn't be the object of that anger. Neither should Morgana. The Lady damaged Shuffle beyond the point of repair. I wanted her head. It also felt very odd using words Arthur might have used to me in the same situation.

Tancred rose and I noticed the black leather of his uniform looked stained. "You are hurt?" I asked.

"I've been healed," he spoke formally, uncertain of his role with Arthur at my side.

No such doubts filled me. I transferred my weight to Tancred's arm. "Find me somewhere to pass out," I begged.

"Shuffle…" Tancred said.

"I'll find someone," Arthur said, simply handing me

over without a murmur. Perhaps he knew I'd be unable to cope with a challenge.

Time blurred and I found myself in rooms I vaguely recognised. Morgana stood in front of me with her hands on my chest, undoing buckles and laces. "If I untie this lot will you just fall into pieces?" she asked.

"I might," I said.

"I owe you a debt for today. I knew it would be hard for you, but heroic doesn't quite cover your suffering."

"Why did Shuffle want you dead?" I asked.

Her hands stopped moving and her head bowed. "I didn't know he still lived. I didn't know he was the same man. I didn't know what she did."

"Just tell me what happened," I requested. A cold lump formed in my chest.

"Aeddan wanted his wife. Shuffle said no. I facilitated her victimisation," the words were quiet, soft. Her hands trembled but she did not make an excuse or beg forgiveness.

"What was his name?" I asked

She looked at me in surprise. "Loci, and his wife was Annabel. They were good people. It happened a long time ago, before Aeddan became King."

"The Lady used him as her first Champion. When he failed she broke him," I said, the cold lump spreading.

"I was barely more than a slave myself in those days. I don't know what deals Aeddan might have struck to rid himself of enemies or to gain allies." Morgana raised her eyes and tears quivered on the edges. Were they real?

"Those days are over," I said.

"Yes, my Lord, they are, I promise you."

"Why were you so quiet in the aftermath of today?" I asked, switching subject. I only had so long left and a great deal to cover.

"You are King and you needed to be more than my husband. You need to be strong without me. I will have my time." She started to undress me again.

"Where is Tancred?" I asked.

"Here, Lancelot," he said coming through a door.

He carried a pile of towels. "There is a bath next door. Come," he smiled and held out his hand. "I know how much you like messing about in water."

I raised a smile and with Morgana's help wobbled into the next room. A huge metal bath sat on a raised dais. Steam rose and drifted. I shuffled forward and stopped for Tancred to finish stripping me of clothing. I didn't bleed anywhere, they'd healed me enough for that, but I did have some interesting new scars. Tancred undressed quickly, his own scars painfully obvious in the soft candlelight. The new wound looked angry but sealed. My hand strayed toward it and the bruises running down his ribs.

"Being able to heal has advantages," I said.

Tancred ignored me, "Morgana, he will need you. We have to have him up and about and able to defend himself."

"I'm not getting into the water with you two." Her jaw jutted out in that now familiar stubborn set.

"It's fine, Tancred, leave her alone," I said. Exhaustion made me feel sick and giddy. I just want to be still and to close my eyes.

"It's not fine, we are pack and you need healing. I can't do it alone. We've all been pushed too far today but we have more work to do." He stood with his arms crossed, his muscles bunched.

I sighed. "We are pack, Morgana and you will be safe. Besides, I think we are both far too exhausted to include you in anything other than the cleaning."

Morgana rolled her expressive eyes, "Fine." She pulled at her simple green dress and in moments, it dropped to the floor. She wore a plain cream shift underneath. She did something with her hair and for the first time I saw it lifted away from her face and into a loose bundle at the back of her head. She looked so vulnerable, except for the scowl on her face. Tancred took one side of me, she the other and together they helped me up the steps and into the water. I actually whimpered in relief. For the first time in nine months, I put my poor aching body into hot water. Morgana's shift grew almost transparent in the water and she pulled me toward her. She sank down and I found myself in her arms, my back to her chest. I felt her heart beating quickly and her breasts, slightly larger than would fit into my hand, pressing into my naked skin.

Tancred sat further away and just watched. I relaxed into the water and let it close over my head. Morgana coaxed me up and pushed my hair back, laying my head against her chest. I closed my eyes and just let her hold me. I'd never felt anything so blissful.

The water moved and I opened my eyes only to see Tancred now very close. I gazed into his brown eyes and my heart ached with love. He'd grown harder, stronger, darker and I actually loved him more because of those changes. A slender hand reached out and touched his chest. Tancred looked down in surprise. Morgana traced the dripping scars over his muscular chest.

"I am sorry this happened," she said.

"You did not order it," Tancred said moving away and closing down. I reached out and realised my limbs were day old foal weak. It stopped him moving though.

"Did she know?" I asked.

"They all knew, including Rafe, but no one could stop it. Or maybe they didn't want it to stop," he said, with a challenge in his eyes for Morgana.

"They were bad times," she said, so quietly I hardly heard her words.

The vision of Shuffle losing the love of his life came into my mind and grief ripped away the peace of Morgana's arms. Whether she supported Aeddan or feared him, she'd been complicit in many crimes against her people.

"I cannot deal with this - I am too tired and too overwrought." I pushed against Tancred slightly to move him, then I left Morgana's arms. "I just want to be clean, warm and asleep." I used the anger now coursing through me to grasp soap and a cloth. I began scrubbing hard, not able to look at either of my companions.

"As you wish, my Lord," Morgana sounded brittle. I heard her move and realised she left the bath. I let her. I needed quiet. Tancred moved toward me, took the soap and cloth. He began to clean me but didn't speak. He knew me too well.

When we finished and another wave of exhaustion hit me, Tancred held my arms and helped me out of the bath. I stood long enough for him dry me off, my right knee very large and bruises everywhere. We hobbled to another room and a large bed beckoned. We didn't speak, but our original relationship had been built on silence; we just climbed into bed. Tancred rolled me onto my favourite side and curled around my back. We were asleep in moments.

CHAPTER TWENTY NINE

When we woke, we made love. Our familiarity with each other made it perfect and I felt whole for the first time in a long time. Just as his sister helped heal me once from a terrible wound, Tancred's strong arms held me all night and I woke more or less in one piece. He's own bruising and scarring had reduced too.

I traced the faint line Shuffle's attack had left. "If I can heal this fast every time, I don't think I'd mind being smashed to smithereens again."

He took my fingers to his lips and a thrill went through my sated body. His beard felt soft, even though it was trimmed close to his jaw. "I have limits, Lancelot, I can't heal everything. A great deal of this repair work is down to Morgana."

I sighed. "Don't remind me."

A soft knock came at the door. I glanced at Tancred. "They can't find you here," the panic in my voice proved me a coward.

He laughed. "This isn't Camelot, love." He rolled off the bed, stood in one fluid movement and grabbed a shirt. He covered his scars while moving toward the door. He swung it open; a small man stood there and bowed.

"Your Majesty," he said.

I blinked and muttered, "This is weird."

Tancred grinned. "What can we do for you?"

The small man, another walnut type fey, or Brownie, I reminded myself, didn't flinch at finding another man in my bedroom. He merely walked in and began tidying up. "Today you are to be crowned, the coronation is this evening so we have time but you cannot waste the day."

"Erm," I said losing control of the day already.

Tancred climbed back onto the bed. "What's your name?" he asked.

"Quilliam, my Lord," he said. "And you will need to be

cleaned up too. We have a uniform for you. We thought black was best but we are uncertain if you want an insignia on the breast."

"Erm," I managed.

"Food and wine are on the way," Quilliam said.

"Wine? It's too early even for me," I finally articulated.

Quilliam looked at me in surprise. "Very well. What would you prefer?"

"Water is fine," I said.

Quilliam closed his eyes briefly and nodded. "Water is on the way."

I glanced at Tancred, who smirked at me. "They run the palace and I suspect the entire country. The Brownie people are all connected to each other and have an innate ability to know what has happened in their environment. Quilliam will be your personal servant, as I suspect he was for Aeddan."

I looked back at the small man. "Were you?" I asked.

"Yes, Sire."

"And now you work for me?"

Quilliam cocked his head to one side. "With you, Sire."

"Lancelot is fine," I said.

Quilliam frowned. "No, Sire, it isn't."

"Oh," I said feeling more fear than I did during the whole of yesterday.

Tancred, clearly used to Brownies, began chatting happily with Quilliam and I vanished into a private bathroom.

The morning became a blur, which made Camelot look disorganised. By the time the midday meal appeared I'd had enough of being dressed, undressed and cleaned up. I'd signed documents, sealed everything placed before me and been nice to all those I needed on my side. Tancred and Morgana helped me play at diplomat until I finally escaped their clutches. My head pounded and I craved peace. Instead I sought out the one conversation I dreaded over all others. I needed to speak to my King.

A Brownie appeared at my elbow when I found myself turning in circles looking for the right direction to take. She said, "May I be of service, your Majesty?"

"I'm looking for King Arthur," I said. I'd given up asking them to use my name not my title. They didn't listen.

"He is with one who died," she said and her eyes grew very large as if she empathised with my pain at the thought.

I nodded quickly. "Show me," I said.

We wove through the sprawling edifice and she left me at a plain wooden door. I didn't knock, I just entered. Nimue stood next to Arthur. They spoke quietly with Shuffle lying on a wooden bier before them. He'd been redressed in proper clothes, washed and his eyes discreetly sewn closed. Both looked up at my arrival.

I approached my friend's body and touched his crown. Someone had tried to brush his hair but it hadn't worked very well. The pain of his loss made my heart swell in anguish. I didn't want to prove weak before Nimue, so manfully wrestled with my need to weep.

"I am sorry about his death," she said. "Regretful considering the circumstances, but perhaps it was a blessing."

"As you say, regretful." I didn't look at her. "I want The Lady brought to book for this and other crimes."

Nimue's breath hissed through her teeth. "Lancelot, that isn't a good idea. Besides, she's already left. She is powerful, stronger than Morgana, and she would have won if you hadn't played the game so well."

My teeth clenched and I had to consciously relax to be able to speak. "For a game, many good men and women died. The fey court needs to consider that their way of life is wrong and will be changing."

"I wish you luck. We've been a debauched, corrupt bunch for centuries." Nimue sounded like she wanted to laugh at me.

"Perhaps you would be kind enough to leave us, my Lady. I have business with King Arthur," I said, dismissing her.

Her face twitched in amusement. "I'm sure you do." She bowed briefly and left without argument.

"That was too easy," I said.

"She's a complicated woman," Arthur said. "You need her as an ally but I fear she will ask a high price for her loyalty and you can't trust her."

I grunted. Nimue was a problem for another day. I reached over Shuffle's body and lay my hand on Arthur's shoulder. He finally raised his eyes to my face. I said, "We need to talk."

The sadness in those eyes made me realise he already knew most of the conversation. "Tancred is back," he said. No bitterness, no anger, just disappointment. "And you are married."

I released Arthur's shoulder and limped away from Shuffle, unable to bear this final silence from my friend. I found a chair and lowered myself slowly. "I'm married as a convenience, you must know that," I said.

Arthur also moved from Shuffle and nodded while placing a chair in front of me. "Yes, I know. The deal is a sensible one I suppose. A year and day to help her establish her power base and gain a child."

"If she can cope with the concept of letting me near her for anything other than an argument," I said, rubbing my eyes.

Arthur chuckled. "She isn't going to make your life an oasis of calm." He paused for some time and I didn't have the courage to continue the conversation. "Lancelot," he took my hands, "I know I am losing you. If Morgana does have a child, you will have the family you always wanted. You can't leave that promise for your future." I thought about the terrible lessons I'd learnt in that cave with Lugh.

I studied our hands. Mine were still stained with blood. Knuckles broken, fingers no longer quite straight, callouses thick and palms rough. Arthur's fingers were straight, most of his knuckles were still whole, the callouses weren't as rough or as thick. He finally dropped to his knees at my feet and held my hands to lips and nose, sucking in my scent. His body trembled and he gasped, trying to control his anguish.

"Arthur," I whispered. I freed one hand and lay it on his head, which he placed in my lap. We sat for a long time with Shuffle on his bier and Arthur on his knees, me stroking his hair.

It hurt so much, far more than I ever considered possible. We were bound together through ties that were deeper than mere words and gestures. We'd bound our souls into one but...

"I need him," I said, when words became once more possible.

"I know," Arthur said, not moving from my lap. "I watch him with you and I am envious of how comfortable you are with each other. There is something different about your relationship. Something I can't give you. I don't know what it is."

I did. He didn't feed my addiction. I didn't need Tancred to validate my existence. He just accepted me. "He makes no demands on me, Arthur. It is simple, safe, we are equals," I said wanting to explain just a little of what I'd learnt and hoping that it would help.

"You and I are equals," Arthur said with anguish. "I bent my knee to you, gave you homage, acknowledged you as my equal."

It was true, the White Hart submitted to the Black Wolf. Arthur sat back and gazed up at me, his blue eyes dark with punishing emotions, his face strained, and I realised he'd lost weight while I'd been away.

"Don't leave me," Arthur requested. His voice remained quiet but I heard the order. I heard my future on those words and it looked a lot like my past.

I swallowed a hard lump in my throat, drawn into his gaze, feeling him moving through my soul to tug on my heart. "Please, Arthur, let me go," I begged. "I love you but how many times have we lain together since my return to Camelot?"

Arthur released me from his gaze. "I don't know, I don't keep score," he said. I held myself in place and didn't tell him I remembered each time, like a precious flower in my memory to hold on the endless nights I was alone. He continued, "But I thought our union meant more to you than just sex."

I sighed. "It does, but I don't like celibacy and it isn't about that, you know it isn't about that."

"It's about Tancred," Arthur drew away from me and stood. He paced, restless and powerful, full of grace and anger. "He left you, remember," Arthur said.

"No, you pushed and he fled, there is a difference." I wanted to remain calm against Arthur's fractious energy. I would not concede. I would break this habit of ours.

"He belongs to Rafe as you do to me," Arthur said.

"No, he died to free himself of Rafe," I said.

Arthur stopped. "Is that what you want? To be free of me?" he asked. The brittle edge to the questions cut me.

"No." I rose on tired legs and crossed the small room to join him. "I don't want to be free of you. I just want to be loved and held and kept safe. You can't and won't do that for me, Arthur, and while I am with you, I can't do it for myself."

"I've been lost without you, these nine months," he said, while touching my hair with gentle fingers.

"I know, but I've been lost without Tancred for the last two years," I said. "It's time for our commitments to each other to change. We will always protect each other, Albion and Camelot will both be safe with me as king here, but our physical love needs to die in peace. Please, Arthur, let me go," I repeated.

He looked to the ground. "I knew, when I woke and they told me what you'd done, that you'd come here, I'd lose you to him again. I've always known Tancred gave you something I can't. I just wish I understood what that is, so I could call you back to my side." He looked up and a sad half smile covered his face. "I had to try, Wolf. I had to try to bring you home."

He turned away from me and left the small room without another word. I approached Shuffle once more and stood vigil by my friend for a while, sometimes weeping for him, sometimes for myself and sometimes for Arthur.

Tancred offered me a chance to be free of the addiction I found in serving Camelot. I didn't have to ease Arthur's conscience. It wasn't my role in life to make his easier, not if it meant I sacrificed myself. I wanted a family because in that I saw hope for my future. I saw life not death. I would serve that objective, not Arthur's. Was I really free of Camelot? Was I really free of Arthur Pendragon? I wanted it to be real, but Arthur had conceded just a little too quickly and he no longer inspired my trust as he had once done, so time would tell.

I left the room, with a final private farewell to Shuffle, and managed to retrace my steps to the rooms we'd been using. I felt pensive and distant. I'd finally told Arthur I would no longer be his lover. I'd finally found the courage, but it was a hollow victory. I thought it would leave me lighter, free of the constant ache and calmer, but it hadn't. I still felt lost.

When Quilliam found me, he voiced his displeasure at my lack of commitment to his care by forcing me to endure more fussing and primping.

The only other person I needed to speak to was Merlin but he stayed out of the way and I grew faintly suspicious; he'd been far too quiet. He knew something and I wanted him to share but trying to force information from the old buzzard before he was ready, felt like trying to pin down lightning sent by the gods.

Now, however, I had to survive my coronation.

I'd been washed, shaved uncomfortably close and had my hair cut but not short after my outburst. They, being the Brownies, had spent the night sewing and I now stood in my new clothes. They'd chosen gold to begin with and I argued until someone produced a something in plain black, with fur trim. Black leather and fur could I handle, but gold? Me? Really? Once primped, or should I say pimped, they hauled me off to an antechamber. When they continued to fuss, I threatened to draw Caliburn until they vanished from the room. One muttered how much more impressive Aeddan was, which proved the final straw. Brownies or not, things were going to change in this bloody city.

I paced the antechamber restlessly. I'd gleaned from various sources Morgana would appear from one side, I from the other. We would walk together across a staging area before taking our places on two thrones. Then we'd be asked to recite various sentences and crowns would be placed on our heads. Job done. I doubted it would be that simple. I'd attended too many high court functions in Camelot to think this would be easy. I reached breaking point in no time and snatched open the door. Tancred stood the other side with his fist raised to knock.

His eyebrow rose. "Planning on running?" he asked. I hadn't seen him all afternoon.

"Yes," I snapped. "Want to come with me?" I asked.

He pushed lightly on my chest, forcing me back in the room. "You look lovely," he said.

"Thank you," I said grumpily.

He grinned, then laughed. "Cheer up, it's not that bad."

"I don't want to be king."

"You won't be forever if you don't want to be. That's the beauty of the fey system, it's just no one ever resigns unless forced."

"Or they're killed," I muttered.

"It's my job to make sure that doesn't happen, remember?" he said, clearly trying to coax me into calming down. I looked at him and realised I'd been missing a treat. His clothing matched mine, but he wore a black shirt not a white one and no fur adorned his doublet. The thongs on my lacing were gold, his silver and his boots came a long way up his thighs. His short hair looked artfully ruffled and his beard trimmed close to his strong jaw. He really did look like the shadow behind my throne. My heart raced with some very unclean thoughts.

"Nice," I said appreciatively.

"Arthur's in Camelot's colours," Tancred said.

"Is he coming?" I asked, needing his support and worrying about his attendance in equal quantities.

"He'll be at the front of the crowd but they won't let him in here. I'm only allowed because I'm your Champion," Tancred said. "He doesn't seem very happy." Tancred's gaze dropped. "I wasn't expecting him to be here."

"You have nothing to fear, Tancred. I've told Arthur where we stand. He knows it's time," I said. I shook myself and tried to change the subject. Talking about Arthur with Tancred just seemed a bit too hard right now. I touched his left breast. A finely embroidered wolf's head nestled in the leather, with an ash tree behind the face, dropping down to form a circle.

"What's this?" I asked.

He blushed, "They insisted on a symbol to use to represent you. It's all I could think of and they wouldn't ask you directly, something to do with etiquette. The Brownies seemed to think they should already know what you would like and the fact that they didn't caused them considerable upset. Angry Brownies are not fun."

"So you chose my coat of arms?" I asked.

"No," he said hastily. "I chose something we can use for the moment."

"I like it, reminds me of home and you are pack, family," I said trying to think sensibly and not with my balls. "This is ours, yours and mine."

"And Morgana's," Tancred said.

I grunted without commitment, still too angry with her on his and Shuffle's behalf to play nice.

A gong sounded.

"It's almost time," Tancred said.

"Already?" I asked my stomach flipping over. I hated public events and the scrutiny that comes with them.

"Come on, hero, time to show your public what they bought into." Tancred pushed me toward a door.

"This is such a bad idea," I breathed, walking through and out into a wave of sound.

Cheering, not a great deal different to the lot at the arena, slammed into me. I think I'd have run then, if Tancred hadn't discreetly blocked off my exit. Light, white light emanated from every wall, filling the vast space. No candles or torches or braziers, just pure light. The ceiling of the throne room swept upward in a vast arc of lead and stained glass. The colour from the dying sun filled the centre, which they'd left a plain circle. I saw a vague pattern of interlaced trees and animals but you'd need an entire afternoon lying on your back to understand all the images. I focused only on the thrones, great chairs carved from white marble. On the surface the same swirling, dancing patterns I'd seen so often in Albion, which drew more pictures my nervous mind didn't interpret. Then I saw Morgana.

I stopped walking until Tancred prodded me. She looked literally breathtaking. I'd always realised she was beautiful but I'd never seen her look like this. She wore the gold and frowned slightly at my perpetual black. But the dress she wore looked like liquid and yet never hinted at anything indelicate. Her black hair lay in thick ribbons over her shoulders and back. Her blue eyes shone from her face with her makeup almost invisible yet blending to enhance her perfection. I approached her transfixed. She stopped, leaned toward me and kissed my lips. I responded without thinking and pulled her toward me for a more thorough exploration. The crowd cheered, which reminded me we were not alone.

She gasped slightly when I let her go. "Interesting," she said.

"Sorry," I muttered.

"Don't be, just sit and let this happen." She took my hand and guided me to the left hand throne. I sat. The damned thing was cold and very hard. It made me feel like a naughty child, my feet hardly touched the ground.

A man, dressed in blue and red robes with a ridiculously pointed hat appeared on my right, making my hand ache to reach for Caliburn. He started to intone words, like pedigree, responsibility and sanctity. I didn't think my dear father cared too much about any of those things. The words began to drown me and I sought out Arthur in the crowd. I found his golden head and he smiled. My panic calmed and I just focused on him, standing next to Nimue.

I repeated words that became meaningless and just kept breathing calmly. Finally, a small boy approached from my left and held a cushion with a very old looking gold circlet. My warrior's instinct started to scream at me. It wanted to escape, it wanted to run and the voices I'd thought I'd left behind started to yell in panic. They didn't want this and didn't want to be trapped into this world of politics.

We needed to run.

I placed my hands on the arms of the throne and started to rise. A hand grabbed the back of my neck.

"Calm, love, it's going to be over soon and we can leave. Don't panic," Tancred said directly into my mind.

"I can't," I cried out silently.

"Just a few more heartbeats, Lancelot." Tancred's grip tightened.

The man in the pointy hat picked up the circle of gold and moved silently to my side. He said some more words and lifted the crown. My hands flexed and my mouth opened to help me breathe. Arthur looked at me, willing me to stay still just as much as Tancred. Why did they want me to do this?

The metal hit my head and the weight felt tremendous. Bile rose in my throat and my head screamed. Tancred's hand moved on my neck, I leaned into his grasp and he tried to send soothing thoughts. I closed my eyes and just tried to make the crown feel lighter. Right in that moment, it was sharp, heavy and cold. It made me so tense I thought I'd adhered to the throne.

Cheering forced a wall against my body and suddenly Morgana clutched my hand. I turned to face her but the terror in my blood did not match the excitement making her eyes dance with joy.

The crowd continued to cheer. I started to notice one particular figure walking through the mass of bodies without touching anyone. The crowd simply melted out of his way but no one paid him a moment's notice. He stood a good three hands taller than myself. His breadth made him vast and his long legs were heavily muscled. He wore a single long strip of cloth tied in a complex way, but it left his limbs and half his chest naked. A vast black tattoo of an eight spoked wheel sat over his left breast. He made me feel tiny. Golden red hair and a long beard, braided and flowing, finished the image of mighty warrior. He carried a short sword at his hip and an axe in his hand big enough to squash me if I tried to lift the thing. A golden torc circled his neck. His eyes were utterly focused and brilliant blue, more like gems.

I stood and pulled Caliburn. Arthur looked at me in alarm, followed my gaze, saw the threat and jumped onto the dais pulling Excalibur. Tancred stepped forward to my other side and drew his own sword. We all stepped in front of Morgana.

The mountain man stopped and bowed. His hair brushed the stage on which we stood. I pushed Morgana back, out of range.

"Welcome, King and Queen of Albion. I am pleased with the final outcome of your challenge. You did well," his voice boomed over the crowd, rendering it silent.

Merlin appeared from the sidelines, approached me, pushed Caliburn down and bowed low toward the great man. "We are pleased to welcome you to the court of Albion, in The City of this land, Greatest of Lords," he said formally.

Arthur and I shared a long look. Neither of us knew a damned thing and neither of us liked it; this was clearly his grand finale.

"You know why I am here, Wizard of Camelot," the giant said.

"I do," Merlin replied. Damned glad someone did.

The man laughed, the sound rolling around the room. Morgana gripped my sword arm like a vice. Not helpful. "They don't know?" the man asked.

Merlin shrugged. "Sometimes you just have to let things play out on their own."

The man shook his great head. "You people are even worse than we are with politics. But it changes nothing. I have created the team I need."

I finally found my voice, "What and who are you?"

The man smiled on his wide open face. "Ask your wizard if you wish, Champion of both Camelot and Albion, but for now just listen. You have the right to pick five to journey with you but you must leave this place and collect the items that will give my brothers the chance to destroy both of your worlds. Do not think for one moment you can separate England and Albion, you are one, you represent one, the worlds are tied together through time." He grinned,

"I love a bit of alliteration for a prophecy. I'll see you in your dreams, Wolf." He vanished and I realised the people of Albion hadn't noticed a damned thing. They were bound in celebration, a frozen moment which now ended in confusion with three armed men standing before their new Queen.

"Fuck," I yelled at the sky.

CHAPTER THIRTY

I pushed past Arthur and Merlin. I strode back into the antechamber, picked up a chair and threw it against the wall. It vanished into splinters. I didn't feel any better. I picked up another and swept a table clean of random stuff, most of which proved to be wine. I overturned a cabinet and kicked the door repeatedly.

"Fuck," I bellowed repeatedly.

Arthur and Tancred stood in the doorway to the throne room. Morgana pushed through the wall of muscle and stood in the centre of the destroyed room.

"Feel better?" she asked, her tone acidic.

"Not really, no," I snarled.

Tancred stepped forward with his hands out to placate me. "Lancelot -"

"No, don't." I pointed at him viciously. "Don't even think about it. I just want it to stop. I want to rest. I am only supposed to be here for a fucking year and now this... Whatever it is... And frankly I don't want to know."

Merlin appeared behind Arthur. My self control, clearly not very good, vanished completely. I lunged for the wizard. Arthur fell sideways, I grabbed the old man and hauled him into the room to slam him up against the wall, his feet off the floor.

"What the fucking hell have you done?" I spat.

Merlin didn't move, his green eyes held no fear. "I've done what was necessary."

"Why do you keep fucking with my life?"

"You have a destiny which is thick and complex. You have a rich soul, still learning its place in the world. There is nothing I can do to change that," he said, holding his bunched hands in his robes.

"But you don't try to help me change it do you? You just keep setting me up. You made this happen. I wouldn't be surprised if you are the one who sold me out to The Lady in the first place," I snarled. His face paled at the accusation. "You did. I knew it. You didn't stay in Camelot at all. You were the fucking surgeon who said Arthur would die."

"He would have done," Merlin said.

"Not if you'd been there honestly. I wouldn't have needed to come to Albion at all."

"But then you wouldn't be here now and I needed you here now," he said very matter of fact.

I drew back my fist.

Arthur and Tancred landed on me in the same moment and I hit the ground. I fought, I fought hard but both knew me far too well and I found no way to escape their grasp. Eventually, I ran out of blind rage and lay still on the floor. All three of us panted hard and Arthur licked a split lip.

"I just wanted to go home," I said, suddenly on the verge of tears.

Tancred stood up, wincing. "Who was that man?" he asked, ignoring my pathetic bleating.

Merlin lifted one of the only whole chairs in the room and placed it on the floor. He sat on it and looked down at me and Arthur. "That was a god, which one, you can work out for yourself. I'll not invoke his name lightly."

"I don't care," I said. I hauled myself upright and helped Arthur stand. I touched his mouth, "Sorry."

"It's alright, you've had a bad week," he said magnanimously. "Keep talking, Merlin," he ordered.

"Since you destroyed Aeddan by using Rhea, I've been having dreams. When I realised they weren't just normal dreams I started to investigate and meditate on the images. Soon enough, mainly because they were looking for me, I reached these gods. They need help. Items of power, such as the Grail, have been sent to the four winds but they are being retrieved and used. We retrieved the Grail but other items must be found in order to stop the madness. By freeing Rhea you caused a crack to form in the world of Death."

"We didn't free her, we asked, he gave," I growled. I stood with my arms over my chest, the anger building once more.

"Regardless of semantics," Merlin said firmly, "a crack in the prison holding the Titans is a problem because the Titans are pushing for freedom. They will want to escape, kill the gods who rule here and still govern huge amounts of our world, before moving on to destroy everything. They will treat us like slaves and break our worlds for fun. They must be stopped and the items stored more safely. We've grown slack over the centuries and now we will pay the price. We are not caring for our world with sufficient vigilance."

"How many items?" Arthur asked, glancing up at his advisor.

"In the old stories there are fifteen," Merlin said looking slightly sheepish.

"Fifteen," I exploded. "It almost killed us gaining just one."

"Being angry isn't going to help." Merlin sounded irritable. I bunched my fists until Morgana lay a hand on my right arm.

"Fifteen isn't so bad if you know where they are and how to deal with them. Many of the items are lost, which means they could be in a market place or even a rubbish dump. They won't all be guarded like the Grail." She spoke to reassure me. It didn't work. I was too fucking tired.

"Bollocks," I announced. "I can't be bothered. I'm off to get drunk." No one tried to stop my move to the door. I stormed into the main part of the palace. People vanished from around me, a sure sign I was scaring the bastards. Good, I thought, make them leave me alone. Unfortunately, I didn't know my way around well enough and failed to find a door which spat me out into The City. I did find a garden and slumped on a bench. A Brownie appeared like magic, which it probably was, and I ordered brandy.

Within no time I felt lightheaded and a great deal calmer. Sometimes, you just need oblivion. I began to wish for a pretty blond when Tancred appeared.

"Is it safe?" he asked.

"Almost," I grumbled. "How did you find me? Brownies?"

Tancred smiled, sat beside me, took the bottle and drank heavily. "No, don't need them," he tapped his skull. I grunted. Great, couldn't hide from him anymore.

"Thought you'd be in a whorehouse somewhere."

"Planned to be, got lost," I confessed. He laughed, which made me smile and I lost the bitter edge.

"We've had a rough few days," he said.

"Yes."

"What are you going to do?" he asked.

I shrugged. "I will probably do as I'm told. I always do in the end."

"Will Arthur come with us?" he asked. I heard his control wavering.

"Don't know," I said, imagining Guinevere's face when someone told her that her husband had vanished with me again on another adventure. "He's no threat to us," I told my lover.

Tancred stared hard at some weird topiary. "Forgive me for not quite being able to believe that statement, my Lord."

I sighed, "I don't blame you, but it's true."

"I know you think you mean it," Tancred replied.

We drank in silence for a while. I finally said, "I can't prove it to you, can I?"

"No, not really."

"And you don't trust me."

"No. Not with Arthur. Anyone else and you could fuck them without hurting me, I think, but not him."

"I don't plan on bedding anyone but Morgana and I'll only do that because I have to," I said in my own defence.

We drank some more.

"I only left you to go to Rafe because I didn't want you to reject me first," Tancred confessed.

"I think I've known that for a while," I said sadly, staring at the ground between my knees. "I really buggered it up."

"I thought we'd have longer together before he became such a dominant part of your life," Tancred said, referring to Arthur. "I didn't anticipate our trip together. If we'd been left to find a new life in Camelot it might have been different."

"It might," I said, and thought it equally might not have been different.

"Do you want me to stay here and care for Morgana?" he asked. I heard a world of pain in those words. A world where Tancred expected to be rejected once more and he'd just live with the agony so he could follow orders. Arthur had done this to me countless times.

"No." I reached out and took his hand. It shook slightly. "Your place is with me. I've made my decision. Truly made it and Arthur knows that, he knows he made a mistake by forcing me to leave you. You and I didn't really trust what we had and I was too broken to make a stand. I'm not broken any more and neither is Arthur. We can do this."

Tancred tried to laugh; it didn't work well. "Just my luck to fall in love with powerful men who can squash me like a noisy insect any time they like."

"No squashing, Tancred. I promise." I held his hand, kissed his knuckles which weren't quite as broken as mine and we just sat, drinking until full dark filled the garden with shadows. I told him about my life since we'd parted, filling the blanks of almost two years. I explained about Kadien and how I thought I'd find something with her if she'd have me. I hadn't had time to think about her or Rhea. I knew I'd need to speak with Arthur about how to deal with both of them. I also needed him to find a new leader for Camelot's Wolf Pack. I might be gone for years.

I realised I knew Arthur would not be coming with us. I needed him to be safe, in Camelot, with his family. I needed him to help Morgana keep the throne. She certainly couldn't leave Albion's City. Considering all the things The Lady taught me I began considering the other people I'd need in the group. Tancred and I were good fighters and he acted as a healer but we'd need powerful help of the more esoteric kind. I thought about Merla. I'd far rather travel with her than Merlin, but Gawain needed his wife and Arthur needed Gawain.

"Stop thinking," Tancred said. "You've been quiet for too long. Come on, let's go and pass out." He stood and hauled me straight. The world wobbled endearingly and we began to laugh. I started some bawdy song and the pair of us walked through the palace singing loudly.

We crashed through the door to Morgana's suite, the only place we knew we had somewhere to sleep, and found my wife in deep conversation with King Arthur.

They both frowned at us, which set off another verse of song and much giggling. Morgana rose to chastise us but Arthur held her arm and grinned. "There's no point. You'll only make him worse."

I swayed and grabbed my friend into a bear hug. "I love you."

Arthur held me. "I know." He sounded resigned.

I pulled back. "But I can't be at your side anymore."

He flinched. "I know, Lancelot. Maybe we should talk when you're sober."

"I never want to be sober again." I headed for the wine.

Morgana stole the decanter. "No, no more. Bed."

"If you insist." I made a lunge for her and fell over a small table. "Bugger." The ceiling had more spiralling patterns over it and rich colour. "Sleep now." I shut my eyes and life drifted away.

EPILOGUE

"Really? This is your hero?" the woman's voice held scorn and despair in equal measure. Her long white hair cloaked her shoulders and back. Her body, tall and strong, turned to the man at her side.

His mighty physique dwarfed the woman. He wrapped a hank of his beard around his index finger. "If drinking precluded you from being a hero we'd never have managed to get this far. Stop being such an old woman, Epona, you used to enjoy a party."

"I used to enjoy a great many things until every mortal and immortal being thought to lay siege to our lives." Epona turned away from the crystal pool, which showed the Queen of the Fey and the Champion trying to take the King to his bed.

The man followed her. "We need him. He is the best of his kind and the Fey. It is the reason we let Aeddan sleep with that mortal beauty."

Epona snorted, "You let him sleep with the woman because you couldn't and you wanted to watch. Taranis, you are a pervert, so don't try and say it was for the cause, you had no idea she'd make someone that strong."

"So you admit he's strong," Taranis said.

Epona poked her husband in the chest. "Don't change the subject."

Taranis threw his hands in the air. "I'm not. I'm trying to find a way of saving our lives and the lives of the Fey who follow our path. Lancelot is our only hope."

"Then you had better hope he sobers up enough to actually go on this quest," Epona snapped. She realised the anxiety which hounded her constantly about the future of her family might be making her too harsh. She needed to support her husband, not reprimand him constantly. "I'm sorry." She walked into her husband's surprised arms and laid her head in his chest.

Taranis stroked her soft hair and she felt his great heart beating strongly. "I know it's hard, love, but we cannot interfere directly. If we do we will just make the Titans stronger. Being in the world is what they want. If we stay here they cannot pull our energy down into their prison and use it to break free."

"You should never have given Aeddan that damned cauldron," she said, looking up at him.

Taranis sighed. "Grail, dear heart, Grail. It is now the Grail, we gave it to the cause, remember?"

Epona waved an impatient hand and pulled out of his comforting embrace. "Whatever it's called, you shouldn't have given it to him."

Taranis' face grew sad. "No, I should not have done. I just wanted the Fey to have the same chance the humans did. But they are too alike and power is more important to many than Grace."

They walked together in silence through mighty caves and into vast halls. "Do you think they will do it?" Epona asked, taking her husband's hand.

Taranis remained silent for a long time. She felt him shrug. "Possibly, if the motivations are there. Lancelot is a driven man. He wants just one thing, peace. If I don't let him have it until he finishes my work, he will just keep fighting."

"He slipped from your control for six years," Epona reminded him gently.

"He needed a rest and I needed to regroup. I genuinely believed they would kill Aeddan. The Morrigan misjudged that episode badly."

"We all did," Epona said. "Aeddan learnt more than we ever thought possible. Let's hope his son proves more stable and less intelligent."

They walked into the night, a perfect moon high overhead. Its soft light lent grace to the vast edifice of the gods. The wooden palace built to house their vast family when called together in conclave. Epona and Taranis looked into the sky and sent out the request for attendance. They needed their family at home. They needed to prepare for war.

LANCELOT'S BURDEN

CHAPTER ONE

The sword rushed down toward my head and I twisted sideways. The twinge in my right knee reminded me I'd only been healed a few days ago. I cut upward and the man dropped, he screamed while trying to stuff his guts back into his body.

"Lancelot, down," Tancred yelled.

I dropped and his knife whistled over my head. I kicked out backward and smashed the knee of my opponent. Bors stood in front of Nimue and Rhea, protecting them from those who managed to slip past Tancred and I. We circled close together, while our enemies organised themselves.

"Who are these people?" I asked. We both panted but we weren't tired, not yet. "We're only two days outside The City."

"You aren't going to like this," Tancred said risking a glance at me. I didn't say anything, I maintained focus on the attackers. "They are Rafe's men."

I did look then, "What?"

"I've fought them, trained with them," he said and I heard his regret at their deaths.

"Is my dear brother trying to kill me because of you or the throne?" I asked.

"I have no idea," Tancred managed before seven men rushed us simultaneously.

We hacked and slashed. The warmth of the dawn spread over the ground. I drove into the crowd and just became Caliburn's partner. She whispered words of joy at her release and my confidence. We became one; dancing in the light and watching the bright red of blood stain the sky before kissing the earth. My body, honed by months of training, performed every task requested with precision.

Tancred moved in his own dance. His fey heritage made him both graceful and powerful.

The last of the men dropped.

Bors approached, "You might have invited me."

"Your job is to protect them," I nodded toward our female companions.

"I think they are going to be able to look after themselves," he glanced nervously at Nimue. She smiled at me sweetly, her pointed teeth shone, along with her red hair. I hated turning my back on that woman.

I ignored her and looked at Rhea, "You alright?"

She nodded, her eyes very big and her skin several shades too pale. I didn't approach, blood covered my hands and doubtless my face. The damned stuff splashed everywhere given the chance. She'd come at Merlin's request to join the madness of Albion. I couldn't believe how much she'd gown in nine short months.

I looked at Tancred. He held a cloth and wiped the blood off his sword. He appeared unruffled by the bout. Cold almost. I touched his shoulder, "Are you alright?"

He turned his perfect brown eyes to mine, "Of course."

"But Rafe attacked us."

"Yes, I think it's time I put a stop to his idiocy," his gaze looked through me, not at me. "With your permission, I'll back track slightly and finish this off."

We'd ridden hard for two days since leaving The City. The aftermath of the earthquake in such a populous area made me pity Morgana and Arthur for remaining behind and dealing with the chaos. We'd travelled south and I'd hoped we circumnavigated Rafe's property, but we'd not gone far enough, fast enough. The rolling hills between the coast and the river delta of The City, were almost exclusively his land and we needed to cross it.

I moved my hand to Tancred's jaw. His eyes focused on me. I smiled, "Do you really think I'm going to let you go alone?"

"You should. Our task is too important for this foolishness," he waved vaguely at the dead bodies.

I frowned, "Tancred, men died today. It is never foolish."

"They threatened you," he turned away from me and

began pulling at the clothing of one of the men. I watched his back and wondered how much colder he could become before he turned into me. I did not want that fate for my lover.

"Regardless, you aren't facing Rafe alone. We all go or we just move on. He's going to give up at some point," I told him.

"I wouldn't bet on it," Nimue said as she picked her way through the corpses. "Your playmate meant a great deal to my son."

Tancred scowled at Nimue. "I am not his playmate. I am his Champion."

I'd been fighting this for the last few days. Nimue liked to pick at me and Tancred. Bors didn't approve at all but wouldn't discuss it, just chose to ignore us for the moment. Rhea accepted Tancred as my lover and treated him like a big brother or uncle. I loved her for that, even if I hated her being dragged into another fight for Albion and Camelot.

"So what do you suggest?" I asked.

Tancred pulled something off the corpse's neck. "If you won't let me go to him, we'll call him to us." He held a gold pendant in his hand. A purple stone in the centre flashed with the sun.

I frowned. Nimue explained, "It is a device those of us with power can use. When someone we give the pendant to calls we can locate them and materialise."

"So we just call?" I asked. "He won't know we are here? That seems like a very dangerous arrangement."

"There is a code to the call," Tancred said. "But Nimue can crack the code and we can trick him here. I shouldn't imagine it is the same as when I lived with him."

"Some people do stupid things, try it," I instructed.

Nimue's mouth twitched, "Still don't trust me?"

"No," I stated flatly. "He is your son, why should I trust you?"

She shrugged, clearly uncaring about my ability to trust her. Tancred held the pendant out and muttered something. Nimue then grasped it, closed her eyes. I watched her lips move silently, while power crawled like ants over my skin.

Tancred pulled on my arm and we backed away, joining Bors who moved Rhea. The four of us started tacking the horses quickly. Mirach, the stubborn and spirited palomino I'd chosen from Aeddan's stable, flattened his ears and I knew I faced another day trying to convince him I remained in charge regardless of his games. He stuck to a pattern until our midday meal, then gave up, making the afternoon peaceful.

Tancred helped me with Mirach's saddle. "I'm sorry."

"For what?" I asked.

"For this trouble. Let me deal with it, ride on with the others and let me finish this…" his voice trailed off when I kissed him. To be together, like this, in public satisfied a deep and lonely place in my soul.

"I love you. Your trouble is mine. You give my breath and heartbeat meaning. Let me help you," I told him.

"You really mean it don't you? This time is different," he spoke quietly.

He referred to Arthur. I'd left him behind. Made him stay behind. I didn't want him destroying my reunion. I didn't want him taking my new life away. For the first time since we'd met in over thirty years I felt free of Arthur Pendragon and it felt good.

Tancred's body blended with mine and his strength held me tight against his horse, who shifted and leaned back toward me. We kissed, deeply.

When he finally released he growled, "I want so much more."

I grinned, "Short rations proving hard?" We'd been together in The City but on the road it was not only difficult, but inappropriate.

"Lancelot," Nimue's voice chimed clearly forcing us apart for good. "I need you now."

We rushed from the horses as the air changed quality once more. It prickled over my skin and lay heavy on my shoulders, feeling like a thunder sky. Nimue stepped back from the colours beginning to swirl in a small space. Tancred stepped forward. The red of Rafe's long hair, so like his mother's, coalesced first. Then the rest of his tall form appeared. Before it finished, I heard his voice, "You have destroy him? My brother is dead?"

"At least we know the orders were for your King and not for me," Tancred said. The cold fury in his voice made me revaluate him again, he'd changed in the two years we'd been a part. "Treason is a hangable offence even here."

Rafe stepped back in shock, the bodies around him made him gasp. "You killed them all?"

"Them or Lancelot, who did you think I would choose?" Tancred asked.

"Me," Rafe cried out. "You wanted me."

"But you didn't want me," Tancred shot back. "And you are but a pale reflection of the man I have always loved."

I watched my brother's hate filled eyes turn to me, "You are a foul poison."

"Rafe," I stepped forward with my hands out, trying to placate him. As assassinations go, it had been both heavy handed and badly executed. They'd come in on foot, just before dawn. We'd set watch on the only direction from which a sudden attack could occur. I'd seen them coming and woken our camp in time for us all to be armed. They thought weight of numbers would be enough. Foolish men.

"Don't, don't pity me, you bastard. You foul bastard," Rafe's face twisted with such darkness I paused. "If I can't have him, neither can you." He pulled a knife and rushed at Tancred. My Champion, caught desperately unprepared, began to pull his sword but too slow. Far too slow. I lunged for Tancred, turning my back on Rafe and fire erupted in my body.

Life slowed. I fell through air turned to treacle, slowing my descent. Rhea screamed. Nimue held her back. Bors rushed forward. Tancred's right arm drew his blade and cut sideways in an arc, one pure movement. Red hair filled my peripheral vision on my left side and my brother's head landed on the ground at the moment my knees hit the same turf.

Rafe's clear green eyes stared up at me as Tancred dropped and pulled me into his arms to stop me hitting the floor. Voices surrounded me but the shock of the knife jumbled them badly.

Lightning Source UK Ltd.
Milton Keynes UK
UKOW051803100712

195774UK00001B/23/P